Welcome to Land of Fright™!

Land of Fright™ is a world of spine-tingling short horror stories filled with the strange, the eerie, and the weird. The **Land of Fright™** tales encompass the vast expanse of time and space. In the **Land of Fright™** series of books you will visit the world of the Past in Ancient Rome, Medieval England, the old West, World War II, and other eras yet to be revealed. You will find many tales that exist right here in the Present, tales filled with modern lives that have taken a turn down a darker path. You will travel into the Future to tour strange new worlds and interact with alien societies, or to just take a disturbing peek at what tomorrow may bring.

Each **Land of Fright™** story exists in its own territory (which we like to call a **terrorstory**.) Some of the story realms you visit will intrigue you. Some of them may unsettle you. Some of them may even titillate and amuse you. We hope many of them will give you delicious chills along your journey as you meet up with fire-spiders, take part in ancient Aztec rituals, battle smog monsters, experience chilling WWII encounters, glimpse into the lives of alien creatures that roam the stars, and spend quality time with a barbarian king.

First, we need to check your ID. **Land of Fright™** is intended for mature audiences. You will experience adult language, graphic violence, and some explicit sex. Ready to enter? Good. We'll take that ticket now. **Land of Fright™** awaits. You can pass through the dark gates and—Step Into Fear!

Readers Love Land of Fright™!

"This is the first story I've read by this author and it blew me away! A gripping tale that kept me wondering until the end. Images from this will, I fear, haunt me at unexpected moments for many months to come. Readers, be warned! :)" – Amazon review for **Dung Beetles (Land of Fright™ #27 – in Collection III)**

"Some truly original stories. At last, a great collection of unique and different stories. Whilst this is billed as horror, the author managed to steer away from senseless violence and gratuitous gore and instead with artful story telling inspires you to use your own imagination. A great collection. Already looking for other collections… especially loved Kill the Queen (God Save the Queen)." – Amazon UK review for **Land of Fright™ Collection I**

"This was a great story. Even though it was short I still connected with the main character and was rooting for her. Once I read the twist I cheered her on. This was an enjoyable short story." – Amazon review for **Snowflakes (Land of Fright™ #3 – in Collection I)**

"Love the freaky tales from the Land of Fright. This one is particularly nasty and dark. A tale of double revenge unfolds in a graveyard where a perceived business betrayal causes the perceiver to enact an insidious plan to impose the ultimate suffering on his partner. The suffering takes an unexpected turn that I did not see coming." – Amazon review for **Cemetery Dance (Land of Fright™ #49 – in Collection V)**

"I absolutely loved the heck out of this story. The whole story was bizarre, and the end? Well, it was perfect!" – Amazon review for **The Throw-Aways (Land of Fright™ #31 – in Collection IV)**

"I like the idea of a malevolent dimension that finds a way to reach into our world… this was an entertaining read and can be read at lunch or as a palate cleanser between longer stories." – Amazon review for **Sparklers (Land of Fright™ #15 – in Collection II)**

"I enjoyed this quite a bit, but then I enjoy anything set in Pompeii. A horror story is a first, though, and well done. I'm become a fan of the author and so far have enjoyed several of his stories." – Amazon review for **Ghosts of Pompeii (Land of Fright™ #14 – in Collection II)**

"Fantastic science fiction short that has a surprising plot twist, great aliens, cool future tech and occurs in a remote lived-in future mining colony on a distant planet. This short hit all the marks I look for in science fiction stories. The alien creatures are truly alien and attack with a mindless ruthlessness. The desperate colonists defend themselves in a uniquely futuristic way. This work nails the art of the short story. Recommended." – Amazon review for **Out of Ink (Land of Fright™ #26 – in Collection III)**

"I am a fan of the Land of Fright series and have found the horror found in the stories diverse and delightfully bizarre. This tale amp's up the gritty to 11. The barbarian warrior king in this short story is a well written, fearsome, crude and believable beast of a man. This story is not for those offended by sex or violence. I was immersed and found it great escapism, exactly what I look for in recreational reading."- Amazon review for **The King Who Owned The World (Land of Fright™ #50 – in Collection V)**

"Another great story; I've become a fan of Mr. O'Donnell. Please keep them coming…" – Amazon review for **Sands of the Colosseum (Land of Fright™ #18 – in Collection II)**

"Perfect bite size weirdness. Land of Fright does it again with this Zone like short that has two creative plot twists that really caught me off guard. I know comparing this type of work to the Twilight Zone is overdone but it really is a high compliment that denotes original, well conceived and delightfully weird short fiction. Recommended." – Amazon review for **Flipbook (Land of Fright™ #19 – in Collection II)**

"An enjoyable story; refreshingly told from the point of view of the cat...definitely good suspense." – Amazon review for **Pharaoh's Cat (Land of Fright™ #30 – in Collection III)**

"A fun thrill-ride into the Mexican jungle, and another great Land of Fright tale. Not enough people have written horror stories or novels about Aztec sacrifices." -Amazon review for **Virgin Sacrifice (Land of Fright™ #42 – in Collection V)**

"This short has a cool premise and was very effective at quickly transporting me to the sands of the coliseum in ancient Rome. The images of dead and dying gladiators are detailed and vivid. There is a malevolent force that very much likes its job and is not about to give it up, ever. Recommended." – Amazon review for **Hammer of Charon (Land of Fright™ #29 - in Collection III)**

"The thing I like about the Land of Fright series of short stories is that they are so diverse yet share a common weird, unusual and original vibe. From horror to science fiction they are all powerful despite of their brevity. Another great addition to the Land of Fright festival of the odd." - Amazon review for **Snowflakes (Land of Fright™ #3 – in Collection I)**

Land of Fright™

Collection V

JACK O'DONNELL

Published by ODONNELL BOOKS

ISBN-10: 1-940118-13-1
ISBN-13: 978-1-940118-13-0

Visit www.landoffright.com

DEDICATION

To everyone who dreams of doing something they love, and then actually does it. Go for it!

LAND OF FRIGHT™ COLLECTION V CONTENTS

Welcome to the
Land of Fright™
A World of Spine Tingling Stories filled with the Strange, the Eerie, and the Weird
'Step Into Fear!'
Terrorstory
#41
The Hatchlings
A Short Tale of Terror
Jack O'Donnell

TERRORSTORY #41
THE HATCHLINGS

They looked like normal charcoal briquets to Calum Rennalis, but they were anything but normal. As he was soon to find out when the hatchlings made their presence known. The grill sat on the driveway just outside of his open garage, the coals inside the grill just starting to turn white around the edges. Calum eschewed the propane tanks and shiny steel pseudo-stoves that fueled the fancy grills everyone seemed to have these days. He had an old Weber grill that used good old-fashioned charcoal briquets. The grill was basically just an oval basin about three feet wide and two and a half feet deep that held the charcoal within it. A metal grid framework stretched across its surface where the steaks would be laid down once the coals were ready for them. The blue grill was a bit rusty around the edges now, but it still got the job done.

The wife and daughter were off at church and it was Calum's job, since he was now officially a non-practicing former Catholic, to get the steaks grilled before they got back. That way, they could all eat right away when they got home and binge watch another few episodes of their new favorite TV show. He forgot the name of the show, but it was some series on some new cable channel they discovered called Lifeline, some show about suburban psycho killers; his wife Katie and his daughter Violet ate those stories up. He thought it was pretty amusing that a channel with that name had so many shows about murder and death on it; he also felt it was pretty ironic that his wife and daughter turned that show on right after hearing sermons about love and peace and brotherhood, but he kept that thought to himself.

Calum dug into a metal garbage can that was positioned just inside the garage along the wall and pulled out his secret plastic baggie. Inside the baggie were his pipe and his pouch of tobacco. He had gotten the hand-carved wooden pipe and fresh tobacco from a local renaissance faire and really enjoyed the stuff. He filled his pipe, tapped the loose tobacco shavings down with his finger, then lit up the pipe. It took a few flicks of the lighter to get the flame going, and a few quick puffs to ignite the tobacco, but he managed it efficiently enough. He exhaled a thick cloud of smoke, immediately feeling the narcotic effects buzzing his brain. He wasn't a short man, but he did have flashes of pretending to be a pipe-smoking hobbit once in a while as he puffed on his long-handled pipe. He snatched at his open beer and took a quick drink, cooling off his throat.

Calum took another mouthful of intoxicant into his lungs and sent another mouthful of inebriant into his belly. His iPad sat on a nearby plastic table inside the garage, playing random Sinatra tunes from Pandora. He breathed a happy sigh. It was so peaceful. This was one of his most favorite things to do. Bask in the warm sunlight, drink and smoke, listen to Sinatra, and grill steaks. Life was beautiful.

And to top it all off, he had one week of vacation. One glorious week of rest and relaxation away from work. Seven days of no responsibility. Okay, five business days of no responsibility and two weekend days thrown in for good measure. Seven days of actually being able to take a deep breath and enjoy a few moments of actual calmness. *All work and no play makes Calum a ripe candidate for the Sutherberry Rest Home.* And he was feeling plenty ripe lately with everything that was going on at the office. He felt the entire weight of their company's success was riding on his shoulders. If he didn't close the Paterson deal next month, they would be looking at layoffs. The financial well-being of over three dozen people was all depending on him to provide them with a large intake of monetary oxygen.

He set his beer down on the table next to his iPad

and moved over to the grill to look down at the coals, absently pulling at the growth of beard on his chin as he studied the briquets. Katie wasn't a big fan of his beard, especially all the white hairs that made him look ten years older, but he was so sick of shaving that he decided to let the beard grow out several months ago despite his wife's disapproval. The white edges on the coals were a little more pronounced now, but they weren't ready yet. Then something caught his eye. Something out of the ordinary. Calum had grilled hundreds of meals in his 52 year life, but he had never seen anything like this before. He looked closer, feeling the heat of the grill rise up to meet his face.

One of the charcoal briquets had a weird crack in it. He had seen cracks in charcoal briquets before, so that wasn't odd. What was odd was that the crack appeared to be growing as he watched it. His mind immediately flashed back to the chickens hatching in their eggs he had once seen at the Museum of Science and Industry in Chicago long ago when he was a kid. The timing of their visit to the museum had been perfect. They had found themselves in the farming display area, moving amongst the huge tractors and fake bales of hay, reaching the chicken eggs just as they were starting to hatch. The eggs were all enclosed in an incubator, a plastic dome covering the eggs, keeping them warm and safe in their little heated house. He remembered a little beak suddenly poking its way through the cracked egg shell. *Boy, I used to love going to that museum,* he thought. *I really should take Violet there more often.*

Calum took a drag off his pipe and exhaled the smoke out of the corner of his mouth. He continued to stare curiously at the growing crack in the charcoal briquet. Then he noticed another briquet had a crack in it, then another, and another. All of them had cracks that were slowly elongating along their surfaces. Were these some kind of new briquets? He looked over to the bag of charcoal on the garage floor. It was the same brand he always used. Nothing on the bag indicated they were new, or some kind of new formulation. It was the same old charcoal briquets he had been using for years.

A car drove by on the street in front of his house and he glanced up at it. The warm sunlight gleamed off the car's surface as it moved past. Someone was walking their dog on the opposite side of the street, calmly moving off into the distance. Far down at the end of the block where the street curved, some of the neighborhood kids were shooting baskets; they were too far away to hear but he could see them jostling about, shooting the ball. Everything looked normal, but there was something in the air that felt odd to him. Something felt off. Calum wondered if it was the pipe and booze making him feel a bit woozy. He had only gone back to smoking his pipe a few months ago, and only on the weekends when no one else was home, so he was still somewhat getting used to the nicotine buzz again. But he instinctively knew neither the tobacco nor the alcohol was the cause of the unease gnawing at him. Something else was going on, something else was troubling him, but he couldn't quite put his finger on it. Calum shuffled back over to the table to grab his beer. He set his pipe down, then took another cooling drink of the pale amber brew.

The grill made a crackling noise and he looked back over to the coals. Even from this distance, he could see that one of the briquets had a very pronounced crack in it. Calum frowned. *That was so weird.* He moved back over to the grill.

When the tiny leg poked its way out of the charcoal, he dropped his beer bottle in startled amazement. The bottle shattered on the concrete floor of the garage, spraying his jeans with splashing liquid and spattering flecks of foam.

Calum stared at the coals. *No, not coals. Eggs.* They were eggs of some kind and his grill had turned into an incubator. *What the fuck?* Another tiny leg poked its way out of the briquet and he took a step back away from the grill, his gym shoe crunching on a piece of broken glass from the shattered beer bottle. The tiny legs were black, shiny, almost metallic looking. *What the hell are they made of? Asbestos? What the hell difference does it make what they are made of? What the fuck are they? Where the hell did they come from?*

Two more coals showed signs of life as tiny legs pushed themselves out of the cracks. Half a dozen more briquets had deep cracks in them now. *Put them out. Put them out, you dumb ass!*

Calum turned and raced back into the house through the garage door that led into the kitchen. He grabbed at a bucket beneath the kitchen sink and started filling it up with cold water from the sink faucet. He moved impatiently from foot to foot, anxiously awaiting for the water to rise in the bucket. "Come on, come on." After the bucket was half full, he slammed the faucet handle down to shut the water off, and turned to race back outside.

He moved quickly back up to the grill, oblivious to the broken glass again crunching beneath his shoes. He raised the bucket over the grill, getting ready to pour the water over the coals, but then suddenly stopped and lowered the bucket. *Son of a bitch.* It was gone. The briquet that had two legs poking out of it was now completely split in half, revealing a hollowed-out interior. The creature that had been inside it was now gone. Calum glanced anxiously around the area. *Where did it go? And what the fuck was it? Worry about that later. Just put out the coals.*

He turned back to the grill and dumped the contents of the bucket into the grill. A hot blast of steam exploded upwards from the grill, showering him in the white vapor and tiny grey flakes of charcoal that erupted from the intense clash of cold versus heat, water versus flame. An eerie screeching noise filled the air, mingling with the sounds of coals sizzling and crackling. Calum coughed and swatted at the steam and white and grey smoke, trying to clear the air to get a better look at the coals. He thought he saw movement in the grill, tiny legs scurrying for cover. He swatted at the air some more, coughing, wincing as his eyes continued to water from the burning, irritating smoke and steam. The smoke dissipated enough for him to get a clear view of the grill. Calum stared with a growing dread at half a dozen charcoal briquets that were split open, their hollow interiors indicating something had just been inside them but were now free of their confines. A hint of movement to his right drew his gaze. A charcoal briquet shifted, a growing crack nearly running along its entire length. A tiny leg appeared from within the crack, extending upwards, twitching as if tasting the air around it. Then, the top half of the briquet shifted, separating itself from the bottom half, sliding open like the top half of a casket sliding open in an old Hammer vampire movie.

Calum stared at the hatchling within the charcoal egg. It had eight, no, ten, ten tiny black legs attached to its round body. It had a black body, almost metallic in appearance. He couldn't see any eyes on the torso, nor did it look like it had a separate head. It was very much like a black spider, but a headless spider with ten legs.

Something struck his shoulder and Calum felt a sharp stinging sensation in his skin. And a hot burning feeling. He glanced down to his right shoulder to see one of the creatures clawing at his shirt. He dropped the bucket and swatted at the creature, crying out in shock and alarm, trying to dislodge it from his body. "Fuck!"

His shirt caught fire and started to burn. He smacked at the flame with his open palm, trying to smother the fire. He succeeded in putting the tiny flame out, but then another fire started near his chest. He slapped at that, quickly putting it out. The creature was still lodged in his shoulder, the burning sensation intensifying. Calum grabbed at the creature and ripped it violently away from his body, ripping his shirt and his flesh in the process. "Motherfucker!" Blood splattered outward as he dislodged the creature's claws from his skin. He threw the hatchling to the concrete garage floor and backed away from it.

He could see the tips of the creature's claws were now a bright red. A hot, bright red. There was an empty cardboard box near the garbage cans that lined one of the garage walls. The creature lifted one of its legs and touched the tip of its red-hot claw to the box and the cardboard burst into flames where the creature touched it.

Three more hatchlings gathered around the box, sticking their bodies into the flames. The flames seemed to move towards their bodies, as if there were some kind of suction coming from their bodies drawing the flames to them. Calum stared at the creatures, watching the flames being pulled towards their bodies. It was as if they were eating the flames.

Suddenly, the flames were pulled sharply towards one of the creatures, as if a very strong wind had just blown through the garage and pushed the flames toward this single creature. But there had been no strong wind. The hatchling had sucked in all the flames into its body and had extinguished the flames with its action. The other creatures made scratchy hissing sounds, and one of them whacked the selfish creature on its back with two of its ten legs, clearly chiding the selfish creature for absorbing all the flames into itself. The selfish hatchling backed away from the strike, hissing back in reply. Calum could see no mouths on the creatures, so he wasn't sure where the sounds were coming from, but they were definitely making noises of some kind.

The striking creature returned its attention to the partially burnt cardboard box and touched a red hot tip of one of its claws to the cardboard. The box burst into flames again. The others gathered around and again started to feed on the fire, sucking the flames into their bodies.

Something touched Calum's arm and he flinched, instinctively swatting at his forearm where he had felt the sensation. There was no creature on his arm.

Something else had hit his arm, something dropping from above. It looked like a loose piece of drywall. Another piece hit his bare, bleeding shoulder and bounced off. He slowly glanced up to see one of the creatures directly above his head, its claws hooked into the drywall ceiling of the garage. It moved steadily across the ceiling, sinking its claws into the drywall as it moved. The tips of its claws were black, not red, so Calum knew the hatchlings could control the heat coming from their claws at will. Calum glanced in the direction the creature was headed and felt his chest tighten up. There were half a dozen pieces of wood resting along the far garage wall, leftover scraps from the shelving unit he had just built. He had a feeling that's where the creature was headed.

He glanced at the burning cardboard box and the creatures gathered around it like kids sitting around a campfire. He would come back to that later, but first he had to stop the creature on the ceiling from reaching the scraps of wood. He scanned the garage quickly, his gaze alighting on the broom in the corner near the garbage cans. He skirted the burning cardboard box and grabbed at the broom.

The creature on the ceiling was nearly at the far end of the garage, nearly over the stacked wood. Calum darted in its direction and swiped the end of the broom at it. He hit the creature on the first swing, but did not dislodge it. He swatted at it again and again. The creature sunk all ten legs firmly into the drywall, anchoring itself to the ceiling as Calum batted at it. He swung again and the creature pulled two of its legs out of the drywall to meet his strike with red-hot-tipped claws. The tight cluster of straw that made up the broom's head burst into flames. Calum shook the broom roughly, trying to put out the flames. He jammed the broom against the concrete, as if he was trying to snuff out a giant cigarette by jabbing it down into an ashtray. He managed to snuff the flames, putting out the burning straw. The head of the broom was charred and blackened, smoking lightly, now useless. He stepped on the burnt head of the broom and quickly twisted the handle, loosening it, and pulled the handle free of the broom head.

Movement caught his eye and Calum turned to see one of the creatures scurrying out of the garage onto the driveway. They just had the driveway re-paved two weeks ago so it was a deep black color. This made it hard to see the creature against the black surface, but its movement gave its position away. It stopped on the driveway for a brief moment, nearly disappearing as its deep black skin camouflaged it well against the asphalt, then scurried off into the grass, vanishing around the corner of the garage.

Shit. Where the fuck is it going? He glanced at the burning cardboard. The box was nearly gone now; only a small portion still burned. He looked up at the creature still lodged in the drywall ceiling. The creature hadn't moved; it was still anchored in the position where he had struck at it. There were a few blackened burnt smears on the ceiling where the creature's red-hot tipped claws must have touched the drywall, but it looked as if the creature had cooled the tips to re-anchor them back into the ceiling. He knew he couldn't let the creature that had raced out of the garage get away. *Who knows what kind of damage it could cause?* Calum gripped the broom handle and raced out of the garage after the black hatchling.

He found the creature huddled beneath a bush on the side of the house. He poked at it with the broom handle, trying to get it to move, trying to push it out into the open where he had every intent to smash it into a pulp. But the creature wouldn't move. It just sat motionless under the bush, nearly invisible in the dark shadows.

Calum looked closer at it. It wasn't motionless. It wasn't really moving, though. It was more like a shuddering motion, as if it were shivering. But soon he realized it wasn't shivering. It was molting. He realized he was staring at the selfish creature that had absorbed all the flames into itself and been scolded by its fellow creatures. The creature's outer skin cracked and started to peel. He could only watch in fascination as this unearthly creature's wings started to unfold. *Wings. It has fucking wings!*

He knew he couldn't let it get away. He stabbed at it with the broom handle, thrusting the end of the handle as savagely as he could against the creature's body. It shifted, but just barely. He realized it must have its ten claws sunk deep into the ground to anchor it. He needed something better than a broom handle. *A shovel.* He tossed the broom handle into the grass and hurried back to the garage.

Calum sprinted back into the garage only to find flames shooting up the far wall. Half a dozen of the creatures were gathered around the burning scraps of wood. Black scorching marks ran up the side of the garage wall. "Motherfuckers!" He thought of getting the hose but they had already put it away for the fall; the green coil lay curled up on a shelf on the back wall of the garage. *Shit.* He raced towards the inner garage door that led into the kitchen, thinking of the fire extinguisher he knew was in the kitchen somewhere.

Two of the creatures were on the wooden steps leading up to the door, getting ready to sink the red-hot tips of their claws into the wood. He kicked at both of them, catching the black hatchlings by surprise before they could anchor themselves to the wood, managing to knock them away so he could get to the door. They hissed and squealed as they flew through the air. Calum flung the door open and burst into the kitchen.

He raced to the small cabinets above the refrigerator and whipped the cabinet doors open, looking for the fire extinguisher. He rifled through the cans of cleaning solutions, furniture sprays, sponges, spare light bulbs, but didn't find the fire extinguisher. It wasn't there. *Shit! Where the fuck is the extinguisher?* He darted over to the cabinets beneath the sink and searched through more cleaning solutions, but still couldn't find the fire extinguisher. There was a beat-up old blue plastic bucket under the sink. He grabbed that and started to fill the bucket with water. *Call the police or the fire department, stupid.* As the water filled the bucket, he moved over to the kitchen phone. The phone wasn't in its cradle. *God damn it. Where is the phone?* He hit the button on the cradle base that made the phone ring so he could locate it. He thought he heard it ring upstairs. Violet probably took it up there to talk to her school friends in her bedroom, or Katie might have taken it up there to talk to her mother or her sister; they were always gabbing on the phone. His cell phone was upstairs, too.

He was about to head upstairs to get his phone when a loud crash came from the garage, making him pause. *Son of a bitch. What the hell was that?* He glanced back upstairs, but another loud crashing noise diverted his attention back towards the garage. *Shit.* He moved back to the sink, shut the water off, and grabbed the three-quarters-full bucket of water. He jerked the bucket out of the sink and water sloshed over the side, splashing on the kitchen floor as he hurried back to the door leading out to the garage.

A dozen creatures huddled around the fire in the garage now, all of them drawing the flames into themselves with whatever sucking mechanism they were using to eat the flames. The thick scraps of wood lay scattered about the garage floor now as the hatchlings had knocked them over, causing the loud banging sounds.

Calum thrust the bucket in the direction of the fire, hurling the water into the flames. The water also hit several of the creatures and they hissed in savage protest, and what sounded like pain-filled cries. The water doused a portion of the flames, but it didn't put out all of the fire.

Another hissing sound coming from just outside the garage drew Calum's attention. He turned to see the selfish creature sitting on the ledge of the grill, its wings folded in against its body. Then, it unfurled its wings, spreading them wide about three inches across on each side of its body. And then it propelled itself straight for Calum, flapping its wings quickly up and down, making a beeline directly at his head.

Calum raised the bucket defensively and the creature flew into the open end, slamming hard against the bottom of the bucket. The momentum of the strike pushed the bucket back hard against Calum's forehead and nose. Calum thought he heard his nose crunch and felt a sharp pain spread across his entire face. But he still was able to react quickly, thrusting the bucket down towards the cement floor of the garage, trapping the flying creature in the bucket. The bucket jostled as the hatchling fought to get free of its confines. Calum put his full weight on the bucket, pressing both hands down on the overturned bucket.

Then he saw one of the creature's claws push its way through the bucket, its tip red and hot. It was melting the bucket to get out. *Damn it, I need this fucking bucket.* He quickly pulled the bucket up off the creature. All ten claws of the black-bodied creature glowed red-hot. And then the creature launched itself at Calum, sinking all ten claws into his chest, scorching his flesh, drawing rivulets of blood from the areas of charred skin around each embedded claw. Calum howled in pain. The bucket clattered to the garage floor, bouncing along the cement, colliding against the other dropped bucket. He grabbed at the creature, tugging at its body, but he couldn't loosen the hatchling's deep grip on his flesh.

Calum staggered towards the inner garage door, the intense pain fogging his mind. *Water. I need water.*

He fumbled at the door, somehow managed to get it open, and staggered into the house.

Calum stumbled to the kitchen sink, reeling from the searing pain radiating out from his chest. He felt like his blood was about to start boiling at any moment. He slammed against the edge of the sink and flipped the water on. He slapped at the running column of water, hitting the water from behind the stream so it would spray onto the creature that was lodged in his chest. A few splashes of water hit the hatchling and some steam exploded off its shell in tiny clouds of grayish white smoke. That only seemed to aggravate the creature further and it sunk its claws deeper into him. Calum gritted his teeth and then howled at the intense pain spearing through him.

He fumbled at a coffee cup in the sink and filled it with water, then threw the water onto the creature, splashing the liquid against his chest. More steam erupted from the creature. But the creature still anchored itself firmly to his chest, all ten claws buried inside his flesh.

Calum staggered over to the refrigerator and yanked the door open. There were bottles of water on the shelf inside the door. Cold water. He grabbed one and twisted off the cap, letting the cap fall to the kitchen floor. He quickly upended the water bottle, pouring the cold water onto the creature. This colder water had a strong effect on the hatchling and it made an angry hissing sound as the cold liquid drenched it. A huge cloud of steam appeared and a sizzling sound filled the kitchen. The creature's wings spread wide and fluttered wildly, beating against Calum's chest. He kept pouring the water, finishing off the bottle. He tossed it aside and immediately grabbed another bottle of cold water from the refrigerator shelf. He upended that bottle, pouring it straight onto the creature. With his other hand, he snatched at one of the creature's wings and managed to get a good grip on it. He tugged at the wing, yanking at it roughly. He heard one of the claws come out of his skin with a sickening popping sound. He kept tugging and yanking and jerking at the hatchling's wing. Another leg popped out of his chest. The water bottle emptied and Calum whipped it aside, immediately going for the last water bottle on the refrigerator shelf. He had to stop yanking on the creature's wing to open the water bottle, and the creature sunk its two loose claws back into his skin. Calum screamed in agony and threw the water bottle down before he could open it. He gripped the creature's body with both hands and jerked at it with all the might he had left, ripping the hatchling off of his body with a primal, ear-splitting shriek of pain and a thundering grunt of extreme effort.

He threw the creature away from him and collapsed to the kitchen floor, panting with the exertion, reeling from the waves of pain flooding over him in a torrent of agony. He put his hand to his chest and felt a liquid ooze over it and through his fingers. He raised up his fingers to see they were coated in blood. Millions of tiny black dots swam across his vision. Calum felt woozy, and knew he was about to faint. He could handle seeing other people's blood, but not his own; he had fainted once at the hospital after seeing a test tube fill up with his blood during a routine check up. He saw the dropped water bottle on the ground near him and he snatched at it. He fumbled at the cap and got the bottle open. He quickly poured the cold water over his head, shocking his body back into an awakened state. He shook his head, trying to shake the water out of his eyes as he kept pouring the cold water over his head. The tiny black dots in his vision faded away and he felt his head clearing as the wooziness went away.

But then he saw a big black dot in his vision. No, not a dot. It was the creature. It was the black hatchling he had just ripped out of his chest. It was sitting near the kitchen table, three of its claws sunk into the wood of one of the table legs. The table leg let off a few small wisps of smoke, and then caught fire.

Calum coughed and tasted a bitter coppery taste in his mouth. He was bleeding internally. *How far had the creature sunk its claws into me? A good few inches? What the hell kind of damage had it done?* He needed to call 911. He glanced up dazedly at the phone cradle that was up on the counter a few feet away. The phone wasn't there. *Right. It's upstairs somewhere. I need to find it.* He knew he had to move, but he couldn't find the energy to get up. He glanced down to see a widening pool of blood spreading around him. *I'm bleeding to death.*

He looked to the open refrigerator. *You'd better close that. The food will spoil.* He kicked at the door, managing to hook his shoe around the bottom, and pulled the refrigerator door closed. A crackling noise drew his gaze and he looked up to see his kitchen table burning brightly now. *At least I'll stay warm,* he thought. *You're losing it. Keep it together, man.*

Calum glanced around the kitchen, fighting back

the fatigue and exhaustion threatening to permanently overwhelm him. That's when he saw the kitchen pantry doors. It was where they kept extra school supplies, garbage bags, the mop, cleaning rags, and other miscellaneous stuff. Calum pulled himself along the floor towards the pantry doors, leaving a smeared bloody trail behind him. He opened the pantry doors and found what he was looking for. Duct tape and feather dusters. He forced himself up to his knees and grabbed one of the feather dusters from the shelf and plastered it against his chest over the bleeding holes in his flesh. The feather duster immediately stuck to the blood and started to absorb it, the strip of material staying in place when he let go of it. He grabbed at the roll of duct tape and peeled off a strip of it, ripping it with his teeth. He slapped the grey tape over his wound, doing his best to make it as tight as possible over his skin. He gritted his teeth as pain speared through him. He ripped off several more strips of the duct tape, slapping them in place on his chest. He then unrolled a length of the duct tape but didn't tear it off the roll. He stuck the sticky end to his chest, and awkwardly worked the roll all the way around his body, twisting and contorting his arms, wrapping the tape around his torso several times and pulling it taut before ripping off the piece to seal it down to his body. He panted heavily as he finished, dropping the roll of duct tape to the ground next to him.

The smoke coming from the burning kitchen table thickened, drifting up towards the ceiling to form low hanging clouds in his kitchen. The smoke detector alarm was beeping loudly. He hadn't heard it before, but now the sound was incessantly pounding in his ears. He reached up and gripped the edge of the kitchen island, pulling himself up to his feet with tremendous effort and with a tremendous groan. He leaned over the island, panting heavily.

Calum glanced over to see the creature sitting very near the burning kitchen table, doing its weird flame-eating feeding motions, sucking the fire into its body. The hatchling looked larger to him now, taller and fatter. Its wings were neatly folded up, curled against its sides.

He glanced over to the other kitchen counter, staring at the knife block through the haze of smoke that was continuing to thicken around him. He coughed, swiping at the air to brush the smoke away from his face. A trickle of blood oozed down over his lower lip, sliding out of his mouth, but he ignored it. *Can I stab it? Could a knife puncture that shell?* Then, he saw the meat tenderizer. It was a mallet with a thick block of studded wood at the end used to pound meat to make it more tender. He stumbled over to the counter and grabbed the meat tenderizer. He looked at the creature through the smoke. It was still busy feeding on the flames, paying him no attention. At least he thought it wasn't paying him any attention; Calum still didn't know if the damn thing had any eyes, or if it did where they were located on its body.

He moved slowly towards the creature, trying to be as stealthy as possible. He struggled to keep his breathing low and shallow, trying not to choke on the thickening smoke that was starting to fog up the entire room. He drew closer. The creature still did not seem to notice him. Its body swelled and pulsated as it continued to feed on the flames. *What the hell were these things eating?* Calum vaguely recalled his science class lessons about fire. He knew water molecules and carbon dioxide molecules were produced by combustion. Was that what they were eating? Water and carbon dioxide? He knew other chemicals were also created when a fire burned. Carbon was one of them, he remembered. *Is that what they are eating? Carbon produced by the flames? Umm, asshole, does it matter? Bash the fucking thing's head in and then you can study it later.*

Calum reached the creature and raised the mallet slowly, trying to avoid any quick movements. And then he swung, bringing the mallet down fast and furious. The mallet thudded against the kitchen floor. The black hatchling had evaded his strike as effortlessly as a vigilant fly evades an attack from a rolled up magazine trying to smash it. The creature flew into the air, going deeper into the kitchen. Calum chased it, swinging. He missed and the mallet head slammed into the microwave, cracking the front door of the appliance. He continued chasing after the creature, swinging the meat tenderizer mallet. He missed the hatchling again, smashing the blender, knocking the blender base and the container onto the floor with a loud crash.

The creature retaliated, dive-bombing at his face. Calum threw his hands up defensively and stumbled backwards. He tripped over the blender base and went sprawling backwards into the open pantry. His arms hit the shelves inside the pantry, sending cleaning supplies and school supplies showering down over him as he fell hard onto his buttocks. A heavy metal cylinder clubbed him in the head and he grunted. He was beyond any pain now. He just pushed it all away.

Then he saw the small cylinder that had just hit him in the head roll across the kitchen floor. It was a small red cylinder with bright white letters, a silver handle, and a slender black hose. The fire extinguisher! He remembered buying one years ago and putting it into the pantry in case of an emergency. He vaguely recalled it was a Class K fire extinguisher for fires that involved cooking oils, trans-fats, or fats in cooking appliances, and are typically found in restaurant and cafeteria kitchens. *Newsflash, asshole. It's an emergency! Get moving.*

Calum dropped the mallet and grabbed desperately at the fire extinguisher. He got to his feet, gripping the fire extinguisher with a growing hope. He pulled the pin, arming his new weapon. He held the fire extinguisher at his hip like a mobster holding a sub-machine gun, feeling a powerful renewal and surge of energy. The acronym PASS flashed through his head. Pull. Aim. Squeeze. Sweep. Pull the pin. Aim the nozzle. Squeeze the trigger. Sweep the nozzle from side to side as you spray. He saw the creature coming towards him and he fired, squeezing the trigger hard, releasing a gentle stream of fine mist straight at the hatchling. He had expected a big blast of white foam to come erupting out of the extinguisher, but then he remembered the Class K fire extinguishers were designed to spray a gentle mist so that the oils involved in most kitchen fires didn't splash up and spread the fire. Despite the lack of a big wave of white foam, at least his aim was true. The extinguisher mist showered the creature in a transparent coating of death. Calum swept the spray back and forth, dousing the hatchling, the misty blend of potassium acetate and potassium citrate creating a solid barrier between the extreme heat source of the creature and any nearby oxygen so the hatchling would not be able to reignite.

The creature dropped like a wasp getting hit mid-flight with a heavy dose of bug spray, plummeting like a rock straight down. It hit the kitchen floor, then flopped about, its ten legs spasmodically twitching in all directions. Calum grinned triumphantly. The extinguisher liquid was like poison to them. He sprayed another blast of liquid on the creature. "Take that, you little bastard!" The hatchling's wings fluttered, then began to withdraw back into its body. Some of the tips on a few of the hatchling's legs glowed red hot, then faded down back into a dull black. And then they, too, began to withdraw back into its body.

Within seconds, the creature was still. It looked once again like a lifeless charcoal briquet. Calum stared at the creature. It did not move. He brought the end of the fire extinguisher down on the black lump, smashing it again and again and again, not stopping until it was a pulverized pile of soot. He stared at the dark smear on the floor. *Where was the blood? Where were its guts?*

The crackling fire from the burning kitchen table drew his attention. Calum quickly moved over to the flames and sprayed the mist across the fire, sweeping the spray back and forth, snuffing out the flames. Thankfully, the Class K extinguisher worked just as well on other types of fires. *Jesus, the garage!* He moved quickly for the door.

The smoke detector alarm continued to blare.

Calum stood just inside the garage, feeling his jaw tighten at what he was witnessing. The stacks of wood were gone, devoured by the creatures. Black lines of soot streaked the walls of the garage just above where the pile of wood had been located. The ten-legged black hatchlings were now all gathered around his corn hole game boards. His bags boards. He gritted his teeth. He had just bought those last week. He had a tournament all set up next weekend with his relatives. And here these fuckers were, burning them and eating the flames. He held the fire extinguisher at his hip and started to spray, screaming at the creatures as he attacked them with the liquid fire-killer. "Heeyahh! Take that, motherfuckers!"

Calum sat on the porch stoop, still clutching the fire extinguisher, his face smeared with blood and soot, his fingers bloody and black. The garage behind him was quiet, the hatchlings destroyed, the smoke detector alarm now silenced. Blackened smears of soot and tiny shards of squashed charcoal dotted the garage floor. He was pretty certain he got all of them. He managed to save one of his bags boards, but the other one was toast, charred beyond use. The aches and pains slowly started to make themselves known again. A spot on his head throbbed mightily. His chest burned. He heard a fluttering sound and immediately raised the fire extinguisher, feeling a tightness grip his heart. He scanned the area quickly, his gaze darting all about, but he didn't see any creatures. A piece of paper floated down to the porch, landing next to him. It was a neighborhood flyer. He picked it up and read it: **"Neighborhood Barbecue. Saturday Night. August 24th. Get Out Your Grills And Join In The Fun!"**

He looked at the bag of briquets sitting on the garage floor. How many bags of charcoal had been sold? How many had his neighbors bought from their local store? How many in the state? How many in the country? How many across the world? Would they just stay dormant until the heat made them hatch? He couldn't just throw the bag of charcoal briquets away. He had to destroy them. He obviously couldn't burn them. He had to smash them. He had to crush them all.

He dropped the flyer and quickly moved back into the garage, grabbing a hammer from its resting place on the pegboard near the back wall. He moved back to the bag of briquets and set the fire extinguisher down next to it. He stared at the bag for a long moment. There was no avoiding his responsibility. The weight was heavy on his shoulders and he knew there would be no break from it. Not now. Not ever. *You cannot escape the responsibility of tomorrow by evading it today.* The quote from Abraham Lincoln flashed through his head. He gritted his teeth and set his resolve, standing tall, embracing the weight on his shoulders. *Who needs a vacation? Bah, rest and relaxation is for the weak. Taking a break is for the timid.*

Calum opened the bag of briquets with his free hand, unfurling the edge of the thick paper that comprised the bag, gripping the hammer tightly in his right hand. He was determined to stay strong despite how exhausted he felt. He hesitated with his hand hovering over the bag's opening for but a brief second before plunging his fingers into the bag to grab a briquet. He took one out, quickly dropping the lump of charcoal to the cement garage floor as soon as he got it out of the bag. He brought the head of the steel hammer smashing down on the briquet, smashing it into a black powder. He half expected some kind of guts to spew out when he smashed the briquet, but only tiny shards of the charcoal filled the area, the ground smearing with black soot as he brought the hammer down again and again. The harsh metallic sound of the hammer hitting the hard cement rang out in the garage.

The sound of a car pulling into the driveway drew Calum's gaze. He looked up to see Katie and Violet getting out of the car. "Dinner ready yet?" Katie asked as she walked towards him.

Calum looked up at his wife, said nothing, grabbed another briquet out of the bag, and resumed his important work. His family depended on him. His neighborhood depended on him. The world depended on him. The harsh metallic clang of the hammer hitting the hard cement again rang out in the garage, mingling with the soothing sounds of Sinatra in the background.

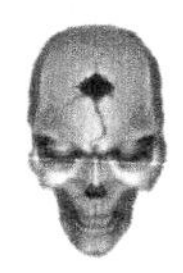

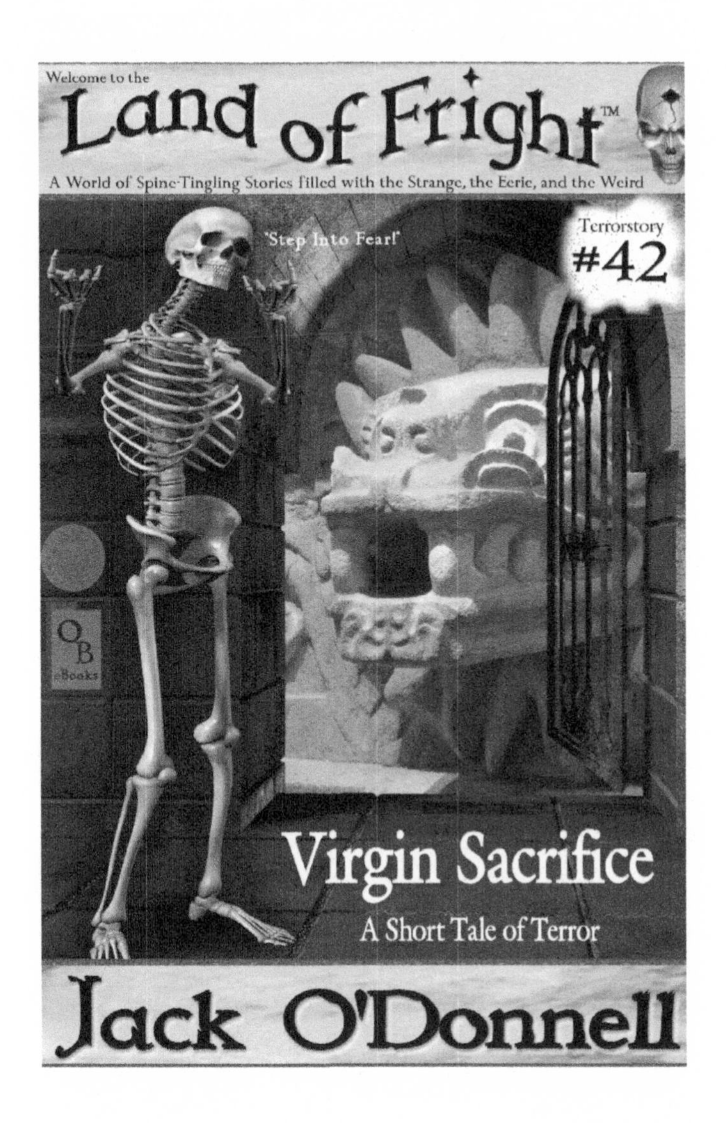
Welcome to the
Land of Fright™
A World of Spine-Tingling Stories filled with the Strange, the Eerie, and the Weird
'Step Into Fear!'
Terrorstory
#42
OB
eBooks
Virgin Sacrifice
A Short Tale of Terror
Jack O'Donnell

TERRORSTORY #42
VIRGIN SACRIFICE

Three virgins were going to accompany him on his trip to Mexico. Professor Ansel Langridge couldn't believe his good fortune. Three virgin women. He only needed one of them, but bringing along three of them practically assured a positive outcome. Ansel stared at the small Aztec ceremonial knife he held in his hand. He was so close! The plane was leaving tomorrow. Tomorrow! The four-inch blade was made of flint, its hard surface rough with irregular edges, the top edge of the stone hacked into a sharpened point. The blade had a light, grayish-brown color to it, with a darker brown at its sharp edge. The handle was made of cedar wood, covered in a turquoise and shell mosaic that represented the Aztec Eagle Knight, a symbol of power, strength, and courage. He wasn't certain of the exact age of the sacrificial dagger, but he surmised it was most likely used around 1400 to 1525 CE.

Ansel thought about what had led him to this point, and it was all rather simple and obvious. The world was going to hell. The crime rate was up. Families were disintegrating. Financial markets were collapsing. Nuclear accidents polluted the oceans. Global warming was devouring the polar ice caps and changing the world's weather patterns for the worse. Reports of terrorist strikes were on the news every night of the week now. Planes were getting shot out of the skies. Innocent civilians were getting slaughtered in theaters, in restaurants, on the streets. Severe droughts crippled vital crop production. A new strain of Ebola had emerged, deadlier than its predecessor. The Zika virus was deforming fetuses. Famine killed millions. Wars ripped apart countries. Ansel knew why. The gods were angry. The 52 year cycle was nearly complete and the gods were angry at the indifference common men showed them. What other explanation could there be? Nothing else made sense. Ansel knew if nothing was done, the world would truly come to an end. Sure, the world was a shithole now, but it was the shithole he had to live in and he didn't want it to come to a fiery climax.

The Aztec way was the only true way. They had the greatest civilization known to mankind — until they stopped following the sacred rituals. That was their downfall. They stopped believing. That was the downfall of every great civilization. They stopped believing in what had made them great in the first place.

Ansel closed his fingers around the hilt of the knife; the handle felt cool in his hand. He believed. He believed in the power of the ancient rituals. He had seen and read too many things in his studies to deny their strength. The rituals worked if they were strictly adhered to. Yes, they worked, and he was going to renew their power by performing them. He would forge a new world based on the grandeur and splendor of the old. Yes, the old ways were violent and filled with bloodshed, but homage and respect had to be shown to the gods. The deaths of a few would save the lives of billions. It was an easy decision to make.

He felt the excitement race through his fingers, making his hand actually tremble as he clutched the knife. He could hardly believe the time had finally arrived. But he really couldn't complain about the wait. It had been one of the best years in his life. No, not just one of the best. It had been *the* best year of his life.

Everything seemed to have come together just at the right time during the past year. The theologians and archaeologists Ansel admired all had agreed to help him with his writings earlier in the year, taking him under their wings, offering him advice and their own words of wisdom. His resulting book, "*Maintain Your Balance*," had been a bestseller, and was still selling strong. He felt like he had become a member in some secret royal society. Being a best-selling author was like being a movie star, but better. He got all the perks, but none of the tabloid or paparazzi nonsense that went along with being a movie star.

He was given preferential treatment at fancy restaurants. Lavish feasts had been a staple for him this year. So many interesting dishes, so many delightful delicacies. He had never known there were so many different flavors in the food chain.

He had been invited to give speeches at dozens of other universities, and had been paid handsomely for each one. Business leaders had flown him around the world on their private jets, seeking out his advice.

And the women. So many women. They were practically throwing themselves at his feet. He never realized how many different sexual positions were actually possible - and he had tried them all this year!

His year had been full of sights, sounds, tastes, and experiences that went beyond even his wild imaginings. All because he had harnessed the ancient wisdom of the Aztecs and turned their accumulated knowledge into practical real-world advice. His book detailed the balanced, middle path one should take in life to avoid excess. The excesses caused imbalance, which caused one to stumble off the path of prosperity and good health and be led into misfortune and ill-being. Far too many people had stumbled off the path. Far too many people had lost their way. The sheer magnitude of the misguided had caused the entire world to go off-center. He knew the book was helping, but he also knew it was not enough. More had to be done to set the world right again.

Ansel stood next to his bed. An opened suitcase was positioned on the mattress near him, some pants and folded shirts already placed neatly inside. Some stray toiletries and plastic baggies were in a pile on the bed near the suitcase. He slid the ceremonial knife between two shirts. Then, he packed his toiletries in various plastic baggies and positioned those around the dagger, placing them between the two shirts as well. He really had no idea what he was doing; he was hoping that any TSA employee who saw the clustered toiletry items on some x-ray machine would just not pay attention to this other item that was scattered amongst the rest. He had no idea how vigilant they were in thoroughly investigating every single piece of checked luggage. Regardless, even if they detected it, he had the credentials to explain why he had such an item in his possession; it was a rare archaeological artifact. He shrugged. The gods would decide the dagger's fate. They would either allow it to get through security, or they wouldn't. It would be out of his control. Yes, the gods would decide. Ansel smiled at the thought, and the anticipation inside him grew. He was determined to put the world back onto a balanced path.

Ansel always had a fascination with Aztec rituals, but that fascination turned into a full-blown obsession after he found the amulets and realized the power they had. He had discovered a cache of them on one of his expeditions into a newly-discovered Aztec ruin over a year ago. He had no idea what the amulets were at first. He thought they were just some discarded jewelry that had no real value beyond being ancient Aztec artifacts, but when he picked up one of the amber pieces and felt it tingle in his fingers he knew they were more than just a scrapheap of trinkets. There were hundreds of them, scattered about on the ground, or stored in stone containers. He knew the Mexican government would claim ownership of them all once the existence of the ruins was made public, so he took a few dozen for himself and stuffed them into his backpack to bring back home with him to study.

That was the best bit of thievery he had ever done in his life.

Ansel studied Lucina as they waited for their flight in the airport. Two of the three virgin women were already present. Lucina sat opposite Ansel, gently sipping on a Starbucks coffee as she read a fashion magazine. Brittany stood before the huge glass windows nearby, watching the movement of the planes outside. Staci hadn't arrived yet.

Lucina Hernandez was a quiet, mousy Hispanic woman who worked in the university library, industriously going about her duties amongst the tall shelves of books, keeping mostly to herself. Ansel didn't really know her very well; he just nodded and politely said hello to her when he saw her. He found it very easy to believe she was still a virgin. She was very plain, almost ugly, with a hint of a mustache running across her upper lip. She was overweight and her hair hung lifeless and limp on her head, dropping flat to her shoulders. It was actually unpleasant to look at her. For a brief moment, Ansel felt the beginnings of pity well up inside of him for her. He wondered what kind of life Lucina had led looking like she did.

He wondered if she thought he was hitting on her when he asked her to try on the amulet. He hoped not, but he strongly suspected she did. When he told her that he had gotten permission for her to travel with them to Mexico for their trip, that probably only added fuel to that misconception. He told her he wanted her to accompany him to Mexico on the expedition because he needed help in cataloging any artifacts they might find, which was complete bullshit, but she seemed to buy it. He was a bit surprised when she had said yes, but she probably felt obligated to say yes. That was just her way. She avoided confrontation and negativity of any sort.

The amulet Lucina wore around her neck still held its pale amber color. The amulet reminded Ansel of the mood rings that had been such a fad in the sixties and seventies, but the amulets he had discovered in the Aztec ruins didn't detect moods, they revealed sexual history, or the lack thereof. He didn't know how the amulets worked in exact scientific detail, but he did know that the pale amber color was the telltale sign of virginity. If the amulet remained that pale amber color after touching a woman's skin, then her body had never triggered a chemical response due to sexual intercourse, and thus she was still a virgin.

He had tested the amulets on two dozen women. Women who had children were the most obvious ones to test it on. When these women wore the amulet, the color of the stone turned a darker gold, nearly a brown. Ansel had given one to his sister as a gift and the amulet had immediately turned a deep, dark gold when she put it on. Then, he had given one to his twelve year old niece. He was terrified in the few seconds before Shannon put on the amulet, afraid it might change colors, but his fears were quickly allayed as the amulet remained the pale amber color when it touched Shannon's skin.

Lucina flipped a page on the magazine and sipped her coffee. Ansel thought of having sex with Lucina, tried to imagine himself plowing the ugly woman in the missionary position, but that elicited no response from his flaccid member in his pants, not even a slight stirring. Which was all for the better anyway. He needed her to stay a virgin.

Now Brittany Hillson was another thing altogether. Ansel glanced over to her as she stood by the massive windows that looked out on the planes and runways beyond. Her jeans were tightly formed around her rear, shaping her buttocks into two ripe handfuls. She was a most luscious piece of ass and he could easily imagine himself plowing her in any position. He knew it was crude and vulgar to think of her that way, but he couldn't help it. His reaction to her was so stereotypical. The aging professor lusting after his hot student. But luckily he had Marjorie Lords and Heather Canyon in his classes, too. When those two lovely beauties had tried on the amulets, the small stones had turned the deepest gold color he had seen yet. They had been fucked quite a few times already, so he had no problem plowing the hairy fields of those two. They gave him a much needed release so he could keep his focus on the task at hand.

Brittany, though, would still be a dangerous temptation on this trip. How she was still a virgin was beyond him. Just the sight of her bare shoulder was arousing. A beautiful blonde with piercing blue eyes like that barely made it past sixteen with her virginity intact, let alone making it to twenty. But the amulet dangling around Brittany's neck was a pale amber, so Ansel still believed she was pure. Of course, the amulet could be misleading, but Ansel didn't want to go there. The entire objective of this trip depended on the amulets relaying accurate information. All he could do was work with the information given him and do his best. The gods would do the rest.

But his own lust was not the greatest danger to the success of the expedition where Brittany had been concerned. Chris Cartier had been putting the moves on Brittany for the last few weeks, so Ansel had thought of flunking him to get him out of the way, but he knew that could have backfired and made Brittany feel sorry for the kid. Chris was smooth enough to take full advantage of that emotion; just looking at the kid interacting with some of the other girls in the class had told the Professor that much. Instead, Ansel had told Chris his work was lackluster and gave him a huge project to complete if he wanted to pass the class. The kid was still probably trying to finish it. Ansel chuckled at the thought.

Ansel looked up as Staci approached the airport seating area where they awaited their flight.

Staci was the third virgin in the group. She was sporty, athletic, a bit of a hipster. She was a nice looking girl with hazel eyes, a pleasant smile, and shoulder length brown hair that was always elegantly styled even when it was tied up in a bun or corded into a ponytail. She certainly had her share of male admirers. Ansel saw her go out on a few dates, but she didn't really seem that interested in the guys. He sometimes wondered about her sexual preferences. Could a lesbian lose her virginity if she had never had intercourse with a man? Would it make a difference to how the amulet detected virginity? He didn't know. Regardless, the amulet was still a pale amber color as it dangled from Staci's neck, so the gem still classified her as a virgin in that regard.

Ansel rose up to his feet, beaming a smile at Staci. "Hey, Staci."

Staci moved over to him, pulling her carry-on suitcase behind her, its wheels clacking on the tile floor. She leaned up to Ansel and gave him a kiss on the cheek. "Hey, Dad. Let's get this party started."

"You are certain this is the way, Chico?" Ansel asked the guide as he pushed his way past the thick jungle growth before them. Their flight to Mexico had been calm and uneventful. No security official had questioned him about the dagger in his luggage, so Ansel assumed they hadn't even seen it, or if they had they didn't recognize it for what it was. The gods were certainly working in his favor so far. They were now on a very old jungle trail, working their way past the heavy foliage, heading for the ruins, heading for his destiny. How ironic that murky ancient Aztec ruins held the key to a brighter future…

Chico Cordage nodded his head without even looking back. "Yes, Mister Langridge. This is the way." Chico was a small, lean man with deeply tanned, weathered skin. Old acne scars pockmarked his face. A slight stroke he had suffered years ago left the right side of his mouth drooping slightly lower than his left, but he could still speak clearly; the slight physical deformity just gave him an odd, twisted smile.

Ansel frowned at Chico. "I told you, you can just call me Professor," Ansel said. He never got tired of hearing people call him Professor, and reminded everyone at every opportunity that is the way they ought to address him.

"Yes, Professor, this is the way," Chico said.

"Chico knows the jungle," Emerico said from behind Ansel.

Ansel turned to look at Emerico. Chico had unexpectedly brought this other man with him, this young man he called Emerico. Ansel was a bit apprehensive about this new man accompanying them, but Chico assured him that Emerico was a man he could trust. Emerico was a bit taller than Chico, a bit more muscular, quite a few years younger, probably twenty years or more. Chico was probably right. They would need more help when the time came, but Ansel just didn't like the squint that Emerico seemed to have permanently etched into the corners of his eyes. It made him look shifty and devious. Ansel pushed that thought away. Emerico had been pleasant and cordial so far, if not even a little dim-witted, so he knew he was just being overly suspicious. He was so close now and he knew his nerves would just get more rattled the closer they got to their final destination. Emerico nodded reassuringly at Ansel.

"Have you been on this trail before?" Ansel asked Emerico.

Emerico shook his head. "No, but I trust Chico. He knows the way."

Ansel hesitated for just a moment, but then nodded back.

They pushed through another thick wall of leaves and suddenly they were in a small clearing. Chico, of course, had been right. The small stone temple sat quietly at the end of the small clearing, its entrance shadowed, the interior beyond murky and dark.

"Wow," Ansel heard Brittany mutter from behind him.

The walls of the temple were hewn from stone, with Aztec carvings etched into the sides of the temple walls. Vines and foliage grew wildly across the walls, criss-crossing the stone, but the entrance was still clear, as if the temple itself would not allow the jungle growth to penetrate it. Ansel had a gnawing fear that the temple would be overrun with slobbering tourists, or worse yet be crawling with officials from the Mexican government barring his access, but to his relief the temple was exactly the way he had found it. No one else had stumbled across it so deep in the jungle. He had paid Chico handsomely to keep it a secret, but he knew it was only a matter of time before the man talked and the secret would be out. But none of those worries mattered now; he was here and the temple awaited him.

Emerico took a step forward, clearly entranced by the sight of the ancient Aztec temple before him. Ansel quickly grabbed his arm, stopping his movement. Emerico turned to look curiously at him. Ansel shook his head and motioned to the jungle ground just in front of Emerico. The ground was covered with large roots, fallen leaves, and other foliage. The soil beneath was not visible, hidden by all the jungle growth. "Booby traps," Ansel said to him.

Emerico looked down at the ground, then back up to Ansel. A quick flash of nervous fear crossed his face and he took a step back. Ansel released his hold on Emerico's arm. Ansel glanced at Chico, showing their guide a look clearly full of disapproval.

Chico smiled his lopsided smile. "I tell him to be careful on the trail, but he doesn't always listen."

Ansel frowned. He was in no mood now to babysit Chico's companion. He looked around at the group. "Everyone follow Chico. Follow his footsteps exactly. And I mean exactly." Ansel looked at the others one by one, stopping on Emerico. "Everyone understand? Exactly."

They all nodded.

"Lucina, you go first behind Chico, then Emerico. Staci, then Brittany, then me."

"I'll go last, Dad," Staci said. She absently fingered the pale amber amulet dangling around her neck.

"What's the… titty trap?" Emerico asked.

Everyone looked at him, frowning curiously for a moment. Then Staci laughed. "Booby trap," she said, correcting him. "It's called a booby trap."

The others twittered and chuckled. Chico glanced down, shaking his head softly.

Ansel pointed to some nearby trees that lined the right side of the small clearing. "There's a blade secured to one of those trees." Ansel pointed up into the trees just above eye level. "If you look close enough you can see the blade. It's a bit rusted, but it's there." He looked back to the ground, glancing about the clearing. "There's a trigger buried here somewhere, but we're not sure exactly where. If you step on it, we think it will release the blade like a pendulum."

They were all quiet for a moment.

"Ready?" Chico asked.

Ansel nodded at the guide. "Ready."

Chico moved forward, gingerly setting his foot down with each step as he proceeded towards the dark temple doorway ahead of them.

Lucina followed Chico, intently staring at his feet, noting where he stepped and very cautiously adhering to his exact path. Chico stepped over a thick root and continued on. Lucina raised her foot to bring it over the fat root when a bird suddenly darted out of the jungle trees, screeching loudly, its colorful wings fluttering wildly. Lucina started and stumbled, losing her balance. Her knee hit the ground nearby, landing off the trail Chico had been setting with his cautious footsteps.

Everyone froze, listening, only moving their eyes, watching, scanning the surrounding area.

Lucina stared wide eyed at the trees Ansel had pointed out earlier.

Ansel stared at the thick jungle growth as well, fearing any moment the blade would come smashing out of the trees, swinging towards them.

The trees remained quiet, calm, motionless but for the faint swaying of their leaves in the subtle wind.

"Lucina," Ansel said with a quiet, coaxing tone. "Get back up on the path."

Lucina continued to stare at the trees, remaining on her knees off the path.

"Listen," Staci said. She cocked her head, looking

off towards the temple doorway.

"What?" Brittany asked. "What is it?"

"Shhh!" Staci said, waving her hand sharply at Brittany.

"I don't hear anything," Brittany said.

"Because you're fucking talking," Staci snapped, doing her best to keep her own voice down. "Be quiet."

Brittany frowned, but kept quiet.

And then they all heard it, coming from within the temple.

"It sounds like something… grinding," Staci said. "Like a heavy gate opening…"

They waited, listening for more sounds coming from within the dark structure, but soon the temple was quiet once again.

"Chico, help Lucina get back up," Ansel said.

"Yes, Professor," Chico said. He turned and reached down towards Lucina, offering her his hand.

At that moment, a dark shadowy shape appeared in the temple doorway up ahead of them.

"Shit," Staci said.

Ansel looked back at his daughter, then turned back to the temple entrance as he followed her gaze. He stared with growing unease at the lumbering shape pacing in the gloom just inside the temple's threshold. It appeared to be a large jungle cat of some sort, a panther or a jaguar. It paced back and forth, but moved with an odd stumbling gait, not with the typical feline grace jungle cats usually possessed. The jungle cat stopped pacing and faced directly at them. It moved to a crouching position, lowering its body down, and then it shifted its rear slowly, swaying it ever so slightly back and forth. Ansel knew what that small motion meant; the animal was getting ready to attack.

"Chico, Emerico, help Lucina up. Now!" Ansel's loud, demanding voice acted like a trigger, sending Chico, Emerico, and the jungle cat all into action at the same time.

Chico looked away from the charging jungle cat and tugged hard on Lucina's arm, yanking her roughly up to her feet. But Emerico also grabbed one of Lucina's arms and tugged her. The sharp motion caught Lucina off guard and she stumbled again as she tried to right herself, again falling off the path. Her elbow hit the jungle floor, but she didn't hit soft earth; her elbow hit something hard and solid. Something hard like the trigger of a booby trap.

As the animal burst into the sunlight and charged towards them, Ansel could see that it was a jaguar, but unlike any other jaguar he had ever seen. Its skin looked molted, nearly rotted, some of its muscles and tendons showing through the decaying outer layer of fur. Then a glint of sunlight on steel caught the corner of Ansel's eye and he saw motion in the trees to their right. The huge blade was moving, the massive pendulum starting to swing loose. Ansel suddenly felt himself being shoved aside and then saw Staci burst past him as she raced towards Chico, Emerico, and Lucina.

The jaguar guardian sped closer, awkwardly galloping across the jungle floor. Bits of dirt and fallen leaves churned up behind its paws.

Staci reached Chico, Emerico, and Lucina, propelling herself forward, crashing hard into them, throwing her arms wide around all three of them, knocking them all down to the ground just as the jaguar leaped at them — and just as the swinging pendulum blade reached them. The jaguar soared through the air, its claws outstretched, its teeth bared, but missed all four of them as they fell beneath the animal's lunging leap. The pendulum blade missed the four of them as well, but it did not miss the leaping jaguar. The swinging blade sliced clean through the lunging jungle cat, cutting the jaguar clean in half. The top half of the jaguar's body hit the jungle floor to Ansel's right; the bottom half skittered across the ground to his left. There was no blood. He supposed he should have been surprised by that, but he wasn't. The animal was clearly no normal jungle cat. It was some ancient guardian left to protect the temple, its life-force probably fueled by some ancient Aztec ritual. Ansel wasn't certain why the jaguar hadn't appeared the first time he had discovered the temple, but it hadn't. Lucina falling off the path had probably triggered its cage to be opened and thus let the beast loose.

Everyone was quiet for a long moment. The pendulum blade swung back and forth, its momentum slowing, its arc becoming less and less pronounced with each swing, the whooshing sound it made growing fainter and fainter with each pass of the blade. Finally, the curved blade stopped and just hung quietly, blocking the path, with Brittany and Ansel on the far side, and Staci, Lucina, Emerico, and Chico on the side of the blade nearest to the temple entrance.

Ansel stared at the still blade. It was much larger than he had first realized, about six feet high, nearly as tall as he was. It was a bit rusted around the edges, but the smooth metal surface still gleamed and he could see Brittany and himself in its reflection. He glanced upward, following the large chain that held the blade suspended, but lost the end of the heavy links in the thick canopy of branches and foliage above them.

Brittany made a move to go around the six-foot high blade, nearly stepping off the path, but Ansel quickly grabbed at her arm, stopping her. "No," he told her. "Go over it. Not around it." The bottom part of the blade was curved and sharp, but the top part of the blade was flat and smooth where the chain was connected to a thick loop.

Ansel helped Brittany climb over the flat top of the blade, inadvertently getting the two handfuls of Brittany's ass that he not-so-secretly craved. Emerico, Chico, and Staci helped Brittany over the blade and down onto their side of the path. Ansel quickly followed, grunting and groaning with the effort of getting himself over the blade, but he managed and soon found himself standing next to the others.

Emerico stared at the top half of the jaguar that lay unmoving nearby. "Is anybody going to speak about this?" he asked.

No one had anything to say. Ansel fought to catch his breath from the exertion of climbing over the blade.

Emerico continued to stare at the severed half of the jaguar. "Madre de Dios, what the hell is it?"

No one answered.

"Okay, let's keep moving," Ansel said. "Just be careful everybody." He paused. "Oh, and stay on the fucking path."

Chico's twisted lips formed a twisted wry smile, but Ansel could see the guide clearly wasn't really finding anything amusing about this at all. This was supposed to be the easy part. Chico continued forward, and the others cautiously followed in his footsteps as he led them towards the temple doorway.

They reached the opening of the temple without further incident. No one stepped inside yet. They all gathered around the opening, watching, listening, trying to peer into the murky depths beyond the doorway.

Emerico pointed up to a carving just above the doorway's threshold. "What does it say?"

Ansel look expectantly at Staci and Brittany, but neither one answered Emerico's question.

"You should really pay more attention in your old man's class," Ansel said, gently chiding his daughter.

"I know what it says," Lucina said.

Ansel looked at Lucina with complete surprise. He squinted at her. "You know what it says?"

Lucina nodded. "I saw it in a book in the library."

Ansel continued to stare curiously at her. He knew what the Aztec symbols meant, but he was curious to hear what Lucina believed they said.

Lucina returned his gaze. "I don't just dust and stack the books. Sometimes I read them, too. Can you believe it?"

Ansel motioned with his head to the carving above the door as he looked at Lucina. "So what does it say?"

Lucina looked up at the carvings. "Honor Quetzeltoltec with blood."

Ansel looked at Lucina with a measure of new-found respect. "She's right. That's what it says."

They all stared quietly at the carvings above the door.

"The Aztec people believed they owed an eternal blood-debt to the gods," Ansel said. "They wanted to avert disaster by paying this endless debt. So the blood sacrifices were made to appease the gods."

Brittany looked at the abandoned temple around them, the overgrown foliage.

"I know what you are thinking," Ansel said to Brittany.

Brittany looked at him curiously.

"Looks like their blood sacrifices didn't work out very well, right? Otherwise, why is everything in ruins and their civilization gone?" Ansel shook his head. "But they did work. They worked very well. It's only when they stopped believing in the sacrifices that the Aztec empire started to crumble."

The air was cooler just inside the gloomy doorway, the heavy stones blocking the sun's harsh rays, the shadowy interior shielding the temple hallway from the heat. The walls were filled with carvings of ancient Aztec gods and men and women. It was all as Ansel remembered it from his last visit. Nothing seemed to be disturbed.

They stepped deeper into the hallway, their flashlights cutting through the gloom. Their footsteps were soft and muted, slightly echoing against the rocky floor and stone walls.

"Look," Chico said.

They turned to follow the light stream of his

flashlight as he aimed it down a side hallway off the main corridor, seeing what looked like metal bars caught in the end of its beam. It was a cage of some sort. And the cage door was open.

Chico crept closer to the cage, keeping his flashlight beam focused on the cage opening. The others followed closely behind him.

"There's something in there," Staci said. She shined her flashlight deeper into the cage, illuminating part of some skeletal object. She moved slowly closer to the cage opening, her flashlight beam revealing more of the skeletal shape laying huddled in the corner.

"It's a jaguar skeleton," Ansel said. "Another temple guardian."

"How long do you think it's been dead?" Staci asked.

"It's not dead," Emerico said. "It's not dead! It's moving!"

It wasn't moving. It was just the flashlight beams and the shadows playing tricks with Emerico's head. They all entered the cage together, moving under the raised metal-gated door, standing nearly on top of the jaguar skeleton, shining their flashlight beams down on the animal's bones. The skeleton did not move.

But the grinding sound of the cage door closing behind them made them move. It made them move real fast. They scrambled for the cage opening, fumbling over each other in their hurry to get out of the cage before the heavy metal door slid back down into place.

They all stood just outside the closed cage door, everyone breathing heavily, everyone a bit frightened by nearly being trapped inside the cage.

"I don't like this place," Emerico said. He wiped a sheen of nervous sweat off his forehead.

"Come," Chico said. "This way." He looked at Ansel. "Oh, and Professor, please remind everyone to stay on the fucking path. Including me."

They moved cautiously through the corridors, keeping behind Chico, following his lead, being careful to step where he stepped.

They reached a room full of small statuettes and their pace slowed as everyone stared at the ancient carvings, shining their flashlights across them to illuminate them. One statue in particular seemed to dominate the room. It was a winged serpent of some sort, a great beast with a long, sinewy body and a forked tail. What made it especially unsettling and disturbing to look at was the human head that sat atop its serpentine body.

"Don't touch anything," Ansel said. "It may look harmless, but you might trigger a booby trap just by touching it."

Emerico put his hand back down to his side.

They moved on.

They found the sacrificial chamber and moved inside. And then there it was. The sacrificial altar. It looked so plain. It was just a smooth slab of stone set atop another square block of stone, sitting at the far end of the large chamber. They moved closer, shining their flashlights before them.

Ansel reached the altar and shined his light down upon it. There were some dark stains marring the stone and Ansel knew those were ancient blood stains. They were the remnants of ancient Aztec sacrifices to their gods. Narrow grooves carved into the stone ran along the length of the slab, several rows of cuts into the rock visible on either side of the altar slab. Ansel knew these were there to drain the blood into the deep, dark pit that loomed neared the bottom of the slab.

That was the only part of the Aztec legend he did not believe. Ansel didn't believe some magnificent beast was lurking deep in the pit, waiting to be resurrected. The beast portrayed in Aztec carvings and paintings had just been a symbol, a metaphor for the power of the ritual.

Ansel fingered the flint blade in his pocket. It was nearly time. But who? He knew the Aztecs sacrificed, and sometimes even ate, their own children. That was considered the most noble and grandest of sacrifices. But he didn't think he had it in him to put the blade in Staci's chest and cut out his daughter's heart. He mentally shook his head. No, the choice was easy. It would be Lucina. She's the one who needs to die so the cycle can continue. She's the virgin who needs to give her pure blood to the gods.

Ansel turned to face the group, his decision made.

But what he saw changed everything.

Lucina and Brittany stood facing Ansel, their faces stoic, serious. Brittany clutched a flint blade much like the one he carried in his own pocket. Ansel instinctively reached into his pocket, thinking she had somehow pick-pocketed the blade from him, but his dagger was still there inside his pocket. The sacrificial blade Brittany held was not his; it was a different blade. Ansel frowned at them. "What are you doing?"

Suddenly, Staci was behind Ansel, strong-arming his hands behind his back, ruthlessly gripping him tight. His flashlight hit the stone floor and the lens shattered. Ansel tried to shake free of his daughter, but Staci's hold on him was like being gripped in a vise; he couldn't break free. "Staci, what the hell are you doing?" Ansel asked, his stern fatherly tone demanding an answer. "Let me go." He shook his body, again trying to get free of his daughter's grasp.

Staci remained quiet, gripping him tight.

Ansel turned his head towards Chico. "Chico," he said. "Chico, what's going on?"

Chico suddenly gripped Emerico tightly, pinning the man's arms behind his back. Despite Emerico's larger size, Chico was easily holding his own with the man, keeping him tightly wrapped up. The guide said nothing in response to Ansel's pleading question.

Ansel looked at Emerico. The young man looked as confused and befuddled as he felt. He didn't know what was happening either. Ansel looked back to Chico. "What are you doing? Why are you holding Emerico?"

"You are going to eat him," Chico said and smiled his twisted smile.

Ansel couldn't process what Chico had just told him. His words made no sense. He just stared numbly at the eerily grinning guide.

True fear filled Emerico's face and he struggled mightily to get free, but Chico had him in an iron grip and the man could not shake himself free. "No, no," Emerico said, a pleading tone immediately coming into his voice. "No, Papi. No."

"It's time," Lucina said.

Ansel looked at Lucina. Yes, it was time, Ansel thought. Time for *him* to begin the ritual. Had Lucina figured out what he was planning? Had she known all along? Had Emerico just called Chico *Papi*? Emerico was Chico's son? Confusion clouded Ansel's thoughts. He looked at Lucina with bewildered eyes. "Time?" he asked. "Time for what?"

"Time to complete the offering," Lucina said.

Ansel shook his body, but Staci refused to relinquish her tight grip on him. "Don't fight it, Dad," Staci said. "You should feel honored."

Ansel looked up to see dozens of shapes stepping out of the darkness, dozens of people gathering around the sacrificial altar, many of them clutching burning torches that illuminated their faces in an orangish-red glow. Ansel saw some of his mentors move closer. Several university professors. Marjorie Lords and Heather Canyon. Some of the other women he had lain with. Chris Cartier. His sister. And Shannon. Oh my God. Shannon, his twelve year old niece. Ansel shook his body violently, struggling to get free.

Then Ansel felt a chill freezing his body. The history of the Aztecs flashed through his head, exploding like a cyclone through a corn field, whipping memories through his brain. A sacrificial victim was often treated like royalty for one year prior to the sacrificial ceremony. Tutored by priests, given a female entourage and honored with dances and flowers, the victim was the god's manifestation on Earth until that final brutal moment when he met his maker. It was so obvious. He was such a blind fool! The book tours, the professionals he had admired giving him guidance and advice, the invitations to all those lectures, the lavish meals, the money, the women.

Ansel was stunned by the magnitude of the implications. How many people were in on it? Dozens? Hundreds? He had been blinded by his own excesses! He hadn't practiced what his book had preached. He had put his own life in a state of imbalance.

Several of the stronger men gripped Ansel, taking him out of Staci's grasp. Marjorie and Heather stepped up to him and began to undress him. There was nothing sexual about it. They went about removing Ansel's shirt in a business-like manner, then stripped him of his pants.

"Staci, please," Ansel said, his voice a pleading whisper.

The men held him tight, waiting patiently as the young women removed the last shred of his clothing, leaving him completely naked. The men then lifted Ansel up in the air, raising him and turning his body flat so they could set him down atop the stone slab of the altar. "Staci!" Ansel cried. "Don't let them do this!"

"Don't fight it, Dad," Staci said again, her voice surprisingly calm. "You should feel honored you were chosen."

Ansel felt his wrists and ankles being bound. He

bucked his body, but the futile effort did nothing but cause abrasions on his skin as his naked body rubbed against the rough stone. Within moments, he was securely tied down to the altar. He could feel the cold stone of the slab seeping through his skin, chilling him to the very core of his being.

"You taught us well, Professor," Brittany said as she stepped up to the sacrificial altar. "You convinced all of us that the rituals must continue, so it was easy for us to join Lucina."

Ansel frowned. "Lucina…?"

Chris Cartier stepped up next to Brittany and smiled softly down at Ansel. "I didn't have time to complete that project you gave me, but maybe you'll consider giving me some extra credit for this."

Brittany fingered the virgin stone amulet that dangled between her breasts as she stared down at Ansel. "And don't worry, Professor," she said. Ansel swiveled his head dazedly in her direction. Brittany reached over and squeezed Chris's hand. "It'll be changing colors tonight."

Lucina stepped closer to the altar. "Haven't you wondered what happened fifty two years ago?" Lucina asked Ansel. "Haven't you wondered how the ritual was completed the last time it was needed?"

Ansel looked up at her. He had thought about it, but he really didn't have an answer. Someone must have completed the fifty-two-year ritual in the past because the world had not been destroyed; humanity had continued on.

"My family completed it," Lucina told him.

Ansel was struck numb for a moment. He stared blankly at Lucina. "Your family?" he finally asked.

Lucina nodded at Ansel. She held up a sacrificial

dagger, pointing at the Aztec Eagle mosaic on the handle. "That is my family's symbol. We are charged with saving the world. And I take that responsibility very seriously, Professor. But the world is so off-balance now that even greater extremes are needed this time. And that is where your part to play really begins."

"How…" Ansel started to say, but his voice just dropped off. "Staci," he muttered. He glanced around, darting his head this way and that. "Staci. Staci!"

Staci stepped up to the altar. "It's okay, Dad." The beginnings of tears started to form in the corners of her eyes, twinkling and gleaming in the torchlight. She reached down and grabbed his hand, squeezing it tight.

"Staci, please."

The tears started to drip down Staci's cheeks, running down both sides of her face. "It's okay, Dad," she repeated. "It's okay."

Lucina raised the sacrificial blade to Staci's face, putting it gently against her cheek, softly catching a few tears on the edge of the dagger. Others stepped forward, the obvious virgins amongst them, all of them wearing an amulet that still held its pale amber color. Brittany, Shannon, and the other virgins put their daggers gently against Staci's cheek, catching more of her tears, wetting the edges of their blades.

Ansel felt the warm blood dripping down his bare chest, dripping down his shoulders, dripping down his legs. He tried to lift his head to watch the blood flow through the tiny channels in the slab, tried to see *his* blood cascade into the dark pit at the foot of the slab, but he couldn't manage to raise his head off the cold stone. He was finding it hard to breathe and his vision started to swim.

Then a huge rumbling sound came from the pit, a tremendous, thunderous booming noise that seemed to shake the entire temple. Ansel felt the stone slab tremble beneath him.

A massive dark shape rose up out of the pit, its wings beating gently as it glided upwards. The great beast had a serpent-like body, glistening with golden scales. The face of the beast made everyone in the chamber exclaim with excitement. It was a face they all recognized. The creature bore the face of Professor Ansel Langridge.

Ansel stared at his own face as his vision dimmed. He felt an immense flooding of love spread through him. Staci had given him a gift. They all had given him a truly great gift. He turned to looked at his daughter as things around him continue to darken at the edges. "Thank you, Staci. Thank you."

Staci reached out and squeezed his hand.

Ansel smiled even as he felt the last shred of life draining from his human body. It was *his* blood that powered the great beast. He would live again as a servant of the gods. He would swoop down out of the skies and cleanse the world with his fire.

Lucina stepped closer to the sacrificial altar. "It is not virgin blood that gives the gods power." She stared down intently at Ansel. "It is virgins who draw blood who give the gods their power." Lucina stroked Ansel affectionately across his cheek. "It's all in the translation."

No one had to translate the tremendous roar that came out of the beast's mouth when the final sacrificial Aztec knives cut deep into Professor Ansel Langridge's human body. Balance was soon to be restored to the world.

The great beast looked towards the trembling body of Emerico and opened its mouth wide.

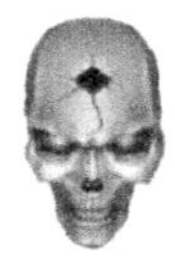

Welcome to the
Land of Fright™
A World of Spine Tingling Stories filled with the Strange, the Eerie, and the Weird
"Step Into Fear!"
Terrorstory
#43
Smog Monsters
A Short Tale of Terror
Jack O'Donnell

TERRORSTORY #43
SMOG MONSTERS

BEIJING — The state-run news media in Beijing announced the first red alert over the capital's unhealthy air quality. Government officials warned residents that the levels of pollution that darkened the skies above northern China this week were dangerously toxic to humans.

It was quite unfortunate for several people that the state-run news media forgot to warn its citizens about what else was in the smog…

Yu Xaing, a 16-year-old student with a love of hot dogs and Pokémon, celebrated when she heard that her school was canceling classes for two days because of air pollution.

But that celebration did not last long.

Yu and her mother sat on the couch in their small apartment, watching the state-run news on their television. Yu was a slender girl, thin arms, thin legs, but already a few inches taller than her mother. Her hair was jet black, cut fashionably with one side short, and the other side flowing over her cheek like the sleek wing of a raven. Yu's school books and her yellow surgical mask were neatly arranged in a stack next to her. She had half a dozen different masks of different colors so she could wear one that matched her mood for the day. Today, she was feeling good and cheerful, and that was even before she had heard the red smog alert warning that had caused her classes to be canceled, so she had plucked her yellow mask out of her drawer.

Shin Xaing, Yu's mother, looked at her with a calm, even face. "No school today." Shin was a petite woman with small lips and a flat nose. She was a serious woman, not prone to smiling, but very prone to keeping her mouth flat and even, betraying no emotion in either direction.

Yu politely nodded her head at her mother, but Yu's own calm face threatened to burst open with the inner smile jubilantly hiding behind the surface. Finally, she would be able to stay up late to watch her favorite Korean soap operas and play computer games with her friends!

But when Yu's laptop beeped at her with incoming messages, she just knew the party was over before it had even started. Yu read the emails and groaned aloud. Her history teacher had assigned 75 pages of reading, including an intricate study of several contrasting Hung dynasties. Her math instructor had assigned them four worksheets. Her English teacher had announced that there would be a three-part exam on Friday when they returned to class.

Yu glanced away from her laptop and looked out the window, staring at the ashen air that clouded the sky from the heavens all the way down to the ground itself. She could barely see more than a dozen yards out the window before everything was obscured by a foggy gray cloud.

Shin reached out and embraced her daughter, pulling Yu into a hug. "At least I don't have to send you out into that filth."

Yu pulled back from the embrace and looked at her mother with a bit of surprise. She felt genuine concern behind her tiny mama's words, and she didn't feel that very often. Yu hugged her mother back.

Not everyone heard or saw the red alert smog warning.

"Papa, it is time for us to depart. I am going to be late for my first class," Chen Xiao said. "I must not be late." Chen was dressed in his school uniform, a blue surgical mask dangling on his chest, held around his neck by a thin rubber band. If there was ever a poster child for a young precocious Chinese boy, Chen was it. He had close-cropped black hair and a round, cherubic face. Patches of acne had already started to form on his ten-year-old face, as if his body was eager to mature much quicker than nature was allowing him to. Black-rimmed glasses, with lenses that were slightly too big for even his wide face, sat atop his nose.

"I'm coming. I'm coming," Jaki Xiao called from another room.

Chen frowned. His father was notoriously disorganized. He glanced out the front window of their apartment. The sky was so dark, so full of thick, dark gray clouds, it made it feel as if the night had never ended. The air pollution was really bad today. He knew he did not even need to check the air quality app he had on his phone; the air condition was obviously poor.

"Okay, let's go," Jaki said as he entered the living room. Jaki was a muscular man, a former boxer, but too many blows to the head had made his brain stop functioning normally. He looked to his young son for help and guidance on nearly everything now as he had difficulty concentrating and making decisions. A white surgical mask dangled around his neck.

"I can walk myself to school," Chen said.

Jaki shook his head. "No, no. I need the exercise."

"I do not want you to get lost coming back home. The smog is very thick today, Papa."

Jaki waved his hand. "I won't get lost. It's only a few blocks."

Chen looked at him for a moment, then nodded. "Okay. Put your mask on, Papa," he said.

Jaki nodded. He pulled the plain white surgical mask up over his mouth and nose.

Chen grabbed his heavy-duty mask and lifted it up to go around his nose and mouth. The front fabric of the mask was emblazoned with a chubby, smiling teddy bear.

And even some of those who heard the red alert chose to ignore it.

Angela Jing stared out the window at the dreary gray sky. It wasn't clouds creating the ashen sky; it was the smog. It was a smog so thick and deadly that the government had declared a red smog alert for the first time ever. A red smog alert. That meant the air itself was dangerously toxic. The very air they all needed to breathe to live! She looked over to her husband and shook her head softly. "You need to stay home today. Stay inside."

Yichen Jing shook his head and set his cup of coffee down. "I have to go into the office. I've got a conference call with the Americans in California. We're going to close the deal today. I have to be there." Yichen was a handsome young man, half Chinese, half Japanese on his mother's side. He was dressed smartly in a three-piece suit, his tie thrown over his shoulder so as to not get stained or soiled as he finished his breakfast.

Angela frowned. "There's a red smog alert. There's never been a red smog alert before. That can only mean the air is really, really bad today."

"I've got my mask. I'll be okay."

She looked at the white surgical mask on the table next to Yichen's breakfast plate. "How do you know it's not one of those fake ones? Zhang said they just caught somebody with over a hundred thousand counterfeit masks."

Yichen glanced at the mask. "It works fine," he said.

"I think you should stay home."

"Angela, I can't." Yichen took a final sip of his coffee and grabbed his mask.

"They cancelled the bus service," Angela said.

"I'll take the car."

"But we've got an even license plate number," Angela said, frowning. "Today's odd. You'll get a ticket."

"The smog's so thick, no one will even be able to see my license plate." Yichen smiled at her and flipped his tie back down into place. "See, the smog is already working to my advantage.

Shin Xaing collapsed in their small kitchen, clutching at her chest.

Yu heard the noise from her bedroom, but didn't really register the sound as being anything important. She was listening to music through her earbuds, absorbed in the chapters she had to read for her English class.

"Yu!"

Her mother shouting her name drew her attention, even through the music pounding in her ears. Her mother never shouted. Ever. Yu pulled out her earbuds and listened.

"Yu," Shin cried out again, but this time her voice was weaker.

Yu leaped off her bed and raced out of her room.

Yichen drove through the smog, absently paying attention to the road before him, his surgical mask dangling down just below his chin. He took a drag on his cigarette and blew the smoke out of the side of his mouth towards the backseat of the car. He thought again about what his doctor had told him at his check up last week. His doctor had prescribed a nature holiday, away from the city, away from the cluster of steel buildings, away from the dirty air. He desperately needed one. Even if he sat in a room wearing virtual reality glasses and looked at a tranquil stream or a quiet forest, that might be good enough to relax him. In his mind's eye, he imagined the scene in the forest. The water bubbled softly as it tumbled over a stretch of rocks that filled the stream. Tall trees filled the area, their leaves a healthy, vibrant green. The air was crisp, clear, clean. A few birds broke the silence with their delicate warbling. Squirrels scurried through the ground cover and made soft noises as their little paws moved through the fallen leaves.

They loomed up right in front of Yichen, as if their bodies materialized within the dense smog out of nowhere. He instinctively jerked on the steering wheel, tugging it savagely to the left as he slammed on the brakes at the same time. The car veered sharply to the left, then stopped abruptly, violently thrusting him forward. His cigarette flew out of his mouth and bounced off the front windshield, showering him with hot sparks. He heard a thud and felt something hit against the side of the car. His seatbelt caught and held, digging savagely into his shoulder as the momentum of the car came to an abrupt stop. Terror filled his thoughts and he hurriedly fumbled at his seatbelt, unbuckling himself, fearing that he had just hit something. He shoved the car door open and raced around the back of the car towards the passenger side.

An even deeper horror clutched at Yichen's throat. He had not struck some thing. He had hit someone. A small body lay in the street, with a larger form hunched over it. Yichen's mask lay about his neck, momentarily forgotten; he usually donned the mask as soon he got out of his car, but he was too frazzled to think about it now. He hurried over to the two figures and stood above them. "Are you okay?" The thick smog swirled around them.

The man, who was Jaki Xiao, looked up over his shoulder at Yichen, his face obscured by his white surgical mask, but said nothing. Jaki looked back down at the young boy laying in the street. Chen's glasses sat askew on his face, but he otherwise appeared unhurt. "You hit my son." Jaki's words came out slightly muffled by the mask, but they were still discernible.

"I didn't see you," Yichen said. "You came out of nowhere."

Chen groaned and rubbed at the back of his head. "There is no such place as nowhere," Chen said from beneath his blue teddy-bear surgical mask. He slowly sat upright and adjusted his glasses.

"Are you okay?" Jaki asked, helping Chen sit up.

"Yes, Papa," Chen said. He looked at the license plate on Yichen's car. "Your license plate has an even number. You are not supposed to be driving today."

Yichen looked at Chen with a frown.

"You must think you are special," Chen said. "Teacher says people who think they are special are wrecking the world for the rest of us."

Yichen moved his lips as if to say something, but then pressed them back together.

"Your vehicle is on fire," Chen stated, his voice flat and matter-of-fact.

"What?" Yichen spun around to look at his car. A small flame flickered from within the car's interior. "Oh shit, my cigarette!"

Then a sound came out of the smog. It sounded like a groan at first, but it wasn't a groan. It was more like a growl. A low, menacing growl.

They all froze, turning their heads in unison towards the disturbing sound coming from within the dirty mist.

"Did you hear that?" Yichen asked, his burning car momentarily forgotten.

Jaki nodded.

Chen stared in the direction of the sound, listening keenly, clearly trying to ascertain the source of the growl.

"What was that?" Yichen asked, turning away from the source of the sound and looking at Jaki.

Jaki didn't answer as he helped Chen back up to his feet. They all stood close together, trying to peer through the dense ashen air, all of them squinting as they struggled to penetrate the thick haze, terrified of the source of the noise but needing to know its origin all the same.

Suddenly, Chen pointed into the distance, into the swirling gray cloud. "There! I saw it."

Yichen and Jaki spun about, looking in the direction of Chen's small pointing finger. "Where? What did you see?" Yichen asked. "Something in the fog?"

"It is not fog," Chen said, his tone clearly corrective and condescending.

"Okay, okay," Yichen said impatiently. "What did you see?"

"Something floating."

"Floating?"

"Or flying," Chen said. "Maybe it was flying. I believe it may have had wings."

"A bird. You saw a bird?" Yichen asked.

Chen shook his head. "I know what birds look like. Had it been a bird, I would have said I saw a bird." His tone was sharp as the words snapped out of his young mouth. "It was not a bird, mister."

"Chen, please," Jaki said, his tone cautioning his young son. "Your manners."

Chen looked at his father, pushing his glasses back up his nose. "I do not know what his name is and he did not introduce himself. I have no other option but to call him mister at this juncture."

Yichen looked at Jaki, giving Chen's father a look that asked *is he really like this?*

Jaki just gave Yichen a slight shrug.

"Papa, we need to run." Chen pointed behind Yichen. And then Chen grabbed Jaki's hand and pulled his father away, forcing the aging ex-boxer into a run to keep up with him.

Yichen turned and looked behind him. The creature was an amorphous blob, a jellyfish-like thing with some kind of thin membrane giving it shape and substance. It did appear to be floating, as if the dense smog was a sea that it could swim in. There was a familiarity to its shape, Yichen realized. It had some resemblance to a cat, a very large cat mixed with a jellyfish. A cat's head with a jellyfish's body. A dozen tendrils dangled down from its body, weaving and squirming in the smog. Yichen just stared, transfixed by the odd creature before him. Nearby, his car continued to burn, the flame inside the vehicle growing larger and brighter, casting an orangish-red glow over Yichen and the creature as it slowly approached him.

And then the creature just split apart, unwinding itself in a double helix shape, separating itself into two distinct creatures. The two newly created halves floated in the smog. A third amorphous blob appeared out of the smog, joining one of the newly separated halves of the first cat-like creature, creating a new merged creature. And then yet another amorphous blob floated into view, joining the other half of the cat-like creature, forming a second new creature.

These two newly created creatures had claws as part of their dangling, jellyfish-like appendages, whereas the first creature Yichen had seen did not. The tendrils dangling from beneath the creatures seemed to have thickened, making Yichen think of octopus arms. Octopus arms with claws on the end of them. Yichen wondered what the claws were for and where they had come from, but he didn't have long to wait before the answer presented itself. One of the creatures struck out at him, one of its dangling arms lashing out, the claws slashing at him like a striking whip, cutting Yichen's cheek, drawing blood. He shrieked and clutched at his wounded face, turning to run after Chen and Jaki as blood oozed through his fingers.

The interior of Yichen's car continued to burn.

Yu looked around frantically for a bus, a vehicle, anything moving, but all she saw was the smog. Her little mama was not doing well. She was not doing well at all. Shin looked very pale, and her breathing was hoarse and ragged. Yu knew she had to get her mama to the clinic, but that was several blocks away. The ambulance crew said they would be there within the hour; a heavy volume of calls was making it impossible to get there any sooner, but Yu didn't think her little mama could wait an hour.

Yu moved down the street, her mother's arm draped over her shoulder.

She heard a loud screeching sound, like tires squealing on pavement, then she heard a thud. She moved towards the sound, carrying Shin along with her as best she could. "Come on, Mama," Yu said. "I hear someone up there. They can give us a ride."

Shin just wheezed.

Chen and Jaki moved quickly through the smog. Visibility was barely more than a few feet in front of them. A streetlight loomed up out of the smog and they nearly collided into it.

Jaki looked back over his shoulder. "What were those things, Chen?" Jaki asked his son.

"I do not know, Papa. I have never seen anything like them in any of my biology books or online."

"Do you still want to go to school?"

"Yes, Papa."

"You are not hurt?"

"No, Papa."

"You are a strong boy, Chen."

Chen paused for a moment to squeeze his father's hand. "Just like my Papa."

Chen and Jaki appeared out of the thick smog, moving quickly towards Yu and Shin.

"My mama needs help!" Yu shouted as they drew closer. She struggled with her mother's weight, fighting to keep Shin upright. "I think she had a heart attack or something."

Chen slowed as he reached Yu. Jaki quickly reached them and slowed as well, stopping next to Chen. Jaki doubled over, clutching at his side, fighting for a breath. The rotten air was clearly taking a toll on his aging body.

"What happened to her?" Chen asked. "Was she attacked?"

Yu frowned deeply at Chen. "Attacked? What are you talking about?"

Yichen appeared out of the fog, running fast, glancing behind him as he moved. The side of his face and neck was streaked with blood. He crashed into Yu and Shin, knocking them both to the ground as he also went tumbling to the ground. Shin grunted as her head hit the pavement hard; the sickening crack of her skull hitting the pavement seemed to reflect off the smog and echo all around them.

Yichen scrambled to his feet. "I'm sorry, I'm sorry." Blood oozed through the fingers on his right hand as he continued to press them against the cuts in his cheek. "We have to keep moving. The damned thing attacked me. They're right behind us."

Chen and Jaki looked apprehensively in the direction Yichen had come from, but did not move. Chen pointed to the mask dangling around Yichen's neck. "You should put that on."

Yichen donned his surgical mask.

Yu crouched over her mother's prone body. "Mama?" Her voice grew louder, more shrill with each questioning call. "Mama? Mama?" She looked up at Chen. "She's not moving. She's not moving!"

"She is dead," Chen said. He adjusted his teddy-bear mask.

The simple declarative sentence came out calmly from the young boy's lips. No one spoke for a moment. They all just stared at Chen and his emotionless eyes.

Yichen finally spoke. "What?"

Chen pointed down at the motionless body of Shin Xaing. "She is dead. She is not blinking and her chest is not moving." Chen looked away from Shin's body, staring back into the smog from whence they had come. "We need to leave this place," he said. "It is not safe here."

"Where should we go, Chen?" Jaki asked.

"There is a fire station one block north. We should go there," Chen said.

"So you are no longer going to school?" Jaki asked.

"Not today, Papa."

Jaki nodded at his son.

Chen started to move off up the block, but Jaki's voice stopped him. "Chen," Jaki said.

Chen stopped and turned back to face his father.

"We cannot just leave them." Jaki motioned to the sobbing Yu crying over the body of her dead mother.

"I fear our lives are at stake, Papa," Chen said. "There is something in the smog that does not belong here. Something very dangerous."

"So is hers," Jaki said.

"I do not know her," Chen said.

"So that is reason enough to leave her here on her own?" Jaki asked.

"Yes," Chen replied without hesitation.

"Have I taught you no compassion?" Jaki asked.

"You taught me how to respect family and how to survive," Chen replied. "She is not family and we need to leave this area if we want to survive."

"You are cold, kid," Yichen said. He moved over to Yu and gently grabbed her arm. "Come on, we need to get out of here."

Yu whipped her head up towards Yichen and snarled at him with a voice full of venom and rage. "You killed her! You killed my mama!"

Yichen let go of her arm quickly as if he had just grabbed the wrong end of a hot fireplace poker. He took a few steps back away from Yu.

"You killed her!" Yu said, the words coming out thick with rage.

"I — I didn't mean to." Yichen pointed towards the smog, motioning with a wild jerk of his arm in the direction of his car, which was no longer visible in the dense, dank air. "I was attacked! I was running away from them. Look at my face!" He pull his mask down with his bloody fingers and turned his face to show her the ripped gouges in his flesh.

"We need to go, Papa," Chen said.

Yichen turned towards Chen, the scowl thick on his lips. "What the hell is wrong with you? We can't just leave her here."

"I am unclear as to the *we* of whom you are speaking," Chen asked. "My father and I are together. We are not with you."

"Are you a little robot, or something?" Yichen asked. "I think I saw you in a video. The Japanese made you, didn't they?"

"Are we not all just little robots?" Chen answered. "Controlled by unknown mechanisms in our brains and our bodies. Subject to their whims."

Yichen's frown deepened. "I don't know who I'm more afraid of. Those creatures out there, or you," Yichen said.

"You should be more afraid of those creatures," Chen said.

"Why?"

Chen pointed over Yichen's shoulder. "Because they are heading right for us."

Yichen glanced over his shoulder and saw four of the smog monsters floating closer.

Two of them were the cat-like creatures that had attacked Yichen earlier. The other two were more rat-like in appearance, but instead of the claws dangling down from their globule blob of a body, they had dozens of tails swishing back and forth beneath them as they floated in the ashen, smog-filled air. They all moved as if they were creatures adrift, floating down a gray-white river.

Yichen turned back to see Chen and Jaki already

moving quickly away. Yichen quickly moved to Yu and grabbed her arm, pulling her away from her dead mother.

"Let go of me!" Yu said, snarling. Her eyes were laced with red, her face smeared with tears. She jerked her shoulder back, trying to get free of Yichen's hold.

Yichen kept a firm grip on her arm. "We have to go," he said.

Yu tugged back, twisting and turning, trying to get free of his grasp.

Yichen glanced up to see another smog monster drifting closer. He could see two fly-like wings jutting out from its sides. It had what looked like huge multi-faceted eyes placed around its bulbous head. This one appeared to have a mouth of some sort and the orifice opened wider as it drew closer to them. He gave Yu another sharp tug, pulling her roughly to her feet, yanking her up and away from her mother.

Yu punched at his chest. "You killed her!"

Yichen knew he should move, knew he should turn and run and just drag the girl with him, but his legs suddenly wouldn't obey him. He found himself in a state of shocked disbelief about what was happening. He didn't even feel the fist of the girl pounding on his chest, didn't hear her screaming at him. His brain felt as foggy as the vile air around them. He looked back at the dead body of the woman on the sidewalk. Had he really killed that woman by running into her and knocking her to the ground? He looked back up at the fly-creature approaching as it floated closer in the smog. The creature stopped and now floated near the dead woman, its wings folded against its body. Then the creature just seemed to split into two parts, separating as if a zipper was being pulled down through the middle of its body. One half of the creature lowered itself toward the woman; the other half floated off.

Was it eating her? No, it was oozing into her. It was moving into the woman's body. And then her eyes weren't empty any more. There was something flickering behind them. She was still alive! It was impossible, but he saw it.

Yichen let go of Yu's arm. "She's alive," Yichen said. "She's alive!" He bolted for Shin, dropping to his knees near her body. He looked at her, not knowing if he should touch her, or leave her where she lay. He held his hands above her, uncertainty freezing his movement. Then, he saw her head shift, saw it turn. She opened her mouth and a horrible wail exploded out of her, a shrill piercing scream as if her death scream was finally released from her body because she didn't have the opportunity to scream before she died. She's alive, Yichen thought and an amazing sense of relief flooded through him. I didn't kill her.

"Mama!" Yu dropped to the street and grabbed at her mother, pulling her body towards her. "Mama!"

Yichen stared at the girl, at the misshapen mass that she clutched desperately in her arms. And then teeth formed on the misshapen mass. Huge teeth. They weren't sharp teeth, but they were very big. They started to move down towards the girl's shoulder like massive clamps ready to take hold. Yichen viciously tugged Yu away from her dead mother. "Run!" he screamed at her.

Yichen and Yu reached the fire station to find Chen, Jaki, and two firefighters inside the building. All four of them were wearing surgical masks over their noses and mouths.

Yu immediately walked up to Chen and slapped him in the face, hard. "That's for leaving me. My name is Yu. Yu Xaing. Now you know me."

Chen slowly raised his hand and put it to his cheek. "Oww," he said after a delayed moment. He straightened his glasses with his other hand.

One of the firefighters moved over to them. "Hey, hey, what's going on here?" His name was Chai JangWei. He was bald, with an old scar running across his forehead that he got when he fell after tripping over a loose fire hose. He told strangers he got the wound when a cross beam fell on his head when he was saving twenty children from a school fire. The other firefighters in the station let him enjoy the fairy tale and always backed up his story. That's just what firefighters did for their fire station brothers.

"Nothing," Yu said to Chai. She looked at Chen. "Just making new friends."

Chen continued to rub at his sore cheek.

The second firefighter stepped back away from the front window of the fire station and moved towards the group. "What's going on out there?" His name was Fang Fengqiao. He was fresh out of training and had only been at this fire station for a few weeks. He was a short young man, but powerfully muscular as his tight-fitting shirt plainly revealed.

"There's some kind of monsters out there," Yichen said.

"Monsters?" Fang asked.

Yichen nodded.

Fang looked to Yu as if for confirmation.

"Yes," Yu said. "We saw them."

"What kind of monsters?" Fang asked.

"Smog monsters," Chen said.

Just then a man in a white lab coat burst into the fire station, shoving the front door open, charging into the room. "You have to help us! They're attacking the lab! They're killing everyone in the lab!" The man's name was Xu Jianpin, but no one was going to find that out since he was going to be dead within minutes.

Chen looked at the symbol emblazoned on the man's white lab coat. It was the DNA double helix with the letters DH stylishly embellished within the double helix. Chen knew what lab the man in the white coat had come from. He had read all about their exploits and experiments online. The man was from a genetic engineering company aptly named Double Helix. Chen knew they were working with CRISPR. CRISPR was a gene-editing tool derived from a bacterial protein that allowed scientists to cut and paste specific portions of DNA. It was a powerful, easy-to-use tool in the science community's quest for new treatments and cures for genetic diseases.

Chen knew Chinese researchers had used nonviable embryos from a fertility clinic to do the first intentional gene editing of DNA in human embryos. The work on human embryos prompted scientific leaders from all over the world to call a summit just last month, bringing together all the top experts to discussed the prospect of altering human sperm, eggs, or early embryos to correct genes that were known to cause specific diseases. It was a potentially frightening, as well as tremendously exciting, prospect to alter the genes of unborn children, and even alter the DNA of their parents sperm and egg before conception even took place. But the ramifications of such power made a lot of people very nervous.

The man in the lab coat waved his arm towards the door. "Come on." He moved towards the door, pushing it open, but no one followed. He looked back into the fire station, looking closer at the firefighters. "Come on! People are getting killed! It's your job to save them! Do your job! Follow me!"

And then the man in the white lab coat was gone. A giant leech-like creature just sucked him up into its pulsating mouth and he was gone. It had loomed up out of the smog like some kind of monstrous stealth fighter, appearing out of the murky haze like an enormous bat with the puckered mouth of a leech.

Chai bolted forward and pulled the door shut, quickly locking it.

Chen looked at the door, at the seams where it joined the frame, the top of the door, the bottom of the door. "Is that door hermetically sealed?" he asked Fang.

Fang squinted at him.

"Is it airtight?" Chen asked.

"I don't know."

"Why?" Jaki asked.

"Because I believe the smog monsters can still get in if there are any gaps between the door and the frame," Chen said.

Chai moved up to Chen. "No, it's not hermetically sealed."

Yichen moved up to Yu. "Tell them what we saw. Tell them what happened to your mother."

Yu shoved Yichen away from her, pushing hard against his chest. "Stay away from me."

Chai moved up to Yu. "You're hitting a lot of people," he said.

"Yeah? I'll hit you, too, if you get anywhere near me." Yu's words came out in a blatant snarling tone.

"You just need to calm down, young lady," Chai said.

"I'm no lady."

Chai held up his hands in a placating gesture. "Okay, okay. What's your name? I'm Chai. Yes, like the tea."

A large smog monster smashed hard into the glass door. The door held, but the glass splintered.

Everyone quickly moved back farther away from the door.

Fang moved up to the group. "Can someone tell me what is going on?" His eyes darted about and a sheen of sweat lined his upper lip. The situation was clearly starting to get to him. He hadn't signed up for anything like this. He looked at Yu. "What happened to your mother?"

"She turned into one of those things," Yichen said.

Yu went after Yichen, shoving him hard again, then pounding her small fists on his chest. "She did not! You shut up!"

Yichen just let her strike him, tilting his head to the side so she didn't whack him in the face, or hit his wounds.

"Easy now, easy." Chai moved over to Yu and

tried to pull her away from Yichen, but Yu quickly yanked her arm out of his grasp. "Don't touch me!"

"I think she needs a glass of warm milk," Chen said. "Do you have any warm milk?"

Yichen and the firefighters looked curiously at Chen.

"It calms him," Jaki said as way of an explanation. "Warm milk calms Chen down when he gets agitated."

"I don't need warm milk," Yu said with disdain. "But I'll take a shot of vodka if you got that. Might as well get toasted since we're all just going to fucking die anyway."

Fang grew more agitated. "Somebody needs to tell me what the fuck is going on."

"We saw one of those things split in half," Yichen said. "It split right down the middle, then half of the thing went after the woman. It went right into her."

"It went into her?" Chai asked.

Yichen nodded. "It just went into her, like it was sliding inside of her." He paused. "And then she screamed."

"You said it split in half? The smog monster split in half?" Chen asked.

Yichen turned to look at him. "Yes. Right down the middle."

Chen turned to Chai. "The Double Helix lab is just around the corner, is it not?"

"Yes, why?"

"I think I know what is happening," Chen said. He instinctively knew Double Helix was somehow involved in the creation of the smog monsters. Some inner voice told him that something had gone wrong in the lab. Terribly wrong.

Fang looked at Chen. "So would you mind clueing us the fuck in?"

"Easy, Fang," Chai said. "He's just a kid."

Yichen laughed. "He just *looks* like a kid."

Chai frowned at Yichen. He looked to Chen. "Tell us what you think."

"Look!" Jaki called out from the front window. "They're doing it now. They're splitting in half."

They all rushed to the window. Except for Yu, who hung back in the interior of the fire station.

Outside in the smog, three creatures floated in the thick ashen air.

"Fuck," Yichen said. "It looks like her. It looks like that kid's mother."

Hearing this, Yu hurried up to the window and stared out at the creature that had a strong resemblance to her mother, except she didn't appear to have human flesh anymore. She seemed to be made of the same substance the other smog monsters were made of. The thin membrane of skin had the shape and appearance of her mother, but it clearly wasn't her mother.

And then Yu screamed a shrill scream as the creature split in two, starting at its head, pulling its face apart, then moving down its body, cleaving itself in two.

Another smog creature nearby, the one with a huge cat-like head, also split itself in two. Half of the Shin creature and half of the cat-head creature moved together, bonding, merging, forming a grotesque hybrid of the two. Creating a new life form.

Chen suddenly realized he knew exactly what he was looking at. They had studied it last month in his biology class. The creature was splitting itself so it could replicate. It was if it were a giant strand of DNA replicating itself, creating more strands of DNA. It was using the necessary components from the smog as if the smog contained the elements it needed to create new life, as if the smog was the RNA it needed to complete the replication process.

But it wasn't creating exact duplicates. It was throwing in changes, mutations, to see if one form better suited it than another. It was force-feeding itself evolutionary changes at a rapid rate, condensing what should takes centuries, even millenniums, to accomplish in a matter of minutes. "This is bad," Chen said, more to himself than to the group.

Yichen looked at Chen with disdain. "You think?"

"What are they doing, Chen?" Jaki asked.

"Evolving," Chen said. "I believe they are trying to find the form which will best help them survive."

Chai looked at Chen. "You asked about the Double Helix lab before. Why? You think they did something?"

"Do you know what they are doing in that lab?" Chen asked.

"I heard they were experimenting on human embryos," Chai said.

Chen nodded. "They are doing much more than just that. They developed CRISPR. It is a technique for splicing genes. They must have had an accident or something. They must have lost their containment. Some form of genetically modified material, perhaps even at the microscopic level, escaped into the air. Maybe even some loose strands of potent DNA even."

"Okay," Chai said, but there was more uncertainty in his voice than understanding.

"You must understand," Chen said. "All DNA wants to do is replicate. That is the sole function of DNA. To live and to replicate." Chen looked outside. "And now the air seems to be full of it. Somehow it is finding fuel, finding energy within the smog, finding some kind of food from the pollutants that is allowing it to grow and replicate. It does not know what shape to take to best facilitate its survival, so it will keep changing, keep evolving until it finds a shape that best suits it."

"That's great, kid," Fang said. "That's all well and good. How do we kill them?"

"I have no idea," Chen said.

"You say they are made of smog?" Chai asked.

"I am not sure what they consist of," Chen said. "But I believe the smog is a component of their structure, yes."

Chai nodded. He looked to Fang. "Water," he said. "We need to blast them with water. We need to disperse the smog particles."

Chen nodded. "Yes. Yes. The water particles will bond with the smog particles and increase their mass."

Fang frowned.

"It's like when the air clears after a heavy rain," Chai said to Fang. "We just need to force it to happen." He pointed to a nearby fire truck. "We've got the water to do it."

"Ready?" Fang asked.

Chai nodded. He clutched a heavy water cannon at his waist with both hands, aiming it towards the fire station garage door. They were in the garage area, standing near the large fire engine that the garage housed.

Fang hit the garage door power button and the heavy metal door slowly started to rise.

"There!" Yichen shouted and pointed. Yichen had a bandage over the cuts on his face now, some red already starting to soak through the cloth.

A hulking smog monster, nearly the size of a car, hovered just outside the fire station garage door on the right.

Chai cranked the switch on the hose and a thick stream of water exploded out of the hose. The water hit the hulking smog monster, but only managed to blow a hole in it the size of the circumference of the water's stream. The smog monster did not seem fazed by the water at all.

Chai moved the hose up and down, left and right, hitting the hulking smog monster all over its body. The streaming water acted like a warm knife cutting through a block of butter, easily cutting the creature up into dozens of parts.

"Yeah!" Yichen shouted at Chai as he continued to slice up the smog monster with the hose's stream.

"Stop!" Chen shouted.

Chai looked at him, frowning.

"Stop," Chen said again. "You need to stop."

"What? Why?"

Chen pointed to some of the severed sections of the smog monster. It was quickly forming up with other severed halves, creating new variations of monsters in the process. The blasting stream of water wasn't killing the creature. It was only helping to speed up the replication process.

"Close the door!" Yichen shouted. "Close the door!"

There were now more than a dozen different variations of smog monsters floating just outside the fire station. One looked like it was two humans spliced together, with half a man's body on the right and half a woman's body on the left. Another one looked like a grotesque combination of a bird and a cockroach. A third looked like a combination of a bird, a cat, a human, and a worm, as if the creature had already replicated several times and had continued to combine different animals into its composition.

Fang hurried over to the fire station control panel and slammed a button with his palm.

The door started to slowly close.

One of the smog monsters managed to get in before the door closed. It was the twisted hybrid of Shin and the cat creature. It had Shin's face but the outline and ears of a cat. It looked as if two human legs had started to form beneath it, the human legs dangling amidst the jellyfish-like appendages, nearly low enough to touch the ground. Its lips moved, opening and closing, as if it were trying to speak, but only gross moaning noises came out of its distorted mouth.

Chen stared with rapt fascination, wondering what kind of final form the creature would settle on. What form would it find most advantageous towards its survival? Was it actually trying to speak?

Yu stared in horror at this thing that sported a

gross distortion of her mother's face. Yu spun towards Yichen. "You did this! You did this to her!" She grabbed Yichen with surprising strength, her rage fueling her muscles, and hurled Yichen towards the monster with her mother's face.

Yichen fought to keep his balance, fought to avoid hitting the Shin-cat monster, but he tripped over his own legs and went down. His flailing hands struck his surgical mask and the bandage on his face, knocking both of them askew, exposing his nose and the raw cuts in his cheek. He fell right into the creature and it looked as if he fell into a thick pillow. The monster's membrane billowed outward as Yichen's weight struck it, but it held together. Some of the tendrils immediately went towards the cuts in Yichen's cheek, sliding right into them. A few more tendrils went into his exposed nostrils, oozing up into his nasal cavity.

The mask still covering his mouth only partially muffled his chilling scream.

"Open the door, Chai!" Fang shouted as he bolted forward with a heavy broom. He pushed at Yichen's body, pushed at the hybrid human-smog monster creature that was starting to form.

Chai only froze for a second, then raced to the control panel to slam the door button.

The door slowly started to clank open.

"You're going to let more in!" Yu shouted.

Fang pushed and poked and prodded at the evolving creature with the heavy broom, successfully shoving it outside the fire station garage.

Chai smacked the door button and the door slowly closed.

Fang stood breathing heavily near the door, leaning on the broom, fighting to catch his breath.

Chen turned to stare at Yu. He had never seen a real-life murderer before. He did not notice the two small smog monsters floating low to the ground behind him, moving slowly towards him. They had come in through the fire station's front entrance, oozing under the doorframe.

But Jaki noticed them. "Chen, look out!" Jaki grabbed at a thick water hose nearby and flipped on the nozzle. The heavy force of the stream of water jetting out of the nozzle caught Jaki off guard, nearly knocking him down.

The spray hit the floor of the fire station, then hit Chen in the back of his legs, sweeping him off his feet. Chen hit the cement floor of the fire station with a heavy grunt.

Jaki wrestled with the wild hose. The force of the water thrust the end of the hose upward, sending the water spraying into the ceiling.

The water burst across the ceiling, then came down in a light drizzle over them.

Jaki fought to get the writhing hose under control, bringing the stream back down to blast at the smog monsters near his son. The spearing water just went right through one of the smog monster as it had done before, splitting it into numerous smaller creatures.

"Wait!" Chen shouted. He was still laying on the floor, staring at something near him. "Papa, point it back up at the ceiling."

Jaki turned to his son.

Chen pointed at the ceiling. "Up. Shoot the water up!"

Jaki did as his son instructed, tilting the nozzle up towards the ceiling, sending the water slamming into the ceiling high above.

Chen stared at the sight before him. The misty spray that had fallen from the ceiling had acted like a heavy blanket, covering one of the smog monsters, pushing it down to the floor, flattening it along the concrete, smothering it, dissolving it. He remembered seeing the massive water trucks spraying the air a few weeks ago when there had been a yellow alert issued because of the smog. The smog hadn't been as dense as it was today, but it had still been thick, still that same ashen-gray color. Chen remembered the water men spraying a mist into the fog, not a heavy stream. A fine mist. The water had helped disperse the fog by pulling the pollutants down out of the air. That was it. They didn't need to blast them with water cannons. They needed to smother them.

"Keep going, Papa," Chen said to his father. "Look, it is dissipating them." He pointed to the small smog monsters near him. They seemed paralyzed by the light shower of moisture falling on them. "The water mist is smothering them."

They were so absorbed in watching the smog monster dissolve that they didn't notice another small smog monster drifting towards them from the inner fire station. It was out of reach of the falling misty spray of water, so it easily floated towards them.

Chen saw its movement out of the corner of his eye and shouted in alarm. "Look out!"

Fang, feeling a presence right behind him, turned to see what Chen was looking at. The small smog creature moved straight into Fang's mouth and he immediately started to choke.

"Papa! Here!" Chen raced to his father and grabbed at the hose, urging his father to aim the stream towards Fang.

Jaki followed Chen's urging, swinging the hose towards Fang.

Fang gasped and clutched at his throat, continuing to make awful choking noises.

"Down his throat! Hurry!" Chen urged.

Jaki directed the heavy spray of water straight at Fang's face.

The force of the water knocked Fang's head back, but a heavy dose of water got into his mouth. Fang lifted his head back to face the water, letting the water power into his mouth. After a moment, he fell to his knees, coughing and gasping. He gurgled, then regurgitated up a blob of ashen-gray substance. He crawled backwards away from it, coughing and gasping, wiping at his lips. "I could feel it," Fang gasped. "I could feel it try to crawl inside me." He staggered to his feet and moved to the creature, stomping on it angrily again and again. The globule split into three chunks under Fang's incensed stomping.

"No!" Chen raced forward and pushed Fang back away from the crushed blobs on the floor. "You are going to spread it!"

Fang angrily wiped the back of his hand across his lips, spitting out more of the wretched taste in his mouth. He stared heatedly at the ashen-gray blobs on the floor, but he did not try to stomp on them again.

"Papa, just spray over it. Do not spray directly at it," Chen said.

Jaki nodded. He directed the spray to strike the ceiling above the smog monsters, creating a light spray that fell over the creatures.

Soon, the creatures were smothered, flattened, dissolved, gone.

"You killed that man," Chen said to Yu.

Yu immediately shook her head. "No I didn't. Those monsters did."

"You pushed him into them."

"Look, it's raining." Fang pointed out the large window and jumped from foot to foot, doing a happy dance. His face beamed with a huge smile. "It's raining."

Chen turned away from Yu and looked out into the smog. Fang was right. It was raining. A light drizzle fell down from the sky. Chen wondered if Mother Nature had decided the smog monsters didn't belong here and had sent the rain down to annihilate them. Such a notion was absurd, of course, but the thought still entered his head.

He saw one of the larger smog monsters, the one the size of a car, sinking down towards the ground as the rain began to weigh it down. The creature touched the ground, then started to flatten out as the rain blanket continued to smother it. Soon, the smog monster was gone, leaving no trace that it had even existed.

Chen turned back to look at Yu, but she was gone. He quickly glanced around the fire station, but she was no longer there. He caught movement out of the corner of his eye and turned back to look outside. He caught a fleeting glimpse of a shape running around the corner of a building. He was pretty certain it was Yu, but he wasn't totally positive. Yu Xaing. That's what she said her name was. He knew he should report her to the police.

Jaki came up to Chen and put his hand on his son's shoulder. "She will have to live with what she did for the rest of her life. I think that will be punishment enough."

Chen pushed his glasses back into place and looked up at his father, but said nothing. He thought about what had happened to Fang. What if he inhaled one of the creatures? What if they could get into his lungs? Would they replicate inside of him? Would they begin to feed on him, working their way through his internal organs on their way out of his body? He instinctively shut his mouth and held his breath, but within a matter of several seconds, he knew not breathing was not an option. He took in small, controlled amounts of air, afraid of breathing too deep. Maybe they were already inside him. He forced that thought away. That would just lead him down a road to paralysis and madness.

Out of the corner of his eye, Chen thought he saw more movement. A blurry shape floating and slithering in the air. But when he turned to look, he saw nothing. He knew life would find a way. It would adapt to survive. Life wanted more life. That was its only purpose: to make more of itself. These new creatures had tasted life and he knew they were not about to just give up.

Chen sat on the park bench, absently eating his peanut butter and jelly sandwich. He really liked the spicy peppermint jelly Papa had made him try; it made his mouth tingle. He absently watched a few stalks of grass on the ground nearby sway gently in the wind.

The wide swath of grass had a sickly color to it, an ashen color to its tips, most likely caused by Beijing's chronically foul air. Then Chen looked closer at the grass as a disturbing realization came over him. The grass was swaying with a wider movement now, the wind making the tips of the stalks wriggle like thousands of tiny snakes. But the true horror hit him when he realized there was no wind blowing. No wind blowing at all.

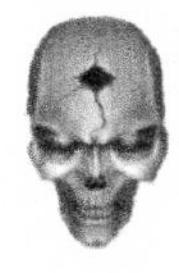

Welcome to the
Land of Fright™
A World of Spine Tingling Stories Filled with the Strange, the Eerie, and the Weird
'Step Into Fear!'
Terrorstory
#44
OB
eBooks
Benders of Space-Time
A Short Tale of Terror
Jack O'Donnell

TERRORSTORY #44
BENDERS OF SPACE-TIME

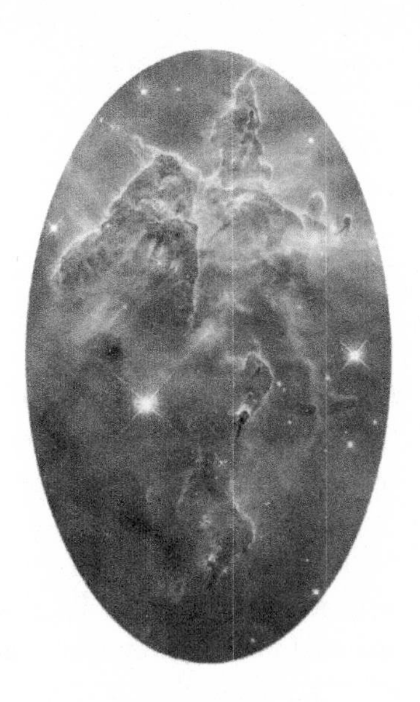

"We can't go down there," Shahree said. She was a soft spoken girl of twelve, with pretty blue eyes and flowing blonde hair. She was timid, prone to bouts of fright over inconsequential things and minor events, except what Ruskurt was proposing was not an inconsequential thing, nor a minor event at all. It was downright lunacy. Even openly rebellious. She didn't have the temperament for rebellion.

"Why not?" Ruskurt asked. He was her age, taller,

much more sure of himself. He shared the same color of blue eyes, but his hair was more of a sandy brown, cut short, well out of his eyes.

Shahree looked at Ruskurt as the frown on her lips spread across her face to tighten the edges of her eyes and draw squint lines on her forehead. Did she really need to tell him the obvious? "That's the deep down. We're not allowed to go down there."

"Who says?"

"Everyone. All the grown-talls."

"You do everything the grown-talls tell you?" Ruskurt asked.

She looked at him, aghast. "Of course. We are ignos. They are grown-talls. Their word is law."

"Their words are just words."

She looked at him with concern, and a hint of gnawing fear. She was having a hard time believing he was actually saying what he was saying. "You need sleep, Ruskurt."

He shook his head. "Sleep is the last thing I need. I need to go into the deep down and see what's there. I can't sleep because I keep thinking about it."

His eyes had an intensity that made them shimmer and Shahree didn't have the strength to hold his stare. He was making her nervous, very nervous. "Come on, let's go play table ball. You need to get rid of some of that energy. Maybe you should run around the med lab twenty times. I remember your mother used to make you do that when you were driving her crazy." She grinned at him.

He didn't grin back. He shook his head. "I want to go down."

She shook her head back at him. "You can't. There's no way down there except through the access elevator, and we don't have the permission. Not even all the grown-talls have permission to use it. *Most* of the grown-talls don't have permission."

"I found another way," Ruskurt said. The shimmer in his eyes changed to a twinkle. A sly, knowing twinkle. A dangerous twinkle.

Shahree just stared at him.

"There's a power conduit in corridor seven. The grown-talls can't fit in there, but we can."

"How do you know?"

"Because I already went in there."

Shahree didn't think her eyes could go as wide as they did, but she felt as if they spread out completely from one side of her head to the other. "You already went to the deep down?"

Ruskurt shook his head. "No. I —" He looked away from her. "I was too scared." He straightened up tall and raised his head. "But I'm not afraid any more. I'm ready to go down." He looked at her face and she felt as if his eyes were magnets pulling her gaze to stay locked on his. "Come with me," he said.

"No," she said immediately. "No! And you can't go down there, either."

"I'm going."

"Why? Why are you acting like a mad fool?"

"I have to know, Shahree," he said. "Haven't you ever felt that way? That you can't stop, you can't rest, until you find the answer to a question that refuses to leave your head?"

"I think you need a day in Tranquility Bay." She looked at him hard. "A day? No, you need a week. A week of rest and relaxation and warm light and soothing music. I'm sure if you explain to the captain how you are feeling, he would grant your request. I'll even vouch for you that you've got a case of the crazies."

Again, he did not return her grin. "No," he said. "I'm going. I'm going now." He stared hard at her. "Are you with me or not?" He held out his hand toward her.

She looked at his outstretched hand, his open palm, but she did not take it.

Ruskurt let his hand linger for a moment before her, then pulled it back. Without another word, he turned and headed away from her.

It was a tight fit, but he managed to make the turn. Ruskurt nearly scraped a layer of his flesh off, but he managed to squeeze past the protruding cluster of tubes and wires. The power cables that ran the length of the starship radiated some intense heat in certain places and he had to stop more than once to wipe sweat off his brow and away from his eyes. His clothes were damp with perspiration.

Why the obsession with the deep down? Ruskurt kept asking himself over and over. He couldn't really say for sure. He just had to know. It was as simple as that. He had to know. It was there and he had to see it. There were too many stories being told, too many rumors, too many lies. He knew the grown-talls told lies. They weren't supposed to, but he knew they did. He wanted to find the truth behind all the stories. And he knew he would only find that truth in the deep down itself.

He both loved and hated Gordin at the same time. If the grown-tall hadn't told him things, hadn't made him try things, he would still be ignorant, blissfully ignorant, of all that was really happening around him on the starship. He'd still be happy viewing the world through his AR lenses, taking his virtual vacations, eating his food pills. But no, Gordin convinced him to take his lenses out, to see the world as it really was. The old Technician always said he regretted helping turn the world into what it was now. Ruskurt thought about Gordin and a wave of sadness washed over him; the old man had died in a freak accident a few weeks ago when a maintenance robot had inadvertently crushed him somehow, and Ruskurt didn't realize how much he had enjoyed Gordin's company until he was gone.

He thought about what Gordin had revealed to him. The ship's walls were not pristine and clean. They were dirty, grimy, beat up slabs of steel. The Augmented Reality projectors created the illusion of cleanliness. The AR lenses altered what everyone saw. He remembered laughing the first time he saw Gordin's shirt. It had the letters AR crossed out with a big red slash through it and the words Just Say No To AR written beneath it. Everyone thought Gordin had just been a crazy old man (nearly two hundred and twelve years old supposedly), but Ruskurt had found his stories absolutely captivating. They were far more entertaining than any holo-shows the Actors were performing lately.

Ruskurt remembered the first meal he ate without his AR lenses in place. It was just a grayish slab of some kind of processed nutrients. With the AR lenses in, it would have looked like a slab of juicy ribeye steak. He supposed it still tasted like a steak when he tried it, but it certainly didn't seem as scrumptious as he had remembered.

He felt sorry for some of the just-borns. All of them had their AR lenses permanently attached to their eyes. They would never see the world as it truly was; the lenses were designed to grow in their eyes as their bodies grew so there was never a need to take them out. His generation was one of the last where the AR lenses were manually inserted into the eyes, like contact lenses in the far-gone days. Sure, he could have gone in for the surgery and had his AR lenses permanently put in place, just like nearly all of his classmates had done, but he had a phobia about anyone cutting at his eyes or sticking needles in them, so he stayed with the old ways. The AR lenses only needed to be replaced once every few years, so it really wasn't that much of a hassle. He wasn't wearing them now, so he was seeing the world truly as it really was. He wanted to see the deep down in all its true glory, not some augmented reality version of it.

Boy, am I thirsty, he thought as he nibbled on a food bar. He had brought several food bars with him, and several water tubes which he had finished off what seemed like hours and hours ago. And I really need to go. He fought back the urge to urinate, squeezing himself tight between his legs, trying to pinch off the pressure.

Ruskurt lost track of how long he had been descending. Had it been hours, half a day? He couldn't tell. He felt like he had been descending for days. He lost track of time. The conduit was dark, nearly pitch black; every once in a while he came across a glowing cable that gave him a brief respite from the sheer darkness that enveloped him. The uncomfortable feeling in his groin grew stronger, becoming almost painful.

He continued his descent. And then he saw it. Finally. A level platform. Was that the bottom? Was he in the deep down? Had he actually arrived at the destination that he had been obsessing about for months?

He reached the platform and stepped onto it. He could see a wide open expanse at the end of the platform, half a dozen yards before him. A very faint light was visible, coming from far below. He moved closer to the edge of the platform, slowly, taking one tentative step at a time. It was very quiet down here, with nothing more than a faint hum discernible. He felt like he was moving towards the edge of a massive cliff; he slowed his steps as he neared the edge, practically just sliding his feet forward. If the stories he had heard were true, the quietness and soft lights made sense. The Benders were said to be very susceptible to loud noises and very bright lights because they supposedly had come into being in the dark and quiet outer reaches of space.

Finally, he had to relent to the intense pressure in his groin and he pulled his penis out of his pants. He urinated into the vast expanse, hoping he didn't electrocute himself by shorting something out. He heard his pee falling down into the darkness but wasn't sure where it would eventually end up. Ha, I'm pissing into the deep down! He felt guilty about what he was doing, but boy did it feel good to go! He thought he was going to burst like an overinflated balloon, except it wouldn't have been just air and rubber spreading everywhere, it would have been piss and penis flesh. He should've worn an EVA suit. He could have recycled his own urine to drink, but it was too late for that now. Besides, the suit wouldn't have fit in the conduit and it was far too bulky to maneuver in the tight spaces he had to contort his body through.

What Ruskurt saw next in the deep down filled him with awe. He stood there with his penis in his hand, just staring.

"I told him not to go," Shahree said. She wiped away a tear from her cheek, brushing her blonde hair away from her face. She felt guilty going to Captain Gevoso, but she knew Ruskurt needed help. He wasn't right in his head. It would have done Ruskurt a grave injustice not to tell the captain what he was doing.

"Where is he now?" Captain Gevoso asked. He was a big man, commanding in presence, his jaw square and strong. He was just like the powerful captains from the holo-movies she loved. Shahree felt very nervous and very safe in his presence all at the same time.

"I think he's there," she said. "In the deep down."

"How long ago did he start?"

"I don't know. Half a day." She looked up at the captain. "I know I should have come to you earlier, but I didn't know what to do. I didn't want to betray Ruskurt's trust in me."

Captain Gevoso reached out and gave her shoulder a gentle squeeze. "You did the right thing, Shahree. You have to believe that."

"Is he… is he in danger?"

The captain withdrew his hand and leaned back.

He glanced out of the small window port in his command office that was situated behind his desk. He was quiet for a moment, staring at the mesmerizing display of lights and textures and colors that made up the bend zones which gave humans the ability to travel quickly amongst the stars and colonize dozens of worlds. "If what you tell me about this boy is true, then we are all in danger."

It was beautiful. That wasn't a word Ruskurt used lightly, or used often. The creature was a marvel to behold as it rose higher out of the deep depths. It was a mass of shimmering light, pleasing to the eye. Not a garish rainbow of color, but more of a soft pastel hue. It had myriad points of light positioned about its body. Not bright, blinding light, but soft glimmering light. There was movement within the creature, as if it had a transparent membrane for flesh, allowing visibility into its innards. Swirls of liquid, or air, he couldn't tell, moved about inside the creature, as if it had gossamer wings beating softly within it. He felt as if he were looking at a miniature swirling galaxy inside the creature, as if parts of the universe were bound inside it.

There was a soft hissing sound coming from the creature, almost a flat hum. Ruskurt knew the sound. They had heard it several times in class during their studies of the cosmos. It was originally thought to be the sound of the Big Bang, the sound of the universe being born so many billions of years ago. But now he realized the sound was something else. It was coming from this creature. But the universe was filled with that sound. Did that mean the universe was filled with these creatures? Was that the sound of their breathing?

He fumbled with himself, stuffing his penis back into his pants. He leaned closer to the edge of the platform, looking, listening, letting his senses absorb everything they could from this alien entity that lived in the bottom of their starship. Was the creature some kind of star-creature? Was this really a Bender? It had to be. So the stories Gordin had told him *were* true. The Benders did exist. And they most likely provided the fuel for galactic travel for their starships, just as Gordin had said. How did it work? How did this creature help them travel amongst the stars? Where did it get its energy? How the heck did it eat? What did it eat? Was it actually alive?

Ruskurt had an absurd thought as he watched the motion inside the creature, watching objects swirl and rotate within it. What if he was looking at an actual galaxy? What if those were solar systems and stars and planets within a galaxy? What if they lived inside a Bender in a similar way? What if they were just part of some massive creature's guts?

He stared at the swirling clouds of color, the lights, the tiny orbs floating inside the entity. Is that how the Benders folded space-time? Is that how they bent one part of space to touch another so space travel between incredibly distant points was possible? By undulating their bodies? He wasn't sure. But clearly that had something to do with their God-like abilities.

Then Ruskurt heard a different sound coming from the direction of the creature, a sound trying to break through the monotonous hiss. It was very faint at first, but he could sense it was a different type of sound. Was it trying to communicate with him? He looked around the length of the creature, looking for some kind of orifice, some kind of mouth, trying to pinpoint the source of the sound, but he saw none.

The sound became more distinct, louder. And then he could clearly discern the sound. And it was a sound that sent a cold chill crawling up his spine. It was the sound of language. The small voice called to him. He couldn't tell if the voice was coming from somewhere in the vast expanse, or if it was somehow being projected into his head. Whatever the source of the sound, it was the sound of words being spoken. The same two words over and over again. There was no hiding the pleading tone in its words. Ruskurt could feel the despair coming from the Bender. It was supposed to be God-like, but this one didn't act God-like; it was scared. God wouldn't allow himself to be trapped like this Bender was trapped. It was trapped and afraid. It was only two words, but they rang in his head with the thundering sound of a gong being struck.

"Help me."

And he had just pissed on it.

Ruskurt did what any rational boy confronted by an alien entity in a place he was forbidden to be in would do; he ran. He ran like hell, and then he climbed and climbed. It may have taken him hours and hours to climb down into the deep down, but it only took him a fraction of the time to climb up and out.

They were waiting for Ruskurt when he exited the conduit. Captain Gevoso did not look pleased to see him, not pleased at all. Ruskurt's father was there, also not looking very happy to see him. And so was Counselor Pirca. Ruskurt knew what that meant; endless boring sessions talking about his feelings. They all continued to frown at him as he finished clambering out of the narrow opening and rose up to stand before them. Shahree wasn't there, but Ruskurt knew she had squealed on him. He was disappointed in her. He knew that was the end of their friendship. He could never trust her again.

They permanently sealed the access hatch the moment after he climbed out. Two maintenance robots were there, waiting with a metal plate and torches. They quickly welded the plate over the opening, and drilled in a few rivets to finish off the seal.

"Tell me what else you saw, Ruskurt," Counselor Pirca said. Pirca was a gentle-looking man with a cherubic face and a weak chin. He didn't have much of a neck and what did show was covered in a thick beard. It was the latest fad amongst the men to grow a beard on their necks but leave their face clean-shaven. Ruskurt assumed the man did it to make himself feel part of the group. He thought it looked rather silly.

"It had beautiful wings," Ruskurt said. "Huge beautiful wings inside of it. It kept… folding them and unfolding them. Like it was trying to fly but not really fly." Ruskurt paused. "It's hard to explain."

Pirca nodded. "It's okay. You are doing fine."

Ruskurt nodded, but said nothing more. The burning embarrassment he felt for urinating on the Bender troubled him, but he kept that to himself.

"And where did you see this — being? This thing with wings?" Pirca asked.

"Deep down," Ruskurt answered. "In the deep down at the bottom of the ship."

"What were you doing in the deep down?" Pirca asked.

"I told him never to go down there." Travain looked disapprovingly at Ruskurt. "But whenever I tell him not to do something, he has a compulsion to go and do it."

Pirca held up his hand at Travain. "Please. Let your son continue."

Travain opened his mouth to speak, but then pressed his lips together, remaining silent.

Pirca looked at Ruskurt, prompting him to continue with a slight cock to his head and a slight waving of his fingers.

Ruskurt remained quiet.

"Is that why you went into the deep down? Because your father told you not to?" Pirca asked.

Ruskurt stared at the floor for a moment. A soft shrug rolled off his shoulders. "I just wanted to see what was down there."

"And did you see what you wanted to see?" Pirca asked.

"I think I saw a Bender," Ruskurt said. "I think that's what it was."

"A Bender? Really?" Pirca looked over at Ruskurt's father, who was sitting in the chair next to his son. Travain said nothing. He fidgeted in his chair slightly, readjusting his position. Pirca looked back at Ruskurt. "And what exactly is a Bender?"

Travain reacted to that question with a grunt. "Counselor, please. He's been down to the deep down. He saw what's down there. The children hear things. They know more than we give them credit for."

"Yes, yes, of course," Pirca said. He leaned back in his chair, looking at Ruskurt quietly for a moment. He leaned forward, casually reaching for his cup that was sitting on his desk. "So what did you think of it?" He took a drink of his coffee.

"It was beautiful!" Ruskurt said, then immediately felt foolish at how quickly his excited answer had gushed out of him.

Pirca smiled and nodded. "So I've heard."

Ruskurt looked at him. "You've never seen one?"

"No, can't say that I have." Pirca took another sip and set his cup down.

"I haven't either," Travain said.

"And do you know what it does? This Bender?" Pirca asked of Ruskurt.

"It powers the ship," Ruskurt said. "Benders can fold space-time and bring two points together so we can travel quickly across solar systems."

Pirca corrected him. "Not just solar systems. Entire galaxies."

Ruskurt looked sheepish.

"You have seen an interstellar map of the reach of humanity in your classes?" Pirca asked.

"Yes," Ruskurt said.

"He has one at home," Travain said. "It's a holo-display. It takes up the entire room. You can stand in the middle of it and pretend you are looking out from

Mother Earth. The colonies stretch on for as far as your eyes can see. They—"

The counselor looked disapprovingly at Travain. "Allow Ruskurt to speak."

Travain closed his mouth.

Counselor Pirca looked at Ruskurt. "Have you been to the Liquid Nitrogen Falls on Einstein?"

"Yes."

"We took him—" Travain began, but one look from the counselor made Travain close his mouth again.

"And the Kepler Crystal Plains on Aldomere?"

"Yes," Ruskurt said.

Pirca nodded. "Beautiful, aren't they?" He paused for a moment, but didn't really give Ruskurt a chance to answer that question. "Do you know how many human colonies there are now?"

"Five hundred and twenty seven. Praxis Colony on Maldair will make five hundred and twenty eight.

"Very good." Pirca nods. "And do you know how many human beings are now alive?"

"Five hundred and twenty eight times two billion on average," Ruskurt said and shrugged. "Something like that. Probably more."

"And you know that they are all interdependent on each other for various things, such as oxygen, food, fuel, building materials?"

"Of course."

"And how would we move amongst the colonies without our ships?"

Ruskurt shrugged. "I don't know."

"I know," Pirca said. "The answer is we would not be able to. Five hundred and twenty eight worlds would be isolated just as Mother Earth was isolated in the pre-GT days. There would be no Galaxy Travel. And without the Benders there would be no way to cross such distances in the short amount of time we need to cross them."

Ruskurt was thoughtful for a moment, then looked at the counselor. "Do they have families?"

Pirca squinted at him. "Who?"

"The Benders," Ruskurt replied. "Do the Benders have families?"

Pirca was quiet for a moment before he answered. "We don't know."

"How do they make more Benders?"

"We don't know," Pirca said again.

"What if a Bender dies? How do you get a new one?"

"They don't die."

"What if they did?" Ruskurt asked.

"They don't die."

"What if they did?"

"Ruskurt," Travain said, his tone cautionary, becoming stern.

Pirca held up his hand, silencing Travain. "It's okay." He looked at Ruskurt. "I have a question for you."

Ruskurt waited for him to continue.

"What if the sun warming Mother Earth went out?" Pirca asked.

"The sun isn't going to go out," Travain said with a scoff.

Counselor Pirca looked at Travain, making no effort to hide his extreme annoyance. "It will eventually. It may take a billion years, but one day it *will* go out. But that is something we don't need to worry about." He turned to looked at Ruskurt. "And so it is with the Benders. Maybe one day they will die, but that day is so far into the distant future as to be incomprehensible to us."

They sat in silence for a moment. Pirca sipped on his coffee.

"I wish I hadn't gotten so scared," Ruskurt said, just suddenly blurting it out. "I should have stayed with it longer. I wish I hadn't run away. Oh, you should see it. It was—beautiful!" He didn't care this time about how it sounded. It was the truth. The Bender had been beautiful. It had been the most beautiful thing he had ever seen.

The two men laughed at his enthusiasm.

"Why *did* you run away?" Pirca asked, his face smiling, the laughter still present behind his question.

"It spoke to me," Ruskurt said.

The laughter stopped as abruptly as a light switch being flicked off turned a room into darkness.

"Benders don't speak," Travain said.

"Your son just said it did," Pirca said.

"Benders don't speak," Travain said again.

"Ruskurt is a bit rebellious, "Pirca said, "but he does not strike me as a liar."

Travain shook his head. "Benders don't speak. He just imagined it."

Ruskurt shook his head. "I didn't imagine it. I heard it talk to me. It wanted me to help it."

"It wanted you to help it? The Bender asked for help?" The tone in Pirca's voice was a level above incredulous.

Ruskurt nodded. "I don't think it wants to be a Bender anymore. I think it wants to be free to fly amongst the stars like it used to. Shouldn't we let it go free if it wants to be free?"

Pirca and Travain looked at Ruskurt, both men clearly absorbing the boy's words. Pirca looked at Ruskurt with a level of seriousness he had not shown up to this point in their session. "What do you feel, Ruskurt? What do you feel right now?" the counselor asked.

Ruskurt lifted his head to look at the counselor and Pirca didn't think he had ever seen a more troubled face in his life. "I feel shame," Ruskurt said. He rose up out his chair, his face flush with agitation. "It was scared and I peed on it! I feel ashamed for all of us!" He turned and bolted out of the room, letting the tears come streaming down out of his eyes.

"You are condemning him?" Travain asked. "We can medicate him," he said, offering the most obvious solution. "Put him in cryo for the rest of the trip."

Pirca shook his head. "He'd have to stay frozen in cryo for the rest of eternity. There is no point to it." The two men sat in the counselor's room, pondering what Ruskurt had just told them. "Nothing works on this. Others have tried in the past, but nothing keeps that feeling back once it takes hold." He looked at Travain with a solemn face. "It always breaks through. This cannot spread. It must be contained. Can you imagine—" Pirca stopped himself. "We're talking the end of galactic civilization as we know it."

"Surely you exaggerate," Travain said. "Yes, it's important to stop it from spreading, but the end of civilization? Really now."

Pirca looked at Travain. "Think about it. Think about it long and hard. Think about what it would mean to all of us. To every colony on every planet. There can be no shame aboard this ship. Or any other ship. Without the Benders, we will all be mud sniffers again. Do you want that?"

"Of course not. Ruskurt knows that. Without the Benders, we wouldn't be able to get back to see his mother," Travain said. "It would take centuries to get back to her. She would be dead before we ever reached Burroughs. Do you think Ruskurt wants that to happen?"

Pirca looked at Travain, but said nothing. "We cannot wish this away. This must be struck down swiftly and severely before it becomes a plague that infects us all."

"How did it happen to him?" Travain wondered aloud. "I am not like that. His mother is not like that. His brother and sister are not like that." Travain was quiet for a moment. "No one we know is like that."

"You have other children?"

"Yes."

"They must be contained and sterilized as well. Are they with your wife? On Burroughs, you said?"

Travain nodded. "I… yes, she… they are on Burroughs. We're heading there in a week."

Pirca quickly put in a call to the bridge. "This is Pirca. I need you to relay a message to the Patrol. They need to find Malory Quaran on Burroughs and contain her. Priority one. Do you understand? And her two children. Priority one. All three of them need to be quarantined immediately."

"Order confirmed," the voice from the bridge com responded.

"Quarantine," Travain said, muttering the word. "Such a delicate way to phrase what it really means…"

Pirca looked at Travain. "You understand what I must do? It must be stopped at its source."

Travain raised his chin. "Yes."

"It's for the good of all humanity." Pirca raised his blaster and fired.

"How are you feeling today, Shahree?" Pirca asked.

"I feel fine, Dad," Shahree said.

Pirca nodded. "Do you miss Ruskurt?"

Shahree shrugged. "Yeah, I guess. Sometimes. He did like to talk a lot. His brain was always going two-forty." She paused. "His funeral was pretty sad, but at least he looked like he was finally at peace."

"Do you ever think about what he told you? Do you ever wonder about the Benders?" Even as he asked his daughter, the question arose in his own mind. Do you ever wonder about the Benders? *Shouldn't we let it go free if it wants to be free?* Ruskurt's questions still whispered at him from the deep recesses of his memory, but he forced them away. The bending of space-time only worked if the Benders were enclosed within the ship, otherwise intergalactic travel was not possible. So what other choice did they have? The citizens of the human race couldn't deny themselves the opportunity to expand across the universe. Could they?

Shahree shook her head. "No, I don't wonder about the Benders at all."

Pirca patted her affectionately on the top of her head. "That's my girl."

In the deep down, the Bender curled its gossamer wings and cried its unheard cries.

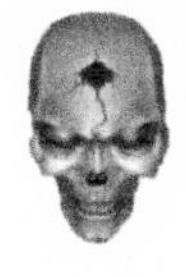

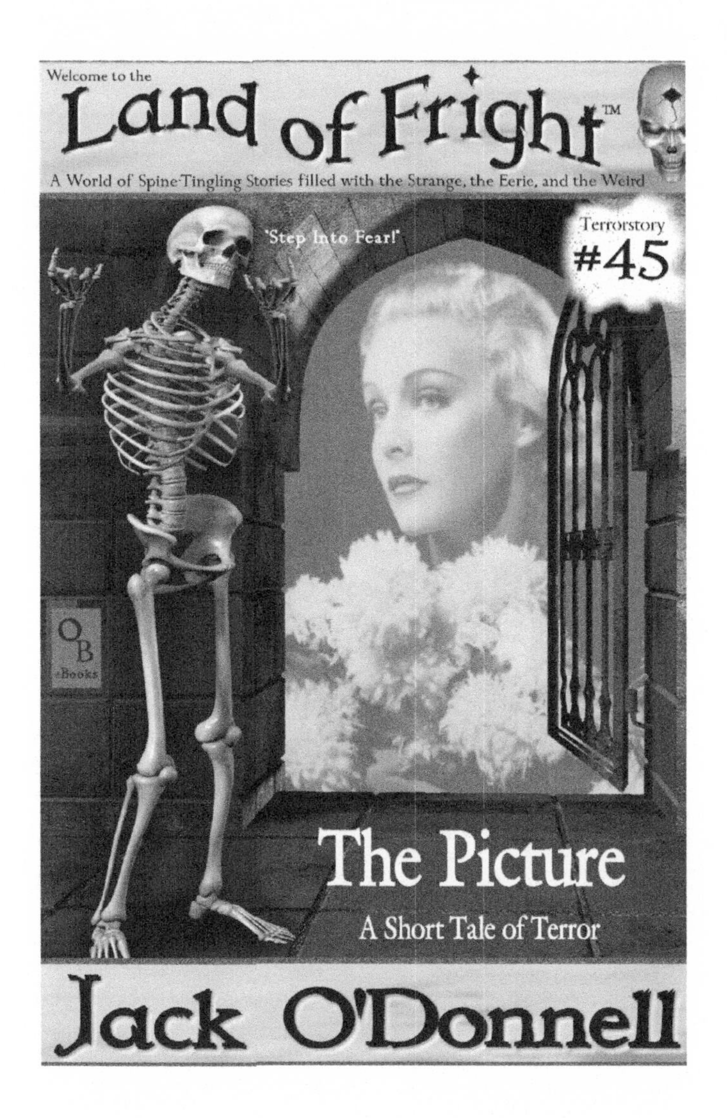
Welcome to the
Land of Fright™
A World of Spine-Tingling Stories filled with the Strange, the Eerie, and the Weird
'Step Into Fear!'
Terrorstory
#45
OB
eBooks
The Picture
A Short Tale of Terror
Jack O'Donnell

TERRORSTORY #45
THE PICTURE

Northern Italy
1944
World War II

"Did I show you a picture of Mareth?" Private Chuck Kincaid pulled the tattered black and white photograph out of his breast pocket. "I'm gonna marry her as soon as I get back to England." Kincaid was a lanky kid, barely nineteen with a few freckles dotting his nose and cheeks. He had joined the unit just as the Allies advanced beyond Rome, taking Florence and closing up on the Gothic Line.

Private Mel Harris took the offered photograph and looked at the picture of the smiling woman. Long, curly dark hair framed a very sweet, very pleasant face. Her smile was bright and cheerful. She had the hint of strong cheekbones and a softly rounded chin. Her eyes were vibrant and lively. "Nice. She's a real cutie." Harris handed the photograph back to Kincaid. "Where'd you meet her?"

Kincaid gently put the photograph back into his breast pocket and patted it softly. "I keep her close to my heart."

Harris gave him a wan smile. "I see that." Harris was lanky as well, but a little more angular in the face, with sharper cheekbones and a stronger jaw. He had only been with the unit for a few days, fresh out of basic.

"I met her at a pub in Wales," Kincaid said. "Sweetest thing you've ever seen. We just hit it off right away. It's like she was just waiting there for me." He paused. "We just finished basic and had two days of R&R. I was dog-tired, let me tell you. Basic nearly killed me. I was pretty damn out of shape."

Harris raised his Garand rifle and tapped it against Kincaid's. "Me, too. But, hey, we're both still here." They were sitting in a foxhole, their backs resting up against the dirt wall. Around them, thick trees towered into the sky. The afternoon sun was bright, the sky clear, the day warm. It would have been a great day to kick back and enjoy a few beers, except for the fact that they were in the middle of the biggest war in human history, and only a few hundred yards away from the enemy.

Kincaid nodded. "Yeah." He paused.

"Shit, keep going," Harris said. "You met her at some pub..."

"Yeah. The Thirsty Whale. So I go into the pub and it's so full of cigarette smoke and bodies and these dim little lights that I can barely make out any faces. So I walk into the pub, heading for the bar to get a drink, but I don't even make it that far. I feel this pull, like somebody's eyes are on me." He looked at Harris. "You ever get that feeling? Like somebody's watching you?"

"You mean like right now with the Germans up on that hill we need to take tomorrow?"

Kincaid smiled. "Yeah, right." He paused, but only for a quick moment before he went back to his story. "So I feel these eyes on me, pulling at me. I just stopped, right there in the middle of the bar. I turn to look to my left and damn if the bodies and the smoke don't just part for me like Moses parting the Red Sea. Like some damn curtain is being drawn open."

Harris leaned in a bit closer, his face clearly full of curiosity, eager to hear more.

"And there she was," Kincaid said, throwing his hand out in front of himself, as if gesturing towards a physical manifestation of her in the foxhole with them. "Just sitting at this little round table all by herself. There's an empty chair across from her and I figure her guy just went to the john or something, or was getting them a fresh round of drinks. But there was no guy. It was just her. She was looking down, twirling her drink with one of them little plastic swords. You know, the ones they stick a cherry on."

Harris nodded.

"And then she looked up. Her eyes nailed me to the spot. I mean, I couldn't move. I just stared at them. Those eyes. Man, those eyes. I could've been staring at them for ten seconds or ten minutes, I don't even know. Next thing I know I'm sitting across the table from her and she's smiling that beautiful shy smile at me. I don't even remember walking to the table. I just remember all of a sudden I'm just sitting across from her. We just started talking and laughing and that was that. I spent all of my R&R with her." Kincaid paused. "Though, I hardly got any R or R.

"Yeah, I bet you mostly got T and A," Harris said. He made no attempt to hide his lascivious grin.

"Oh, man, don't be crude. She's my girl."

"Sorry." Harris wiped away his grin and sat quietly for a moment. "Sounds too good to be true," Harris said.

"It was too good, all right," Kincaid said. He patted his breast pocket and sighed. "Too good."

"We're moving up." Sergeant Ilirio looked down at them in their foxhole. He was a big man with a big head and a big Italian nose. "You guys ready?"

"Hell no, Sarge," Harris said. He nervously gripped his Garand rifle. His helmet was on his head, the chinstrap tight against his stubbled chin.

Kincaid gave Harris a rough nudge with his elbow. He looked up at Ilirio. "Yeah, we're ready."

Sergeant Ilirio nodded. "When you hear the whistle, you move. Don't think. Don't hesitate. Just go and start shooting at anything that moves in front of you. Got it?" Ilirio looked at Harris. "Unstrap that helmet. Any concussion will break your fucking jaw if you got that strapped on so tight."

Harris just looked at him with a vacuous stare.

Sergeant Ilirio returned Harris's vacant look with a quick shake of his head, then moved on towards the next foxhole, keeping low, running fast.

Kincaid looked at Harris. "You good?"

"Yeah, yeah," Harris said, a nervous snap to his voice.

Kincaid looked at the helmet strap that remained tightly bound to Harris's chin, but said nothing.

The shrill whistle rent the calm air, and all around them the sounds of men scrambling, running, charging, guns firing tore through what had been nearly dead silence just seconds before.

"Let's go," Kincaid said and climbed out of the foxhole. Harris followed him out.

They charged forward, hearing men shouting, bullets cracking, the woods filling with an insane cacophony of war. Their objective was to reach a low line of small hills just outside the woods, a small incremental move forward towards the ultimate objective of taking the town that lay just beyond. Over a thousand German troops were garrisoned in the town, and the town had several high buildings the enemy was using as lookout towers. They needed to take the town to clear the way for their armored vehicles to move forward.

It didn't take long for the screaming to start as men started to go down all around them.

Harris took a bullet in the chest and went down hard, his body tumbling as the momentum of the bullet blew him sideways. He hit the ground with a thick thud, dead before his body even stopped moving.

Kincaid saw him go down. He quickly moved over

to him and kneeled down next to his motionless body. Harris's eyes were open, glassy. His helmet was still strapped tightly to his head. It wouldn't have mattered either way. Kincaid reached down and snatched at Harris's dog tags.

Sergeant Ilirio moved up to Kincaid's bunk. They were stationed inside an abandoned warehouse, the men's bunks all lined up in neat rows. "You grab his tags?" Ilirio asked Kincaid.

Kincaid nodded. "Yes, sir."

Kincaid reached into his left breast pocket and produced one of the battered metal dog tags that had been hanging from Harris's neck, handing it to the sergeant.

Ilirio took the offered tag. "You leave the other one for Graves Registration?" Ilirio asked.

"Yes, sir." The lie came out smoothly and easily.

Ilirio nodded, closed his fist around the tag, and moved away.

Kincaid watched Ilirio walk away, then reached into his other breast pocket and pulled out another dog tag. He glanced down at the thin slip of metal, staring at the embossed letters on the tag that spelled out the name of Mel Harris. There was a small "A" in the upper left corner denoting Harris's blood type, and a small "M" below that which denoted his gas mask size was medium. Thankfully, they never had to use their gas masks so far. Kincaid stooped down to open his foot locker and added Harris's dog tag to the half dozen other dog tags he kept hidden beneath his extra pair of socks.

"Kincaid, you got mail."

Kincaid glanced up to see a private fling a letter at him. The letter sailed towards him and Kincaid caught it cleanly.

"Oh, man," private Dean Grayson muttered. "I hope you didn't get one of them dear John letters. Some of those bitches back home can be real ball busters with those." Grayson was older than most of the men in their unit, still itching to kill Germans after the Krauts had killed his younger brother six months ago.

Kincaid lifted the letter up to his nose and sniffed it. "Smells too good to be one of those."

Grayson shook his head. "Don't be too sure. Sometimes they do that just to soften a guy up before the final blow. Just ask O'Conner. He got one of those last week. Crushed his fucking spirit is what it did. Smelled just like fucking roses, too."

Another soldier standing nearby, private Arnie Sanderson, shook his head. "Oh, man. You don't want to read that now. Not right before we go into that Kraut shit storm ahead of us." Sanderson was a tall kid with a deep tan. He had spent a lot of time at the beaches in his hometown in Florida, and lifting weights in the local gym, before enlisting.

Kincaid opened the letter anyway and started to read. He squirmed and shifted uncomfortably.

"Man, I told you not to read it," Grayson said.

"Is it one of them Dear John letters?" Sanderson asked.

"Sort of," Kincaid said as he continued to read.

Grayson frowned.

"It's a Dear Johnson letter," Kincaid said.

"Johnson?" Sanderson frowned at Kincaid. "Your name Johnson?" he asked.

"No." Kincaid glanced down at his crotch. "But his is." He made his dick move beneath his pants. "That's Mister Johnson."

The two privates took a startled jump back from his twitching member and stared at Kincaid incredulously.

"Fucking thing almost bit me," Grayson grumbled.

"She wrote a letter to your cock?" Sanderson asked.

Kincaid nodded. "She misses him." He handed them the letter and Grayson took it.

The two men read it, Sanderson maneuvering to read it over Grayson's shoulder. "Hot damn," Grayson said after finishing reading the letter. "I think I'm gonna fuck one of you in your sleep tonight and pretend it's her. Hot fucking damn."

Grayson started to hand the letter back to Kincaid, but Sanderson grabbed at it. "I need to read that again," Sanderson said. He moved off a few feet away from them to read the letter by himself.

"Hey, you got a picture of her?" Grayson asked. "I'd like to put a face to that letter. Especially to go along with the wet fucking dreams I *know* I'm going to be having tonight."

"Me, too," Sanderson said, without even looking up from the letter as he continued to read it again.

Kincaid dug his picture of Mareth out of his breast pocket and handed it to Grayson.

Grayson stared at the black and white photograph of the pretty young woman smiling at the camera.

"You've had those lips wrapped around your dick?"

Kincaid nodded.

"Hot fucking damn," Grayson muttered.

"Did you fuck her?" Sanderson asked, looking at the picture of Mareth over Grayson's shoulder.

"Of course he fucked her," Grayson said. "A letter like that. Shit."

Kincaid shook his head. "Not yet. But I will when I get back. She promised. She's still a virgin, but she promised I'd be first."

They were all silent.

"Hot fucking damn," Grayson muttered.

"I'd do anything for her if she promised me that," Sanderson said. He shook his head. "Anything at all."

Kincaid nodded. He understood exactly how Sanderson felt.

The message suddenly spread down the line. "We're going over the road. Get ready."

Kincaid quickly took the picture of Mareth out of Grayson's hand and put it back into its safe place inside his breast pocket.

Kincaid looked at the two dog tags in his hand. One had belonged to Dean Grayson, the other had belonged to Arnie Sanderson. A grenade had landed near them and had taken them both out, along with three other soldiers. Sanderson's tag had his wife's name stamped onto it. For a moment, a brief twinge of guilt threatened to hit Kincaid as he read Betty's name over and over, but he pushed it away. He opened his foot locker and set the dog tags down inside to join the others. There were ten tags now in his collection. He wondered how many she needed.

He took out the picture of Mareth and stared at her. Her beautiful eyes stared sweetly back at him. Sacrifices had to be made in war. There was no need for guilt. Just a feeling of purpose. That's what filled him. Purpose. He considered what he was doing as a mission within his regular missions. He was actually quite proud of himself for accomplishing two things at once. Fighting for his country and fighting for his woman. What more noble acts could a man accomplish, after all?

Kincaid sat motionless in the bathroom stall, listening to the two men talking at the urinals. He couldn't see who they were, but their words came through the gap between the stall door and the stall wall very clearly.

"His foot locker's full of them," the guy with the huskier voice said. Kincaid recognized the voice of Corporal Morrow. Morrow was new to their unit, supposedly being groomed as a replacement for Sergeant Ilirio, who had died in a skirmish with a German paratrooper unit.

"So? He's doing the right thing." The second guy had a nasal whine to his voice, but Kincaid didn't recognize who it belonged to.

"No, he's not," Morrow said. "He's collecting them!"

"What? Why the hell would he be collecting them?"

"You tell me," Morrow said.

"That's crazy."

"Just because it's crazy don't mean it's not happening. Something just ain't right. Isn't he supposed to give those to the Lieutenant or something?"

"Man, I don't know," Nasal-voice said. "Maybe he's just holding on to them for him."

"Go ask him," Morrow said.

"I'm not asking him. You ask him. What the hell you snooping around in his foot locker for anyway?"

"I don't know," Morrow said. "Just something don't seem right about him, is all."

The Germans were holed up in the remains of an old castle with three Tiger tanks patrolling the grounds. Two of the massive tanks circled the moat, the Tigers moving in opposite direction from each other. The third one sat in front of the lowered drawbridge, blocking any easy entrance to the castle. The Germans had filled the moat again with water after it being dry for centuries. It was most likely laced with floating mines and underwater booby traps. Nobody had even tried to cross it yet.

British bombers were supposed to make a run over the castle, but the Germans had somehow caught wind of the mission and had ambushed the bombers in the sky with their fighters, knocking ninety percent of them out of the air before they reached the castle. The two bombers that got through dropped their payloads in a frantic haste to get the hell out of there, but their bombs missed their target, landing a hundred yards away from the castle and blowing up an empty field and taking out a few old barns.

So now it was up to the 92nd to take out the Tigers, take out the castle, and destroy whatever secret weapons the Germans were rumored to be working on within. Their unit was positioned behind buildings, behind rocky outcroppings, or hunkered down in foxholes. Kincaid and a few other men were positioned behind a large outcropping of thick boulders.

"Got a smoke?"

Kincaid look over to see private Lawrence eying him. Lawrence was from Naperville, somewhere in Illinois or Indiana, he couldn't remember what state the kid had said. A farm kid, all freckled and carrot-topped.

"Sure." Kincaid pulled out a pack of Lucky Strikes and shook it towards him. Two cigarettes popped up from the open slit in the pack and Lawrence grabbed one of them. "Hey, did I ever show you a picture of my girl?" Kincaid asked.

"Keep that flame low and cup it," Corporal Morrow snarled. He was positioned nearby, hunkered down behind a pile of stones. Morrow was a stocky guy, big and beefy with broad shoulders and big hands. Kincaid didn't like being around him, not since he had overheard Morrow talking about him in the john. "I don't feel like taking fire 'cause you need a smoke," Morrow said. "And blow your smoke down, into the ground. Those fucking German snipers see everything."

"Sure thing, corporal," Lawrence said. He cupped his flame as he lit the cigarette. He looked back over to Kincaid. "So you got a girl?" He started to blow out a cloud of smoke, then quickly lowered his head to blow the rest of the smoke gently down towards the ground.

Kincaid nodded. "Waiting for me back in England." He dug into his jacket pocket and pulled out the picture of Mareth. He handed it to Lawrence.

Lawrence whistled as he studied the photo of the pretty girl. "Nice. What's her name?"

"Her name's Mareth," Kincaid said. He thought he caught Morrow glance at him with an odd stare, but he wasn't sure if he was just projecting that onto Morrow's features. Kincaid realized he really didn't like Morrow, not one bit. He looked back to Lawrence. "You can stare at her rack if you want," Kincaid told him. "I don't mind."

Lawrence looked closer at the picture. "Those are nice."

"I'm gonna marry her when I get back," Kincaid said.

Lawrence shook his head. "You shouldn't say stuff like that. You're gonna jinx yourself."

Kincaid said nothing.

"Hey, what the fuck are you two doing?" Corporal Morrow snapped at them. "Keep your fucking eyes peeled. The Germans are crawling all over this fucking place."

"Hey, Morrow, you seen Kincaid's girl?" Lawrence held up the photo towards Morrow. "Says he's going to marry her."

Morrow did not turn his head to look at the picture, keeping his gaze focused into the distance on one of the Tiger tanks that was making a slow patrol along a road up ahead. "You shouldn't say shit like that. You're gonna jinx yourself."

Lawrence turned to Kincaid and gave him a smug

smile. He looked again at the picture, obviously admiring the pretty young woman.

Kincaid grabbed the picture out of Lawrence's hand. "Jeez, don't drool on it." He put the picture back into his breast pocket.

Kincaid put Lawrence's dog tag with the other dog tags in his foot locker. Command had called off the assault on the castle, but a German sniper had taken the carrot-topped farm kid out with one shot right through his neck before they completed their withdrawal.

The squad huddled down in the gully along the side of the dirt road. The Germans were dug in on the opposite side of the road, not more than thirty or forty yards away. Their objective was a German 88 on the top of a small hill about a hundred yards in the distance. The huge gun was contained within a barricade of stones the Germans had moved to the top of the hill. The gun was raining murderous fire down on an approaching tank battalion and they had to knock it out.

But for now they just waited orders to move out.

"Hey, did I ever show you a picture of my girl?" Kincaid asked a soldier named Palmer crouched next to him.

Corporal Morrow, who was on the opposite side of Kincaid from Palmer, shot Kincaid a most incredulous look. "Are you fucking kidding me? You want to show him a picture of your girl now?"

Kincaid shrugged. "I might not get another chance."

"Why?" Morrow asked. "Because *you're* going to die, or because *he's* going to die?"

Kincaid didn't answer. Then he shrugged. "I just like looking at her before we go into a fight. She helps calm me down."

Palmer continued to give Kincaid a hard stare, but then his look softened and the muscles in his face loosened. "Yeah, okay, sure. Show me a picture of your girl."

Kincaid dug into his jacket pocket and produced the picture. He showed it to Palmer. "Her name's Mareth."

Palmer looked at the picture. "Wow, okay, I see why you wanted to look at her," Palmer said. "She's very nice to look at."

"Yeah, she's a real sweetheart," Kincaid said. "I'm gonna marry her when I get back."

"Sure you are."

"What? You don't believe me?" Kincaid asked.

"Sure, I believe you. You're going to marry her. Sure."

Palmer looked at the picture for a moment longer, then looked over to Morrow. "Hey, Corporal Morrow, you seen her? Kincaid's a lucky man."

The sound of a whistle filled the air. The attack was on! Kincaid put the picture back into his pocket and everyone scrambled forward.

They burst across the road and the air was suddenly thick with bullets. Soldiers fell on either side of Kincaid, but he kept going. He saw the top of a Kraut helmet peering over a boulder and fired. The helmet disappeared. He kept going. He spun left and fired at a German soldier aiming his gun in his direction. Kincaid got his shot off first and the German crumpled to the ground.

Another German suddenly appeared and fired at Kincaid.

Palmer stepped in front of Kincaid, not seeing the German on their left. The stream of bullets took Palmer down, his body shielding Kincaid from the rain of metal slugs. Kincaid fired at the German, lacing his chest with bullets, sending him dead to the ground to join Palmer.

"Give me the picture, Kincaid." Corporal Morrow held out his hand, his big palm up and waiting. His head was oddly turned to the side, only looking at Kincaid out of the corner of his eyes, not square on. They were alone in Morrow's tent. A lantern illuminated the interior in a faint reddish-yellow glow. A small shaving mirror positioned on a table nearby reflected the light.

Kincaid frowned at him. "What are you talking about?"

Morrow gritted his teeth. "Your girl. Give me that fucking picture."

Kincaid made no move to turn over the photograph to the very angry corporal standing at an odd angle before him.

"I know what Mareth means," Morrow said. "It's a Welsh name. I talked to a Brit from Wales and he told me what it means." He thrust his hand forward, insistently, but kept his head turned to the side, as if fearful of looking at Kincaid straight on. Instead, he stared at Kincaid's reflection in the small mirror. "I know what she is."

Kincaid remained motionless.

"I kept asking myself, how is this guy surviving all these battles when no one else in his squad lives?" Morrow said. "How? How is that possible? Lawrence, Palmer, the others. They were all better soldiers than you. Then I remembered the one thing they all had in common." Morrow paused. "They were around you. They were around you and that fucking picture you kept showing everybody. It's that fucking picture. It has to be. It's like looking at the head of Medusa, but instead of turning to stone, you die."

"That sounds a bit crazy, don't you think, Morrow?"

"It's Corporal. And it's not as crazy as sacrificing your fellow soldiers to some goddess of death, is it?" His voice went high and tight as he nearly shouted, "Is it?"

Kincaid reached into his pocket and pulled out the picture. He stared at Mareth, at her smiling eyes. "No, it isn't," Kincaid said as he turned the picture around to face the small mirror.

Morrow realized what Kincaid was doing as he stared at him in the mirror's reflection, but it was too late. He saw her face. He saw Mareth's face in the mirror. He froze, unable to look away, unable to tear his gaze away from her sweet, smiling eyes. It was just a reflection. It shouldn't have had any power over him. Wasn't that how Perseus defeated Medusa? By safely watching her in the reflection of his shield? But Morrow knew seeing Mareth's reflection held as much power over him as looking directly at the picture would have. He could feel the dread seeping into his bones. "She's a devil," Morrow said, his voice barely above a whisper. "You made a deal with the devil."

"She might be a devil. But she's *my* devil," Kincaid said.

It was early in the morning and the pub was mostly empty, but not completely empty, as Kincaid stepped inside. Two patrons hadn't made it home after the prior night's heavy rounds of drinking; both were asleep in a booth. Another man was enjoying an early cup of tea. Two women were busy cleaning off tables and wiping down chairs.

Mareth was waiting for him, sitting alone at the table where he had first seen her. Just as she had promised. He stopped before he reached her. He just wanted to look at her. She was achingly beautiful. He felt stirrings in his chest that had been long absent. But now here she was, and those wondrous feelings had returned. He set his foot locker down on the table in front of her. Mareth looked at him with eager, expectant eyes.

He couldn't wait any longer. He moved up to her, grabbing her in his arms, pulling her to her feet and twirling her around, lifting her up, laughing. She laughed right along with him. He set her back down and motioned for her to open the foot locker, giving her the go-ahead with a soft toss of his head towards the metal case. Her eyes brightened and she reached for the latch, flipping it open. She raised the lid and a very faint silver glow emanated out from the interior of the foot locker. She reached into the foot locker and moved some of his socks aside. The glow brightened tenfold, bathing her face in a shimmering silvery-white sheen. "Oh, Chuck," she said as she stared at the pile of dog tags, his name coming off her lips with a reverence that stirred his very soul. "These will last me awhile."

He smiled at her.

"Now we can spend some time together. Just like I promised."

His smile grew.

She closed the lid. "Bring it up to my room."

He wasted no time in following her up the stairs and into her room. He set the foot locker down on the small table near the large bed and opened it for Mareth.

Mareth reached into the foot locker and shuffled through the dog tags, looking at the names as she went through them: Harris, Ilirio, Sanderson, Grayson, Palmer. She pulled out one of the dog tags from the pile and raised it up. The tiny rectangular shape of the dog tag glowed with a soft white light. The name Morrow shone up at her. She raised the glowing dog tag to her chest and touched it against a silver chain that hung from her neck. The dog tag merged onto the chain, as if the act of merely touching the dog tag to the chain hooked it into the chain. She placed her hand over the dog tag, pressing it against her chest. The glow from the shimmering dog tag seeped through the gaps in her slender fingers. Then, suddenly, the dog tag bloomed brighter, hotter, the silver-white glow turning to a golden-reddish hue. Mareth threw her head back and moaned in what could only be a sound of pleasurable bliss. She kept her hand tightly pressed over the dog tag, holding it firmly to her chest. The golden-red light pulsed and throbbed. She looked over to Kincaid and her eyes were lidded, her mouth slightly open in a sultry pout. "Now," she said, her voice nearly a desperate pant. "Now, Chuck." She reached for him and pulled him to her, kissing him with a passion that was pure lust now. Her lips tingled against his and he felt his body fill up with a strange energy he had never felt before, an energy that was intoxicating.

They made love for hours, moving all about the room, until he fell to the carpeted floor, exhausted, satiated beyond even his wildest fantasies.

"Oh, Chuck," she said in a breathy moan as she lay down beside him. "That was wonderful. I'm so glad I waited for you." She reached over and gently stroked his manhood, his member still moist with her sweet dew.

"You're going to get me started again."

She batted her eyes playfully at him. "Am I?" She took his hand and moved it between her legs. She was hot and wet.

"I have news," he told her after they finished another lengthy, passionate bout of lovemaking, this time ending up on the bed.

She looked at him with bright, expectant eyes.

"I enlisted. Full time."

Her eyes grew even brighter. "Where will you go?" she asked.

"We," he said, correcting her. "Where will *we* go?"

She looked curiously at him.

"Heck, you said you were going to marry me."

A bashful, shy look covered her face. "How can I marry you if you don't ask me?" she said, her voice demure.

"Will you marry me?"

She nodded and smiled, gently touching his bare chest. "Yes, yes I will marry you."

"Hot damn." He grinned and pulled her down to kiss him.

"So where will we go?" she asked.

"I don't know for sure. Things are heating up with the Russians. Maybe somewhere over there." He paused. "There's no war with them yet, though."

She lost a little of her smile.

He grabbed her hand and smiled at her. "Don't worry. There will always be another war. Always." He kissed her fingers.

She nodded back. She was quiet for a long moment. "I think it's time for a new picture. Maybe something a little racier this time. Times are changing, after all."

"What did you have in mind?"

She leaned forward and whispered in his ear.

He pulled back with wide eyes and a huge grin. "Now *that's* racy. They'll look at that one, that's for sure," he said. "We might need to make a few extra copies because I have a feeling some of them might not give that one back."

She smiled.

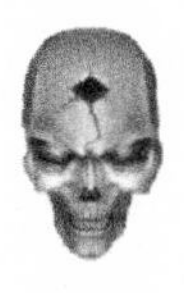

Welcome to the
Land of Fright™
A World of Spine Tingling Stories filled with the Strange, the Eerie, and the Weird
'Step Into Fear!'
Terrorstory
#46
OB
eBooks
Black Ice
A Short Tale of Terror
Jack O'Donnell

TERRORSTORY #46
BLACK ICE

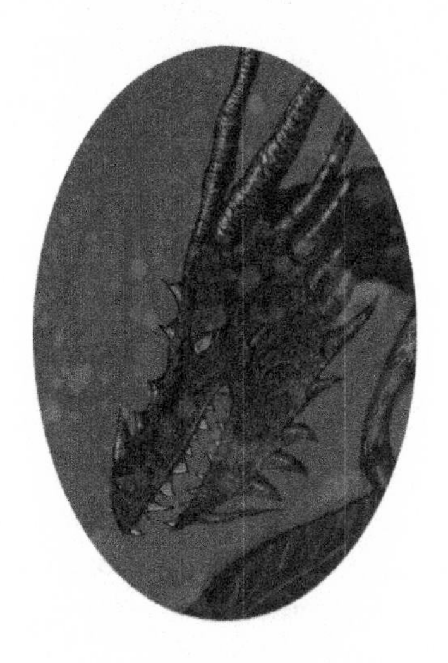

This is a tale of how the fire of the great dragon of Kilajomir Mountain was extinguished by a clever dwarf.

Everyone knows the stories of the great dragon Red Breath, but many have not heard the true tale of Gungu the Great. This record hopes to rectify that. As you all know, Red Breath was the black-scaled beast who once ruled over Kilajomir Mountain and the peoples who lived on the mountain and the great fields surrounding it. Red Breath's reign of terror lasted for generations. Sacrifices were made to appease it. Sacrifices of human flesh. It was far easier to choose sacrifices and offer them to Red Breath than to wait in fear for a random strike from the great beast.

The process of selecting a sacrifice was fair and just. If there were prisoners on hand, one of the prisoners would be offered as the sacrifice. This worked well for years, but soon the deterrent of possibly being fed alive to a dragon greatly reduced criminal activity amongst the peoples of Kilajomir Mountain and those who lived in the great fields surrounding the majestic peaks. The children of Kilajomir Mountain were some of the best behaved children in all the world, I can assure you of that. Every so often, a stranger would wander into the Kilajomir territory and do some misdeed and would be captured and offered up to the dragon. But this sort of activity soon dwindled as word spread of Red Breath and the sacrifices being made to keep its hunger under control.

There has been no crime in the Kilajomir territories for quite some time now.

Of course, that lack of criminal activity led to the eventual complete depletion of prisoners on hand that could be used to feed Red Breath and keep it satiated. It was in the best interests of the residents of the Kilajomir territory to keep the dragon fat and lazy and satisfied. The great beast had gone on a few legendary rages when its needs were not met, destroying entire villages, ripping people apart, burning miles of crops, and no one wanted to re-live any of those destructive times. Once in a great while, someone volunteered to be a sacrifice and offered themselves up to Red Breath. These volunteers were those who were gravely ill, or someone who was just tired of living, or someone who felt it was their duty to protect their loved ones. But that had happened less and less as time went by. Soon, the idea of volunteering to be devoured by a dragon wasn't even given a second thought.

And so the Choosing process was born.

The residents of the Kilajomir territories had hotly debated at what age someone should be considered a candidate for sacrifice. Many argued that the children should be exempt from sacrifice, but they could never agree on what age the cut off should be. Should it be seven? Ten? Sixteen? There was never a consensus on the age. Others argued that everyone, no matter what the age, had to be considered fair game to be chosen.

Others argued that only the fattest should be chosen as sacrifices because their meaty bodies would appease Red Breath greater than someone who was thin. Why only give it a snack when it can have a full course meal? That was rather crude, but the argument had been put forth in just such a manner. This proposal did not pass, but it certainly had an effect on everyone in case one day it was resurrected and put to another vote; there are very few portly residents in the Kilajomir territories these days.

Others argued that the old and the frail or the crippled should be chosen first. Their lives were either at an end, or they served no useful purpose in the running of the villages if their injuries were severe enough. This proposal did not pass, as it was deemed too cruel and too cold-blooded, too heartless.

None of these arguments ever ended in a satisfactory conclusion. They only had served to create animosity amongst themselves, pitting one group against another. It was a rough time for awhile, but soon the anger faded and they all realized they had but one option. They had to make everyone part of the Choosing. Newborns. Men on their death beds. Young children. New parents. The town elders. The strongest. The weakest. Farmers. Hunters. Everyone.

And so everyone brought their name rock to the center of town when it was time for a Choosing. No one dared cheat because to be caught cheating meant you were instantly chosen as the sacrifice. Some had tried to cheat in years past, but they had been caught. One young couple in decades past had tried to hide the birth of their daughter just days before the Choosing was to take place, so her name wouldn't be entered into the Choosing, but their newborn baby girl had been discovered. The young father, who nobly took the blame for the crime to save his young wife and daughter, was chosen as the sacrifice and offered up to Red Breath.

Ting Vala stood atop the platform, looking out at the gathered throng of people. He was dressed in his ceremonial robe, the black fabric symbolizing the dark ebony scales of Red Breath, the red stripes running down the length of the robe symbolizing the dragon's fiery exhalations. Ting was a village elder, his hair and eyebrows gray, his skin wrinkled with age. There were thousands of people gathered around the square. He had made the last call for name rocks moments ago, so only a few people remained on the platform. Three young women dropped their name rocks into the huge tumbler one at a time, and then moved back down the stairs. Each name rock was a flat, circular stone of equal circumference and weight, the resident's name inscribed on the rock with exactly the same amount of dark black ink. They had once carved names into the rocks, but soon realized that residents with shorter names were getting chosen more often because their name rocks were heavier than the others; their short names caused less of the rock to be carved away, thus making the rocks heavier and more likely to settle at the bottom of the tumbler first.

Ting moved to the end of the platform and stared out at the throng. "It is time for the Choosing." The elders used to make long speeches about the nobility of sacrifice that often went on for hours, but now this simple sentence was enough for everyone. They all just wanted to get it done without fanfare.

Ting looked down and motioned for the big man standing near the lever to begin. He was part of the local meat-cutters group. A strong man was always needed to power the tumbler, so most often men involved in heavy labor jobs were selected for that part of the ceremony. The big man was dressed in a black shirt and black pants, standing near the large lever that powered the tumbler. He grabbed the lever and pulled on it, his muscles bulging with the effort. The massive tumbler filled with thousands of name rocks began to turn. The big man pushed and pulled on the lever and the tumbler picked up speed. The sounds of the name rocks crashing against each other as they mixed inside the massive drum filled the area.

"Twenty seven, twenty eight, twenty nine," the crowd shouted as the tumbler made its revolutions. Soon, the shouting of "One hundred!" filled the air, followed by a nearly absolute silence as the big man stepped back away from the lever and the tumbler came to a stop.

Ting looked down at the woman standing near the tumbler gate. She was dressed in a black robe as well, most of her face hidden by the black cowl that was pulled up over her head. He motioned for her to proceed and she slid the thick piece of wood out of the way, allowing space for one name rock to fall out of the tumbler and into the basket below. The woman picked the name rock up out of the basket and turned it over to read the name aloud for everyone to hear.

"Gungu Froslut."

Sympathetic eyes all turned to the small dwarf standing near the town well. The dwarf was four feet tall, dressed smartly in a brown tunic and leather breeches. His brown leather boots were clean, the leather new and crisp. A small sword and coin pouch were attached at his waist.

Gungu looked up, feeling the eyes of the entire village on him. He was an attractive young dwarf, with curly brown hair, well-groomed, his face clean and a vibrant pink. "Well, that sucks fucking ass," Gungu said.

Gungu had never even seen the dragon before, but he knew Red Breath was real. He had heard it bellowing in the sky several times when he was young, and thought he caught a glimpse of its huge black bulk soaring over the village one night, but the night had been very cloudy so he couldn't say with absolute certainty that it had been the dragon. It didn't matter. Red Breath was real all right. And he was about to be its next fucking meal. He would go to the dragon's cavern tomorrow and face the great beast.

He thought about what he would do on his last night. He knew he could fuck any woman in the village he wanted to. That was one of the traditions that had taken root over the years and was still practiced to this day. No woman would deny him, not even the married ones.

He did have a thing for one of the Elders. She was far older than he was, and wrinkles had started to line the corners of her eyes and her mouth, but damn if there wasn't something sexy as hell about her. His cock twitched. *Why not? You're going to die tomorrow anyway.*

He headed off for the home of Elder Grace.

Grace's husband answered his knock on their door. The man, Gungu couldn't recall his name, hesitated before speaking. It was only the briefest of hesitations, but it was awkwardly obvious. "Gungu, hello. Come in."

Gungu entered.

"What can I do for you, Gungu?" the man asked.

"I haven't come to see you," Gungu said. He already felt awkward, and just talking to the man made the feeling even more intensely uncomfortable.

The man paused once more, but again only for a brief second. "I see." He looked towards the kitchen.

"Grace, Gungu is here to… see you."

Grace stuck her head around the kitchen doorway, looking at her husband, then shifting her gaze down to look at Gungu. She stared at him for a moment, then stepped fully into view, wiping her flour-covered hands on a towel.

Gungu admired her beauty. She had piercing blue eyes that shimmered even from this distance. Her skin was pale, her flesh still smooth because she had wisely protected herself from the ravages of the sun. From this distance, he couldn't even see the slight wrinkles that lined the corners of her eyes and lips. Her long blonde hair fell nearly down to her buttocks. There was just a hint of white streaks in her hair that started to show her age, but he thought they made her look even more stunning. He felt pangs of guilt surfacing, like apples bobbing up to the surface after being thrown into the lake. No matter how hard he tried to push the unwanted feelings under the water, they kept rising back up to the surface. *It's not fair. I shouldn't feel this way. I am going to die tomorrow! There is no time for guilt!* He hesitated a moment, but then moved to Grace and took her hand, leading her upstairs.

Grace kissed Gungu fully on the mouth and he headed off into the night air. That had been nice. Grace had been sweet and tender and so lusciously hot. It had been all that he had hoped for. He did her twice, once from the front and once from behind, and then felt fully satisfied. He avoided looking at her husband as he left. That would just spoil his mood.

He wondered how many times he could cum in

one night. His previous record was four times with Silvana, but that had been years ago. He wondered where Silvana was right now. Last he had heard, she moved across the Churning Sea and had two sets of triplets. He shrugged. Right now he just needed a drink, and he knew exactly what drink he was going to have.

"Today's the day, Fank," Gungu said as he clambered up the stool and sat at the table near the fireplace. A low flame burned in the hearth, casting a soft glow around the dwarf. "Give me a shot of fireball."

Fank looked as if he was about to ask Gungu if he was sure about that, but then realized the dwarf was absolutely certain. The bald tavern owner gave Gungu a hearty slap on the back. "And a fireball you shall have." Fank moved off to prepare Gungu's order.

Everyone was polite and cordial to Gungu, nodding at him, giving him soft smiles, but no one really wanted to be anywhere near him, nor did they glance at him for more than a brief moment. Everyone knew he had one day to live. There was something about looking at someone you know is going to be dead in a day that doesn't sit well with most people. Gungu could feel their surreptitious glances hitting him and then bouncing away, but he didn't care. What the hell did he have to care about? It was his last night alive.

Fank returned with a small shot glass filled with a reddish-orange liquid and set it down in front of Gungu. A thin oily film floated atop the surface of the liquid. Fank took the long, thin stick he held in his hand and stuck it into the fire burning in the hearth, waiting for the tip to catch fire before pulling it back out. He held the burning stick over the table and looked at Gungu. "Would you like to do the honors?"

Gungu waved him on. "No, by all means, light it up."

Fank touched the tip of the stick to the shot glass and a fireball of flame erupted upwards as the fire hit the oily liquid. The burst of flames dwindled quickly until a very low flame crackled just along the surface of the drink. Gungu stared at the drink, watching the tiny flames dance along the top of the liquid. He had always wanted to try a fireball but had never gotten up the nerve to actually drink one. He wasn't a big fan of spicy foods or spicy drinks, and this was the spiciest drink known in the entire Kilajomir Mountain region. *What are you waiting for? Don't be a coward.* He grabbed the glass and downed the fireball shot in one gulp.

And then he yelped as the burning sensation seared his throat with an intense pain the likes of which he had never felt before. He whooped and hollered, waving his hand frantically in front of his mouth, desperately trying to cool the volcanic heat burning his tongue and lips and throat. Gungu jumped off the stool and ran about, still whooping, spasmodically waving his hands in front of his mouth, wretchedly trying to fan away the heat.

The tavern became very quiet as everyone watched the dwarf with one day to live dart about like a man trying to run away from a stinging wasp in a crowded room. Except the wasp was already inside him. First, a lone chuckle broke the silence, but that was quickly followed by another and another until soon the room was filled with raucous laughter. Gungu didn't really hear it at all; he was far too focused on the intense burning feeling that was now in his chest and his stomach. He continued to whoop and holler. Then, a hand appeared in front of his face, a hand holding a block of something, something blueish-white with frosted edges. Ice. A piece of ice! Gungu snatched at the offering and shoved the ice into his mouth. Immediate, nearly orgasmic, relief spread through his mouth. He sucked eagerly on the ice, moving it around with his tongue, bringing the ecstatic soothing sensation to every corner of his mouth. He absently backed up, not really watching where he was going, and bumped into the tavern wall. He slid down the wall to sit on the tavern floor. He swallowed some of the cold liquid and the immense feeling of pleasure spread down through his chest, then into his belly. It was incredible. He had never felt such pleasure in his life. He regretted waiting so long to try a fireball.

But then he had the greatest epiphany in his life and realized he had waited for *exactly* the right time to drink his first fireball.

"You sure this is what you want to do, Gungu?" Fank asked.

Gungu nodded. "Just put it into the wagon."

"How will the horse get back from the cavern?"

Gungu looked at him. "Well, you can always accompany me and bring her back down yourself."

Fank said nothing.

"I'll unhook her and send her back. She's smart."

Gungu rubbed the horse's neck affectionately. "She'll find her way back."

"It's a hard trek to Red Breath's lair. You think it will last?"

"Just get me the biggest block you can find. Some of it will melt, but I think I can make it to Red Breath with a lot of it still intact."

Fank shook his head. "Seems like a lot of work."

"So? What else do I need to do?" Gungu asked. "Rest? Ha, no thank you."

And so Gungu rode towards Red Breath, sitting atop the wagon's berth, pulling a huge block of black ice in the wagon behind him. Small droplets of water dotted the ground behind them as moisture slowly dripped off the huge rectangular chunk of ice and splashed to the dirt road. The ice had been carved out from the frozen waters near Sable Lake, so it had a black hue to its surface, caused by the dark sediments that gave Sable Lake its name. It wasn't exactly what Gungu had wanted but Sable Lake was the only place where they could get such a large block of ice in such a short time.

"I bring you a great gift from the cold high mountains and the precious waters of Sable Lake." Gungu stood before Red Breath inside its massive cave. Stalactites dangled down from the cave's ceiling far, far above the enormous chamber. Piles of human bones were scattered about the cave in dozens of different places. The first moment he had seen the dragon had filled him with intense fear. Red Breath truly was a magnificent beast. Its coal-black scales shimmered as if they had their own internal light. The claws on its feet looked so sharp Gungu felt like they could cut his eyes just by glancing at them. How did he hope to survive this encounter? His plan had no chance in succeeding. But he quickly reminded himself that he had nothing to lose. Nothing to lose at all. So he forged on.

The dragon narrowed its gleaming golden eyes. Its sinewy, black-scaled tail slowly waved in the air behind its massive bulk. "I have no interest in jewels. I don't need any black diamonds."

Gungu smiled. "It is not a black diamond, dark king of the lands and master of the sky. It is something I believe you have never seen before."

The dragon moved its head closer to the large rectangular block of ice that sat in the back of the wagon. A trickle of water dripped down the block's side, and the wood beneath the large block was clearly damp with moisture. The dragon flicked its tongue towards the ice block, but did not touch it. The great beast sniffed a loud, obscene sniff, its nostrils flaring as it tried to get the scent of the object. It turned its head to glare at Gungu. "What is it?"

"It is a delicacy, oh magnificent one. Something for you to eat." Gungu motioned to the black block of ice. "Go ahead. Taste it."

The dragon growled. "Perhaps I should taste you instead."

Gungu smiled a condescending smile. "Oh, great one, surely you already know what human flesh tastes like. Mine is no different. But you do not know what this marvelous treat tastes like. I have braved the great high cold mountains where you fear to go to bring you this gift."

The dragon's eyes narrowed into thin slits. "You think I fear the high cold mountains?"

"Those who live there say they have never seen you. I can only assume that you have never been there for them to say such things. And the only reason I can think of for you not to visit the village in the high cold mountains is because you are afraid."

The dragon growled a low grumble. "You stand there with a gift for me, yet you insult me."

"Saying you are afraid is not an insult. I am afraid right now, and I have no desire to insult myself."

"I do not fear the high cold mountains."

Gungu remained quiet.

"I do not like the smell of the air up there. Nor the taste of the sky up there. It displeases me, so I stay away from it."

Gungu wondered if the other dragons felt the same way. They all seemed to avoid the great heights of the mountain tops. Perhaps they should relocate all the human villages to the high plateaus in the mountains. But then he shook his head. The air was too thin, the living too harsh for most. Grand in theory, but not practical for real world existence. He knew personally he could never live at those high altitudes; he could barely walk two steps without gasping for a breath.

"I do not see you humans bathe in the steaming springs in the great forest." Red Breath leaned its large head closer to Gungu. "You must fear them."

"They would boil us alive if we entered them," Gungu said.

"So you fear them."

"They are dangerous to us."

"So you fear them."

"Yes."

The dragon pulled its head away from Gungu with a satisfied grunt. It looked at the block of black ice in the back of the wagon. Droplets of condensation rolled down the sides of the object. "Tell me more of this gift you offer me."

"It is ice, oh great one. It is a delicacy brought down from the high cold mountains."

"Ice." The word hissed off the dragon's tongue. "Iccceee."

"It is something to eat."

"You bring me poison."

Gungu shook his head. "No, it is not poison." Gungu produced a small dagger and chipped off a thin piece of ice. He raised it up so the dragon could clearly see the sliver of frozen water. He popped the ice into his mouth and sucked on it for a moment. He swallowed the remnants of the melted water and smiled pleasantly at the dragon. "It cools the mouth and the throat."

The dragon stared with keen interest at the block of black ice. It flicked its long tongue towards the ice but did not touch it. It turned its head towards Gungu. "And what do you think this gift will buy you?"

Gungu opened his mouth to reply, but he knew the dragon would call him a liar if he denied he had an ulterior motive. "I want peace for my village. I wish to bring you this delicious treat on the first day of each week. It must be brought down fresh from the high cold mountain straight to you lest it melt and become nothing more than plain water. In return, you leave my village and my people in peace."

The black dragon studied him. "And what if other villagers bring me offerings to leave their village in peace? Then which village do I choose to take my meals from?"

"Those are decisions I leave to your wise mind. I can only offer you this delicious treat and hope that you agree to our bargain. We are powerless against your might."

"You strike a bargain for my compassion? Perhaps I have none to bargain for."

"That you speak of compassion means you understand the meaning of it and of my offer. I can again only bow to your wisdom and hope you are willing to strike a bargain. I offer you something you cannot get for yourself."

"I can fly up into the high cold mountains whenever I feel like it."

"And yet you do not." Gungu knew the dragon did not like the thin air or the cold, cold winds that blew high up the mountain. It was a creature of comfort. A fat, lazy dragon with no desire to exert itself more than necessary. After being catered to for so long, it had become slothful and self-indulgent.

The dragon hissed a soft hiss.

"Taste the ice, great one. Experience it and tell me it does not feel like anything you have ever experienced before." Gungu rubbed at his throat. "I can still feel the coolness soothing my throat. I can only imagine the pleasure such a feeling would bring to your throat. A throat that roars with magnificent fire must need to be cooled. At least I can only imagine it must be so."

The dragon looked at him, then turned its

attention back to the block of ice. It brought its snout closer to the ice, sniffing and snorting at it. "It has very little smell."

"Nor does it have much flavor. It's the coolness that makes it a treat for the mouth and throat. It even cools my belly."

The dragon flicked its tongue towards the ice, but again did not touch it.

"It melts even now and will soon be naught but a puddle at your feet. Then the pleasure is lost forever."

The black dragon flicked its tongue again, just letting the tip touch the surface of the ice. It quickly pulled its tongue away from the ice block and hissed angrily at Gungu. "You trick me!"

Gungu threw up his hands. "No, no, great one. It is no trick! That is the cold." Gungu quickly chipped off another block of the ice and put the end in his mouth, sucking on the sliver. He pulled it out of his mouth and held it in front of the dragon. "See. No trick. It's cold. I can feel the cold in my hand and on my lips."

The dragon stared at him warily.

"Surely, you must tire of the constant fire that burns your belly and your throat," Gungu said. "I know I tire of the blistering heat during the day so I seek the shade to cool my skin."

"What do I care what you tire of? You are a walking bite of meat."

Gungu nodded. "That I am, oh breather of magnificent fire. I am meat. And I do walk. And my puny legs take me from the heat of the bright sun into the coolness of dark shade. That is a pleasure that is hard to describe unless you have experienced it yourself."

"I have experienced plenty of shade," the dragon said.

"Yes, of course you have." Gungu bowed to the beast. "I was just trying to make a comparison that you would understand. The ice is like shade for the heat in your mouth and throat."

The dragon's eyes narrowed. "You think I need a simple explanation to understand you?"

"Only because *I* am the one who is simple," Gungu replied after a moment of nervous hesitation.

More droplets of water continued to drip down the side of the block of ice, hitting the ground in tiny explosions of liquid.

"Your gift continues to fade," Gungu said.

Finally, the dragon ran its tongue slowly along the ice. The great beast hissed again, but Gungu knew that was not the sound of anger that issued forth from its mouth. No, it was the hissing sigh of a beast who had just discovered a great pleasure.

Gungu smiled. The dragon's pleasure would soon turn to misery.

Gungu's return to the village caused quite a stir. Grace did not appear pleased to see him, nor did her husband. Gungu was wise enough to avoid them as best he could, though he did find himself looking at Grace whenever she was near, hoping for at least a surreptitious glance from her, but she never looked at him.

Many villagers questioned him, and some even demanded he return to the dragon immediately and fulfill his role as a noble sacrifice. Gungu told them

Red Breath demanded it be brought a fresh chunk of ice every day; the lie came easily and without guilt. Gungu had offered to bring the ice and Red Breath had agreed, but no one needed to know that.

And so every day Gungu brought the icy offering to the great black dragon, and the great dragon hissed with sheer delight. Red Breath no longer just licked at the big black slabs. It bit them with great relish, swallowing large chunks into its belly, moaning with immense pleasure as the soothing cold slid down its hot throat and filled its hot belly with cool bliss.

And then it was time for Gungu to put his plan into action. It would be a dangerous plan, but he knew he would eventually have no choice. He knew he could only delay his inevitable demise for so long. The gifts of ice would only amuse and satisfy the great beast for so long. Drastic, desperate action was needed. The dragon had to be destroyed.

Gungu hoped he would survive long enough to carry it out. And he hoped Fank the bald tavern owner would have enough nerve to do his part.

"Where is the little man?" Red Breath asked. The great dragon stood at the entrance to its massive cave, eyeing Fank with clear disdain and annoyance.

"He ran away," Fank said. "He was afraid of you." Fank heard his voice crack and he berated himself for his weak nerves. The big dragon was an awesomely frightful thing to behold from up close. Beads of sweat formed on Fank's bald head. The beast could easily just devour him with one mighty snap of its jaws.

Red Breath snorted. "Yes, I smelled the fear all over him." The beast looked at Fank. "Are you my meat? I smell the fear on you, too."

Fank felt a trickle of wetness in his loins, but he successfully fought back the urge to completely wet himself. "No. I brought you this." Fank stepped aside to reveal a large block of black ice on a wagon. The block was about four feet long and a few feet wide. It was a muddy black color, an opaque block created from the sediment rich streams running off Sable Lake high in the mountains, similar to the ice blocks Gungu had been bringing to Red Breath for weeks.

Red Breath's eyes widened. "Yessss," the dragon hissed with obvious pleasure at the sight. "Icccce. I like icccce."

The dragon snaked out its tongue and licked at the block of black ice. Its big eyes closed and Fank could have sworn he saw a smile cross the beast's features.

"Yessss," Red Breath hissed again.

"Eat it," Fank urged. "You can eat the whole thing. It's much better that way."

"The whole thing?" the dragon asked. Red Breath eyed the block of ice, slithering its head over the ice, looking at it from several different angles.

"Yes," Fank said. "It will cool your hot belly much more if you just swallow it whole."

"Yessss," Red Breath hissed. "My belly is hot. It's always so hot."

Fank nodded in understanding and tried his best to put a sympathetic look on his face, but he was pretty certain he failed miserably.

Red Breath looked closer at the block of ice,

studying it very intently. "I see something inside of it."

Fank froze for a moment, not knowing what to say or how to react to that statement. "What do you see, great one?"

"Something plump and juicy," Red Breath said. The beast snapped its head towards Fank. "You brought me the little man!"

Fank hesitated. There was no denying it now. They had thought the opaqueness and the black coloring of the ice would hide Gungu's body from the dragon, but the crude outline of his shape was still visible if one looked hard enough. And Red Breath had looked hard enough. "I—yes. Yes, I did," Fank said; he knew he had no choice now but to tell the truth. Fank thought about Gungu's plan and the absurd hopelessness of it all. The dwarf had taken two spoonfuls of sleep root and that had been enough to put him on the verge of death. It usually took five or six spoonfuls of sleep root to knock a full grown man out, but Gungu only needed two before it put him under. They had brought him to Sable Lake and let the cold waters freeze around his body, creating a block of ice that encased his small form. For all Fank knew, Gungu was already dead inside the ice. Others had survived for days in the death-like state that the sleep root induced, some even weeks, before coming back around, but there weren't many stories of people being frozen alive under the spell of the sleep root and then coming back around. In fact, there were no stories of such a thing happening. But he had promised his little friend he would see his mad scheme through to the end, so he went ahead as planned. The dwarf had already been Chosen as a sacrifice, his life already forfeit, so there was nothing to lose in trying his desperate proposal.

"That is wonderful," Red Breath said. "I did ssssooo want to eat him."

Fank nodded. "And now you can. You can swallow him whole."

The block of black ice Gungu had been frozen inside thawed quickly in the heated belly of the great beast. The air was foul, reeking strongly of the stench that poured out of a freshly slaughtered cow when its belly was sliced open for its meat. He still felt the lingering effects of the sleep root, but he knew the wooziness would fade soon enough. He was amazed and delighted that he was actually still alive. At least, he felt alive. Maybe he was dead and this was the beginning of his journey into the hellish lands of the Underneath.

He had to find the source of Red Breath's flame. Did it begin in the dragon's gut? Is that where its fuel was stored? Perhaps, but he knew he still needed to get into the beast's lungs and find the area from whence the dragon breathed its fire. He wondered if he should just hack his way through the beast's stomach, slash his way into the dragon's lungs, but his thoughts were still too muddled by the sleep root to make a command decision.

The darkness was disorienting at first, but Gungu saw a tiny glow shining at the far end of the dragon's gut and his eyes started to adjust to the gloom. He squeezed and unsqueezed his fists, trying to work out the chill in his stubby fingers. The inside of a dragon's belly was a strange place. Several fleshy sacs protruding from the interior stomach wall of the dragon were filled with some kind of oily liquid and Gungu realized those must contain the fuel that fed the dragon's scorching breath. He didn't know how he knew, but he felt pretty certain of his assessment. The dragon chewed and minced human flesh, and in the process extracted all the oils from a human body it needed to keep its fuel sacs full. At least that was the immediate theory his mind formulated as he took in his surroundings.

Thin, tube-like structures ran down out of the fleshy sacs, leading back towards the tiny glowing light. His eyes continued to adjust to the gloom as he moved closer to the glow, following the lines of the tubes as they ran along the stomach wall of the dragon, his boots squishing faintly on the spongy surface of the dragon's stomach. He moved slowly, hoping his movement didn't cause Red Breath any discomfort, or least not enough discomfort for the beast to try and vomit him up. He reached what looked like the opening of a slit, the glowing light coming from somewhere beyond the gap. The slit had two thicker folds of flesh on either side of its opening, and the memory of Grace's vagina flashed through Gungu's mind. He pushed himself through the slimy curtain of flesh, following the glow.

The glow grew hotter, brighter as he stepped through the slit. He thought he now must be standing inside the dragon's lungs, or at least in some body cavity that was somewhere near them. He saw a tiny flame burning a few feet away. The fire was encased in some sort of orb and Gungu immediately realized that the flame was probably what ignited Red

Dragon's fiery blast. He stared at the tiny flame. The orb surrounding the fire looked like glass, but he was pretty certain it wasn't made of glass. He could feel the small flame's intense heat as he neared it. He quickly saw the orb wasn't glass; it was some kind of membrane, some kind of fire-resistant layer of transparent tissue. And as he neared it, he could see that the orb wasn't fully enclosing the flame; there was a small opening at the top of the orb. Gungu reached out towards the orb membrane, but didn't touch it. He only got within a foot of it before it felt like his hand was going to burst into flames. He quickly pulled his hand back and stared at the bright redness suddenly coating the flesh on his fingers. Beads of sweat started to form all over his forehead, the thickening perspiration dripping down his brow, stinging his eyes.

He glanced around the area and saw another dark opening near the orb. It looked like the entrance to a tunnel, its sides blackened and charred. Instinctively, Gungu knew this connected the orb cavity to the dragon's lungs. The dragon's fireballs and flaming breath were most likely created here in this body cavity, fueled by human oils fed in from the dragon's stomach, then propelled forward through the tunnel, up and out through the dragon's lungs, ultimately producing the deadly fire from its mouth.

Suddenly, the surface beneath his feet rolled and shifted. He nearly fell, but managed to keep his balance. He had a dread feeling that the dragon knew he was inside it. Was it trying to cough him up? Gungu knew he had a decision to make. He wondered if putting out the flame would forever prevent the dragon from breathing fire again. Or did it have a means of re-igniting the flame somehow if it went out? He studied the orb, the fire, glancing around the area, but he saw nothing at first to indicate that the flame could be rekindled. He looked closer, wiping away the sweat that continued to rain down over his eyes. And then he saw them. They looked like two pieces of flint lodged in the flesh just above the orb. He remembered the dragon sometimes making clucking sounds and he realized those weren't clucking sounds at all; those were the sounds of the dragon striking the two flint-like objects together to re-ignite his internal flame. If he doused the flame and cut the flints out of the dragon's flesh, would that do the job? Would that make the dragon's breath nothing more than a blast of foul-smelling air?

Gungu drew his sword and looked to the wall of the dragon's belly. That was the other option. To kill the beast from the inside. Could he even cut through that thickness? The histories said the dragon's scales had been impervious to every weapon they had ever tried to wield against it. No swords, no spears, no arrows had successfully penetrated the dragon's scales. What made him think he could do it from the inside? He knew he could most likely cut some of the soft flesh inside the dragon, but he didn't know if he could cut all the way through to the outside. He looked at the soft surface beneath his boots. Should he just hack and slash and do as much damage as he could before the dragon coughed him out?

The dragon retched again, this time much more violently. The motion knocked Gungu to his knees and he nearly lost his grip on his sword. He had to act now!

Gungu went for the flints first, hacking savagely at

them. He could feel the intense heat of the orb burning at his skin as he stood near it to strike at the flints that were positioned above it. The first piece of flint came out with one quick strike and dropped to the spongy surface at his feet with a faint plopping sound. Blood spurted out from the slashed area of flesh, spraying him with the warm liquid of the dragon's life fluid. The second flint was more deeply embedded in the dragon's flesh; it did not come out with the first strike. He hacked and chopped at it, desperately trying to cut it out away from the orb. The heat of the flame burning within the orb started to ignite the hairs on his arms and singe his flesh.

He heard a deafening sound and he knew the dragon was bellowing in pain. The surface of the dragon's orb cavity roiled beneath him and he struggled to keep his balance, bracing himself against the spongy wall of the cavity.

The orb suddenly grew brighter, hotter. Gungu could see tiny undulations in the tubes that led to the orb. The fuel! The dragon was pushing fuel towards the fire. The dragon was getting ready to breathe fire! He hacked at the transparent orb that shielded the flame, cutting through the membrane, going for the flame itself. His blade melted as it cut through the intense fire. His arms burned. His face burned. His shirt sleeves caught on fire.

He threw the sword down, desperately slapping at his burning clothes, putting out that fire. The dragon's fire grew brighter, hotter. He needed to put that flame out, and put it out fast! Blood continued to spill out of the ragged cut he put in the dragon's flesh in the area where he had chopped out the piece of flint. The blood. The blood was wet. He moved over to the cut, ignoring the blood pouring down on him, fighting back the pain the intense heat was causing him, and grabbed the ripped pieces of flesh. He formed a funnel with the torn pieces of skin, aiming the flow of blood towards the burning orb. The blood hit the flames and a huge blast of steam erupted out of the fire, adding more scalding burns to his body. He screamed in pain, but held on to the flesh funnel and kept directing more and more blood onto the flames.

Then he heard a loud sucking noise, like the dragon was inhaling a huge amount of air. A rush of wind raced past him. Red Breath was getting ready to exhale a huge blast of fire. Gungu kept at his work, pouring more and more blood onto the flames. He glanced over his shoulder to look at the dark tunnel; the entrance was wider now. He adjusted his body, positioning himself in the direct path of the dark tunnel, knowing that at any second the huge intake of air would reverse itself into a surging blast of exhalation. Just as he extinguished the flame, Gungu felt himself being propelled backward at a violent pace, the force of the air ripping his hands free of the flesh funnel he had been holding, pushing him towards the dark tunnel. Red Breath was trying to breathe fire and the dragon's action was expelling him as if he were the ball of flame.

Darkness surrounded Gungu for a few very long seconds as he felt himself being propelled up Red Breath's long neck, his body accelerating, the force sending him tumbling end over end inside Red Breath's throat. And then he was flying outside of the dragon's mouth, pushed forward by a heavy force of violently expelled air. There was a warmth to the air, but no heat, no fire. No flames!

Gungu hit the ground hard and grunted as he continued to roll, his dwarven body tumbling head over butt, again and again and again before coming to a stop. He lay motionless for a moment, fighting to catch his breath. Every muscle in his body ached, but he knew he had to get up and move. He could feel the burns covering nearly every inch of his body. He reached up to feel a patch of bare skull where the hair had been completely charred away. He grunted and groaned and grimaced as he moved to his knees. He had to pause to catch his breath, and wait for the agonizing, searing pain to pass. He struggled to his feet and looked up.

Red Breath towered above him, its beady eyes full of hate, glistening with a sheen of liquid venom.

Gungu stared at the beast, his dwarf body covered in blackened streaks and dark red smears.

Had Gungu been a tall man, the dragon's teeth would have snipped him in half, but the chomping teeth just missed him, the great beast's jaws snapping shut inches above his head, only biting on air. And then the great beast collapsed to the side, gurgling and gasping, blood spilling forth from its long snout. The ground in the cavern shook as the heavy bulk of the dragon hit the rocky floor. The damage he had done inside the black-scaled monster had been more than enough to extinguish its fiery breath. It had been enough to slay the dragon. The great beast was no more. Red Breath was dead.

And that is the true story of Gungu the Great who

was born of ice and fire and dragon's blood. He found happiness in the arms of his secret lover Grace for many long years. And the fireball became his new drink of choice.

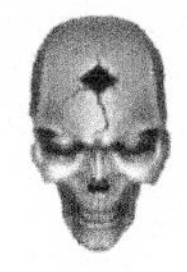

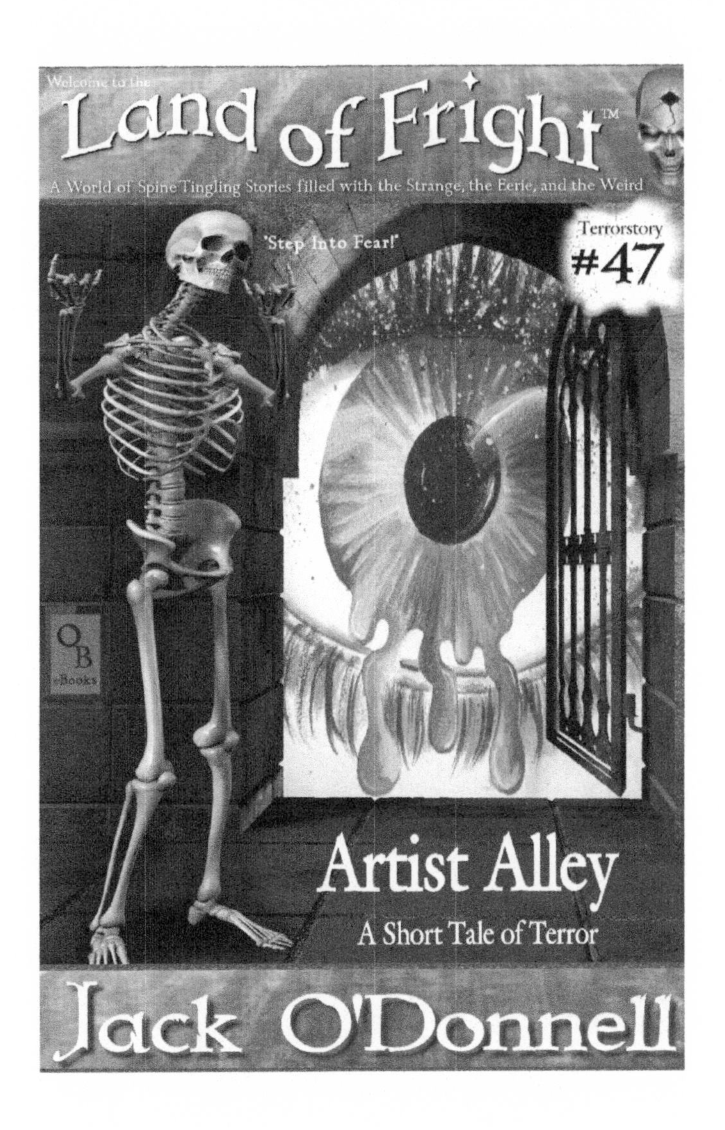
Welcome to the
Land of Fright™
A World of Spine Tingling Stories filled with the Strange, the Eerie, and the Weird
Terrorstory
#47
'Step Into Fear!'
OB
eBooks
Artist Alley
A Short Tale of Terror
Jack O'Donnell

TERRORSTORY #47
ARTIST ALLEY

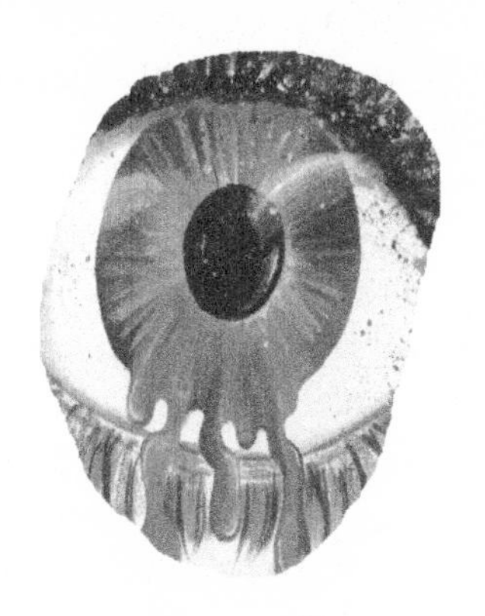

The comic con! Judd Patcher breathed it all in, a big smile brightening his face. Had he known it was going to be his last convention, his excitement surely would have been tempered. But he didn't, so his level of enthusiasm remained high. The con was filled with all the things he loved about entertainment, all in one place. Bright banners filled the massive walkway of the hotel, the splashes of color extending up and down the entire length of the long corridor. There were banners for super heroes, anime, movies, television shows. Throngs of people filled the walkway, every single one of them waiting anxiously to get into the main convention hall. The dazzling display of cosplay costumes everywhere he looked was a treat for the eyes. Look, there was Thor. And over there was Wonder Woman. Yowza, what a rack on that one! Aww, look a little Tyrion over there. How cute. Stormtroopers were in abundance. A few Obi-Wans, too. He already counted half a dozen Batmans. And I have no idea who the hell that guy is supposed to be, Judd thought as he stared at a guy who was dressed in a costume that looked like a cross between a lobster and a rat. Ahh, a scantily clad barbarian woman. Always a pleasure to come across a few of those. She wore a tight leather halter that augmented her already large breasts. Her hair was long and black and wild, a tight headband holding it all back from her face. Her face wasn't so great, but her body more than made up for that shortcoming. He turned his head as he walked past her, blatantly ogling her buttocks as he moved by. Jesus, that is one tight ass.

He absently fingered the publisher badge that dangled from his lanyard as he moved past the attendees all awaiting for the doors to open to the general public. His publisher badge allowed him to get into the show an hour earlier than the masses and he always liked to take advantage of that little perk. He could feel their envious gazes on him as he strode past them. He flashed his publisher badge at the security guard standing at the entrance and she waved him in.

The con used to be only about comic books, but now it was a grand mixture of comics, movies, toys, video games, tech gadgets, even crafts and clothing. He had to admit he preferred it this way. There was so much to look at, so much going on. It was easy to spend an entire day just walking amongst all the vendor booths. It had always been a goal of his to be part of the show instead of just an observer. And here he was, now a publisher and not just an attendee. Life was fucking great.

Judd moved deeper into the main floor area of the con. The place was huge. There were at least three dozen rows, intersected by dozens more. Hundreds and hundreds of dealers and vendors filled the room. He walked amongst some of the comic dealers, moving past table after table filled with comics for sale. Golden Age. Silver Age. Modern comics. He paused to look at some original EC comics from the 50's and marveled at the price tags; the original issues were well into the thousands of dollars. Wow. Too stiff, even for him. Well, maybe later he'd indulge himself with an old Tales from the Crypt or Haunt of Fear issue. He looked at the original price on an old issue of Haunt of Fear. 10 cents. 10 friggin' cents for a comic. And nowadays new issues were $3.99 for one issue, if not more. Even for black and white comics. Hell, I'm charging $4.50 a pop sometimes for my comics, he thought. But the readers were still buying them.

Judd walked into Artist Alley. The Alley was row after row of small tables set up for independent artists and small publishers. Some of the artists had very elaborate back drops set up behind their tables, or displayed their artwork on elaborate easels; some artists had no backdrops at all and just laid their comics or artwork down in haphazard piles on their tables. There was still a half hour to go before the con opened to the public so many of the tables were still unmanned, or in the process of being set up.

He passed one table where some crude first draft sketches were on display. He continued right past the table, but then suddenly stopped. He felt a slight wincing pain in his chest. It only happened for the briefest of moments and then was gone, but he still felt it. He pinched at his chest where the pain had pricked him, but felt nothing more. Probably from working out, he thought. He had done a lot of bench presses yesterday in the hotel gym. Okay, seven. But for him that was a lot.

He looked toward the artist table he had just walked past and something in one of the sketches caught his eye. It was a sketch of a man about to be under attack, or perhaps currently under attack, but his enemy was unseen, not yet drawn by the artist. Only the crude pencil outline of the man was visible, but his face clearly portrayed fear. His eyes were wide, his lips drawn back in fright. His hands were up near his face as if he were trying to ward off his impending attacker. The artist had talent. Even with just a few slashing strokes of his pencil, he had been able to convey a sense of fear in his subject. Judd glanced around for a name tag, or some indicator of who the artist was, but the booth wasn't finished yet and the artist wasn't around. He made a mental note to come back this way later and find out more about the artist.

The convention was a great place to sign hungry talent. They were often so distracted by the throng of people and the prospect of getting a paying gig that they often just skimmed the contract before signing it. The pressure he put on them to sign immediately always helped that along. He told them he only had one slot left and he was looking to fill it today. That always worked. None of the young, hungry-for-work artists he approached ever wanted to miss a chance at a paying gig, even if the pay was minimal and he bought all of the rights to their work.

Judd bought a Starbucks and sipped at the hot coffee, absorbed in his own greatness, thinking of the success he was currently enjoying.

It was a great technique. He learned it from some of his friends in the eBook market. Start your series off with either a free issue, or a very low price. Get people to sample it. Give 'em a taste that doesn't cost them much to partake. He likened it to drug dealers giving out free samples of their wares to get users hooked on the stuff. Then price the next two issues low, get them really hooked into the series, set up some serious drama, some tension, some action, get the suspense going, leave some questions unanswered. Then jack up the price! He had success even going as high as $4.50 an issue on two of his most popular series. Sure, some people would complain and moan, send in nasty e-mails, scrawl obscene comments on their Facebook page, but most of them would keep on buying the comics to keep up with the story because they were hooked. The nasty emails he just marked as spam. He had one of his assistants delete any comments he didn't like on the social media portals they could control. The fury would pass and the next issue would come out, sometimes selling even better than the last issue.

The old adage really was true. There was no such

thing as bad publicity. No publicity was far worse. In these times, discoverability was the key. Readers had to know about you. If they didn't know about you, then no comics would move. Even Amazon was touting something like 38 million books, movies, TV shows, songs, apps, and games available on Amazon Prime. And that didn't even count the competition coming from all the other sources of entertainment. Judd wondered exactly how many individual pieces of entertainment were available to a single person at any given time. It had to be in the hundreds of millions, if not in the billions. That was a helluva lot of clutter to break through. When he sat down and really thought about it, he was amazed they even sold anything at all. *What am I even doing in this business?* He used to find himself asking that question a lot. *It's just crazy.* But then he would look at his bank account statement and all that doubt faded away to be replaced by a contented smile.

And then there were the artists and the writers and the musicians who were continuing to create even more pieces of entertainment. The hundreds of millions of individual entertainment pieces currently available to consumers didn't even count the millions of entertainment pieces being worked on, waiting in drawers to be reborn, hibernating on hard drives, gestating in the subconscious waiting for the right time to rise up to the surface. No, if there were hundreds of millions of pieces of entertainment currently available, there were most likely billions of pieces of entertainment that had not seen the light of the public day. They were languishing on USB disks, hiding in notepads shoved into drawers, stuck in people's imaginations. He thought of the Island of

Misfit Toys from the classic show Rudolph the Red Nose Reindeer. There was probably an Island of Misfit Manuscripts somewhere, too. A place where all the abandoned stories and songs and artwork and movies went to die. What a weird place that would be. He imagined a writer's half-chewed pencil fighting a drummer's drum stick over a spot of land to claim. Or a half-typed page of manuscript wrestling a coffee-stained song sheet for some scraps of food.

Judd thought of the actual artists he dealt with. They were young and hungry. Eager to get any kind of work in the business that they could get. It was easy to manipulate them into signing any contract he put in front of them. If one of them balked, he just moved on from that artist to the next one waiting in line. There were plenty more starving artists to take his, or her, place. He didn't discriminate based on gender or ethnicity or religious belief. If they could draw, he'd work with them. If they were self-proclaimed neo-Nazis and they could draw dynamic panels, he would work with them. If they were gangbangers from East L.A. with drug-dealing and murder on their rap sheet and they could draw facial expressions that popped, he would work with them. If they were lesbians who donned strap-ons and pegged sissy men in the ass and they could ink in subtle details, he would work with them. In fact, the troubled ones were most often the easiest ones to manipulate.

Just sign right there, sweetheart. Right above where it says your signature. Print your name right there, and sign right there. Here's your two hundred dollar signing bonus. Oh, do they love that! For two hundred bucks, I can practically buy their souls. My contracts even give me the right to change their names! Ha, that's one of my favorite bullet points. If no one knows their real names, they can't become a fan favorite. And if they don't become a fan favorite, that keeps their ego in check and their paychecks small. The worst thing that could happen was for an artist to become a fan favorite. That immediately swelled egos and heads. It wasn't long before they were so full of themselves that they were asking for raises, or worse yet, *demanding* raises.

Of course, Judd made sure everyone knew who *he* was. His face and name were plastered on the cover of every issue. His face adorned the Letters pages. He made sure his name was mentioned at least five times somewhere in every issue. It was pretty hard to miss that Judd Patcher was in complete control and in charge. He rubbed at his protruding belly. Large and in charge. He nearly laughed aloud.

"Hey, check it out. It's Judd Patcher."

"Who's that?"

The two men were keeping their voices low, but Judd could still hear them. He was in one of the dealer aisles, standing at a display booth across from the two comic book dealers on the other side of the aisle. Judd was looking at some old movie collectibles, some old Universal monster movie stills and movie posters, when he heard his name.

"You kidding me? He just launched three new lines of comics last month. The guy's ambitious as hell. From what I hear, his sales are on fire."

"Really?"

"Yeah. Oh, I forgot, you're still stuck in the Silver Age. You'd better go back to your Captain Marvels. I doubt you'd even recognize Stan Lee if you saw him."

Judd smiled and moved on, feeling very pleased that people were starting to recognize him and talk about him. In fact, he was feeling so pleased with himself he knew he needed to get to his booth and share some of that pleasure with one of his booth girls.

Judd found his publisher booth, nodding at the Patcher Publications sign that rested on an easel near the entrance to their booth, as if greeting an old friend. He said hello to the two pretty women working the booth. They were handing out free issues of his latest comic to anyone who passed by their booth. And looking lusciously hot while doing so. Jesus, Mandy wasn't even wearing a bra and her nipples were blatantly visible, hard and sharp, poking at the thin fabric of her costume. She was loving all the attention, that's for sure. He wondered if she would give him some later tonight in their hotel room. She looked at him with a hint of hunger in her eyes and he knew he was most definitely getting some tonight. Hell, maybe he'd even get some at lunch time the way her nipples were working overtime.

Jessica dropped a handful of comics she had been holding and they spilled all over the carpeted floor. She got down on her hands and knees and started to pick them up. She glanced up at him over her shoulder, then glanced at her own rear, inviting him to take a deep look at her sweetly tight ass. He accepted her invitation and ravaged her butt with his gaze.

He looked over to see Mandy frowning at Jessica. Judd smiled. A cat fight would be awesome right about now! But he knew they wouldn't throw down right here. They might bicker and argue back in the hotel room later, but they were professional enough to keep it under control while under the close scrutiny of the public eye.

He looked at their display booth, taking it all in. He really never got tired of looking at it. The artwork was gorgeous and he owned it all. The young artists he hired were willing to sign away all rights and he owned every bit of the artwork, even the original sketches. The original art panels alone on the 11x17 bristol boards that the artists used to make their final drawings on were making him a small fortune. And he didn't have to share one red cent with the artists. Sure, he could have. But why? They had willfully signed away all their rights to it. Some of them may not have understood the intricate language in the contract, but that was their problem, not his. He was running a business, not a charity.

Some of the pencilers were miffed when he explained the realities of the contracts they had signed, and had refused to sign up for another project with him, but he didn't much care. There were enough hungry young artists looking to crack into the business that he knew he would never run out of supply. A few inkers were already practically begging him for a chance to do some layouts.

He grabbed Mandy by the hand and pulled her behind the black curtain that they used as a backdrop for their booth. There was no waiting. He'd be obsessed with thinking about getting pussy all day if he didn't get some right now and spurt that obsession out of his body in a thick glob of white goo. There was a cardboard wall behind the curtain that the booth behind them was using for their backdrop, so there was a small area where they could stand and no one could see them. He pulled his dick out and put it into Mandy's mouth. She was already on her knees before him, waiting for it. Have a taste of the Pud of Judd, he thought, and nearly laughed aloud at himself. He knew this would really drive Jessica nuts. She was the one who flaunted herself, yet here he was giving it to Mandy instead. Mandy sucked him eagerly, getting him hard, full and long, immediately. He raised her back up, turned her around, bent her over, slid her costume aside, and plunged his cock into her wetness. Damn these girls were horny! It was probably from all the guys ogling them all day long. There were literally thousands of men fucking them with their eyes all day long. If he was a chick, he knew that would certainly get him horny.

He reached beneath Mandy and fingered her clit while he pounded his prick into her. It was a bit awkward with his big belly pushing him away from her, but he managed it all the same. He felt her cum, heard her gasp, and then he released into her, squirting a healthy load deep inside her. That made her cum again. Man, these con babes are fucking hot! He felt himself getting hard again immediately, but he knew he had work to do so he pulled his glistening cock out of Mandy's very wet pussy and shoved himself back into his pants.

Judd took a bite of his cinnamon churro and sipped on his Starbucks. "You two ever do any modeling?" he asked the two barbarian women standing near him. He made no attempt to stop looking at their ample cleavage. He was back in Artist Alley, on the prowl for talent.

"No," the brunette one said. The blonde shook her head.

"That's a shame," he said. He took another bite out of his churro.

"Are you a photographer?" the brunette asked.

Judd laughed a small laugh. "No. I'm a publisher. I own a publishing company. I publish comics."

"Ohh, that's cool," the blonde woman said.

Judd nodded. "Yeah, I think so, too."

"Do you need models?" the brunette asked.

"We're always looking for beautiful women. That's one of our specialties. We feature hot women on a lot of our covers."

"We're not hot," the brunette said.

Judd smiled at her. "Oh, please, you're both hot and you know it."

He got both of their numbers. "I'll call you," he said and forgot their names five seconds later as he moved on. If Mandy or Jessica weren't accommodating tonight, he was pretty certain one of those two would be.

Judd stared at the drawing he found himself standing in front of. It was very similar to the drawing he had seen earlier, but he was pretty certain he was at a different booth now. It wasn't the same artist table he had stopped at earlier. Or was it? All the tables in Artist Alley tended to blend together. Maybe it was this table.

It was a drawing of the same terrified man he had seen earlier, but now there were more details in the drawing, more fine lines. The enemy was still unseen, but the man now had gym shoes on, jeans, and a T-shirt.

He stared at the man. The man's features had a vague resemblance to his; his clothing was similar as well. Judd frowned. That was odd. He was probably just projecting himself into the drawing.

He suddenly felt light headed for a moment and his vision swam. His stomach gurgled. Damn churro, he thought. I knew it wasn't fresh.

There is no way I am at the same table again, Judd thought. Yet there was the drawing again. This time, the drawing was fully inked. The details were really starting to shine. And it *was* him. The figure now had his beard, even the ghost of the scar above his lip where he had been hit by a shovel when he was ten years old. Why the fuck are they drawing me? He reached up to rub at his beard, a habit he had picked up over the years, but then pulled his hand away sharply from his face. His beard felt practically non-existent. He tentatively reached up and touched his chin again. There was still some hair present, but it was much thinner than he had remembered it being yesterday. Did I get a trim yesterday at the hotel barber shop? No. I didn't even go to the hotel barber shop. Did I get one last week and forgot about it? He rubbed again at his chin and jawline, only feeling a bare bristle of growth. That was fucking strange…

He took his hand away from his face and turned

his attention back to the drawing. Rough outlines of the objects that were attacking the man were now starting to show in the drawing. Judd couldn't make out what they were, but they looked like some long, cylindrical objects coming at the man. Some kind of projectiles? Rockets? Arrows? Or spears, maybe? He couldn't tell.

The chair behind the table was empty. Judd glanced around, but the artist wasn't anywhere in the area. He looked over to the next table and saw a portly guy working on a sketch behind his table. Several sketchbooks, a few completed comics, and some flyers were positioned on the portly guy's table. "Hey," Judd called out to him.

The portly guy looked at him.

Judd pointed to the empty chair behind the table in front of him. "Do you know where he is?"

"She," the portly guy said, correcting him. He shrugged. "I don't know. I think she went to get something to drink."

Judd looked at the name on one of the drawings. Jamie Horn. He ran the name around in his head. It had a vague familiarity to it, but he couldn't be sure. He thought he might have worked with someone named Jamie in the past, but he was pretty certain it had been a guy. Or had it? Shit, he couldn't remember. There were so many artists and inkers and writers and pains-in-the-asses flowing through his life he couldn't possibly remember all of them.

Judd looked at the huge line of people waiting to get a glimpse of their favorite movie and television stars. Some of the actors weren't scheduled to make their appearance for hours, but there were already eager fans waiting in line for them. Some of the more popular actors were charging fifty bucks for an autographed photo and a chance for a selfie with them. Hell, some of them were probably charging even more than that. Some of the two-bit character actors could only get away with charging ten bucks a pop. He felt a jealous pang as he continued on past the rows of stanchions and guard ropes. He knew he'd never reach that level of popularity. Or would he? People were starting to recognize him. He had heard those two comic book dealers talking about him. Maybe it would happen one day. He just had to stay the course. Keep hiring talent on the cheap and taking as much credit as he possibly could for all their hard work. He grinned. Yeah, that could be his ticket to an autograph booth. Stay the course. Keep costs down and profits up. Keep the talent in line and reap all the glory.

He felt a wave of wooziness wash over him and he bumped into two teenagers. They quickly apologized, though he had clearly been the one not paying attention to where he was going. One of the teens dropped a few of his comics and he hurried to pick them back up. Judd noticed that one of the comics was one of his, the name of his company Patcher Publishing splashed big and bold across the front cover.

"You guys like that?" Judd asked, pointing to the comic the first teen had just picked up.

The first teen looked at the comic, then back up to Judd.

"Yeah," the second teen said. "It's pretty good. I

really like the artwork."

"I like the stories," the first teen said, finally speaking.

"Yeah," the second teen said. "The stories are pretty good, too."

"You want me to sign it?" Judd asked.

They both just stared at him, both frowning.

"Dude, that's him," Judd heard the second teen say after a moment of realization swept over the kid. "That's Judd Patcher."

The first teen gave his friend a stupid look that said *what?* without any words.

The second teen took the comic from his friend and opened it up to the editorial page. He pointed to a picture of Judd on the page. "Him. That's him."

"Oh, shit," the first teen said. He looked up at Judd. "That's so cool."

Judd stood there, starting to feel very awkward, but not letting himself show it.

"You can sign mine," the second teen said. He reached into his bag and pulled out an issue of Spine-Tinglers, the newest line of comics from Patcher Publishing.

Judd signed the comic, and the teenagers moved on. That had been awkward. Not quite the way he had imagined it happening. It would get better over time. Pretty soon, he wouldn't even be able to move through the con without getting mobbed. He would just have to work harder on exploiting better talent. He glanced down at his fingers. They had looked odd to him while he was signing the comic. The fleshy color of his hand had faded down to a pale pink. I must be coming down with something, he thought. He loved the con, but the place was probably crawling with germs with so many people packed in.

He suddenly felt very tired, drained, as if he had just spent a day in the hot sun. He walked slowly over to the cafeteria area and sat in one of the plastic chairs, easing his bulk onto the seat. What the hell? He looked again at his fingers; they were still very pale.

Judd headed out of the cafeteria area, moving through Artist Alley on his way towards the comic con exit. The lightheaded feeling was getting worse. He needed to go to his hotel room and lay down.

But then he stopped cold as a painting ensnared his gaze. It was the most beautiful artwork he had ever seen. It was a painting that would stand the test of time. The colors, the textures, the use of light and shadow, all showed keen understanding of the nature of art and true mastery of the craft. And to make it all the more entrancing to him, the painting was a full color portrait of him.

Several people gathered around Judd, forming a semi-circle around him as he stared at the painting. Each person held some form of drawing utensil in their hand, be it a graphite pencil, a colored pencil, an ink pen, or a paintbrush. Judd felt their presence, but didn't really look at them. He was too bewitched by the painting to look away for more than a second. One of the artists reached out and pointed the tip of his pencil at Judd's hand.

Judd felt a tingling in his fingers and looked down at them. He turned his hand over and realized with a sickening churn in his stomach that he was able to see right through his fingers. What the hell was happening to him? Was he hallucinating? Did somebody put something in his coffee when he wasn't looking?

The artists standing around Judd raised their implements, pointing them towards him.

Judd felt a discomforting chill flood his entire body and his gaze was again drawn to the painting, some power compelling him to look at the canvas. It was the most life-like painting he had ever seen. He felt as if he were looking into a mirror. It was also the last thing Judd Patcher ever saw before he completely faded away.

The gathered group of artists who had been standing around Judd lowered their arms, pointing their drawing implements back down towards the ground. They silently dispersed, moving away from each other without saying a word. The spot where Judd Patcher had been standing was now empty.

Every year, the comic convention held an auction, selling off various pieces of original artwork, rare comics, collectible action figures, and other memorabilia. The auctioneer stood on the stage, calling out the bids as they came in. The winners came up to the stage, exchanged money with the auctioneer, and walked away with their prizes.

"Next up is an anonymous donation to the auction. It's a beautiful painting of Judd Patcher." The auctioneer pointed to the painting resting on the easel next to him. "From what I've heard of Judd, it was probably commissioned by himself for himself so he'd always have his number one fan close by."

The audience didn't give the auctioneer much of a response to his quip.

"The painting is not signed, so it truly is a mysterious work," the auctioneer said. "It could be worth something someday if the artist ever does step forward and reveal his or her self."

"Look at the eyes. They look so— alive, don't they?" a man in the crowd said as he looked at the painting, talking quietly to the woman sitting next to him.

"It's kind of creepy," his female companion said. It's like one of those paintings where the eyes follow you wherever you go. I don't like it."

"It's definitely creepy. That's exactly *why* I like it."

"Bids start at one hundred dollars," the auctioneer announced.

The painting of Judd Patcher sold at the comic con auction for $720. All proceeds went to the Starving Artists Charity Fund which supports struggling artists. Unfortunately for the painting's owner, Patcher Publishing suddenly stopped producing comic books, so the value of the painting quickly went to zero.

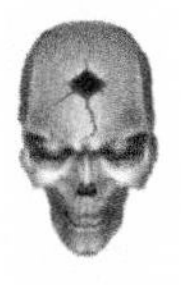

Welcome to the
Land of Fright™
A World of Spine Tingling Stories Filled with the Strange, the Eerie, and the Weird
"Step Into Fear!"
Terrorstory
#48
OB
eBooks
Dead Zone
A Short Tale of Terror
Jack O'Donnell

TERRORSTORY #48
DEAD ZONE

Champagne glasses clinked with a soft tinkling sound as their rims tapped together in a triumphant toast. Sales for their new app were through the roof. Over four million paid downloads, with another twenty million trying the free 30-day demo! They knew from their statistical analysis that anywhere from two to five percent of those trying the demo would pay the buck ninety nine to get the full version. Who knew that an app comparing real-life penis sizes would be so popular! But it shouldn't have been so surprising. So many men liked to brag about how big their dicks were, while so many others were terrified of how inadequate their small cocks were. It was a win-win app. The boastful and the fearful all had an interest in it. They knew only ten percent of users actually uploaded their cock photos, while the other ninety percent were just looking to compare their equipment with everybody else, but that was still enough pictures to make the app very intriguing to everyone who tried it out. And new cock photos were being uploaded every day.

Louisa Reynolds gazed out into the calm waters of the Gulf of Mexico as she rolled her champagne glass between her elegantly manicured fingers. She was a slender brunette woman with a petite body. She had unfortunately been born with a bitch-face, but she had long since gotten over that. People who didn't know her would take one look at her and think she was in a foul mood, even if she wasn't. It was just the way the muscles in her face were laid out.

She sipped on her champagne. As an added bonus, the program was turning out to be a killer dating app for all the size whores who were out there looking for a big dick to fill them up. The dating portion of the app was an in-app download and they charged five bucks a month for that. They already had twenty thousand monthly subscribers. Louisa was certain many of them were gay men, but she also knew a healthy portion of them were women. She didn't care who they were, as long as they remained paying subscribers.

Now they just had to figure out a way to better filter out the Photoshopped phonies and some of the other fake images. Their software caught most of the forged phalluses, but not all of them. She took another sip of her champagne. It was a good problem to have. It would only make the app that much better when they nailed the solution.

The waters beyond the ship seemed oddly dark. She thought they would have been bluer or greener, but they were almost black. Louisa frowned at the sight as she took another sip of her drink; the champagne bubbles tickled her nose. Now that she thought about it, she hadn't seen a fish break the surface for some time now. There had been a ton of flying fish earlier, jumping and leaping about, splashing up out of the gulf waters, as if they were racing the yacht. But now there were none. She glanced over to the wheelhouse and saw Captain Carlyle standing at the wheel, staring out at the waters ahead of the ship. The captain's white-flecked beard fit in perfectly with his white outfit and white cap. Louisa had to admit he did look pretty sharp; Carlyle very much had the look of a captain you might get if you ordered one out of a captain catalog. "Hey Captain, what happened to all the fish?" she asked.

"We're in the dead zone now. No fish here."

"No fish?"

He shook his head. "Hypoxia."

She frowned and repeated the word back to him. "Hypoxia?"

The captain nodded. "Low oxygen," he said. "There's not enough oxygen in the water to support living aquatic organisms."

Her frown remained.

"Fish can't breathe here," Captain Carlyle said.

"Are you serious?"

"Dead serious. In fact, that's what they call them. Dead zones. We're sailing through the biggest one affecting the United States right now."

Louisa looked at the captain for a moment longer,

and his serious expression led her to believe he was telling her the truth. Dead zones. Water without enough oxygen for fish to live in. She had never heard of such a thing. She turned to look back out at the lifeless swath of sea they were moving through and took another sip of her champagne. She didn't even bother to ask what caused it. It was most likely pollution of some sort, something mankind had done to disrupt the natural order of things.

Even sharks wouldn't swim into a dead zone. Even sharks needed to breathe. But the four beings who were once UDT men didn't need to breathe. They didn't feel the stinging bite of the cold sea. Their eyes didn't need to penetrate the deep gloom of the dark waters. The only thing they felt was the unwavering desire to continue their existence. One could call them alive because they had motion, because their limbs still moved as they once did; their arms still stroked through the water and their legs still kicked. And one could call them alive because they still had a need, a craving you might call it. A craving for energy that would keep them from the only thing any of them truly feared: the true end of their existence. Meager as their current existence was, it was far better than the alternative of letting the whisper of life that still fueled them fade into absolute silence. This energy they craved could only be found in food. They could get energy from fish if they caught them, but the dead zone offered them no opportunity to even try. There were no fish here.

But now there was food nearby. Now there was

meat. Meat that would give them energy to continue on as they were. They didn't need much. One meal could last them for years. But their last feeding had been years ago, so the time had come to replenish their energy.

The only alternative was to not eat. To allow themselves to sink into the dark, dark depths of the sea and never rise up again. But that was not something any of them even considered. It was simply not an option. Such a suicidal decision was not in their nature. These were men, or at least they were once men, of the Navy's Underwater Demolition Team, men who had strong wills to live.

Theirs was a brotherhood that defied logic. It was not friendship. That was far too simple of an explanation. It was not love. That was reserved for biological family or members of the opposite sex. It was a bond. A bond stronger than friendship, stronger in its way than love. It was trust, camaraderie, respect, and concern all rolled into one. No other experience could bring men together like fighting for your very life did. No white water rafting adventure. No sky diving adventure. No hunting adventure. No athletic competition. No business partnership. Nothing. How could it? The fight to stay alive was the ultimate adventure. Nothing else could come close, not by a long shot.

There was an intangible power borne of their bond. A power that defied even death itself. No soldier worth his salt ever wanted to leave a buddy behind. No soldier worth his salt ever gave up the fight. These four men of the Underwater Demolition Team were such men. And then some.

Together, they swam towards the surface, towards

the boat that floated atop the waters, towards the meat that called to them.

"My phone's not working," Louisa said, poking her head into Gregor's stateroom. "I can't call out." She flashed her screen in Gregor's direction.

Gregor Moscowitz was sitting in a chair near his bed, book in hand. He was a portly fellow with a thick growth of beard covering most of his face. He put his finger in the book to mark his spot and closed it. "We are out here to relax and celebrate. Not to work," Gregor told her. "It's only for a week. Just relax. Hey, read a book. I mean a real book. You know that thing with a hard cover and that stuff they call paper. They fill the paper with words and it's actually very relaxing to look at them." He raised the book he was holding in his hand and waved it at her. "You should try it some time."

"You're no help. I never should have agreed to this," she muttered. "This isn't relaxing me at all. It's only stressing me out."

"Jeez Louiz—uh. Jeez Louisa. Get it?"

Her frown made it clear she got it.

"Just unplug," Gregor said.

Louisa said nothing and moved on, heading along the narrow corridor where all their staterooms were located, oblivious to the ornate golden decorations that made the hallway shine with an almost obscene sheen of glittering luxury. This whole dead zone thing was really starting to get on her nerves. Not only were there no other ships visible in any direction, nor any sea life for miles and miles around, now they had no cell service. Relax my ass, she thought.

The Germans had tried to infiltrate the Gulf of Mexico during the early 1940's after the bombing of Pearl Harbor brought the United States into the war, during the time when their wolf packs of submarines were roaming the seas with wild abandon and striking fear into every Allied ship that was on the water. The Germans brought over small submarines, sometimes even one-man submersibles, in an attempt to disrupt shipping lanes and create havoc near the American coast.

Groups of Underwater Demolition Team men were assigned to patrol the waters in the Gulf, keeping a keen eye out for any mines, or any other destructive sabotage the Germans might try to inflict on US ships. Their job was to demolish any devices or obstacles they found and keep the water lanes clear.

One afternoon, in the spring of 1943, one of these four-man UDT teams went out on an assignment. They never came back. At least not as the humans they were when they set out on their mission.

Louisa paused outside Jennifer and Liam's door. She raised her hand to knock, but then decided to listen for a moment first. She put her ear closer to the door frame, trying to hear through the tiny crack. She heard the moaning and grunting she had heard so many times before. They were going at it again. Those two really liked to fuck. She wondered if they would let her watch again. It had been only that one time before, and they all had been shit-faced drunk, but they had let her watch while Jennifer mounted Liam and rode him until they both came. She had cum, too, rubbing her clit through her panties beneath her dress. She had never seen another couple actually fucking right in front of her. She had watched plenty of porn, sure, but she had never seen anyone actually doing the act live right in front of her. It had been very erotic, very hot. She thought about just opening the door and barging in, but she didn't have enough alcohol in her yet to completely knock out all of her inhibitions. Ha, she chided herself, you helped develop an app that compares penis sizes and you think you actually have any inhibitions?

Victor brushed by her, making no effort to avoid rubbing himself against her ass as he moved past her in the tight confines of the corridor. Victor was a handsome young man, almost pretty, with black hair that naturally formed tight curls at their edges. "They going at it again?"

Louisa pulled away from the door, still feeling the lingering effects of his crotch touching her buttocks. "Do you mind?" she snapped at him.

"You know I don't mind." Victor glanced down at his crotch, then back up to her face. "I'm still number eight on the charts," he said.

"I'm only interested in the top five," Louisa said.

"Ouch," Victor said.

"When I lower my standards, I'll let you know."

"Double ouch."

There was a sudden change in the ambient noise in the corridor. Both Louisa and Victor noticed it. "You hear that?" Louisa asked.

"Sounds like the engines stopped," Victor said.

The sounds of Jennifer and Liam's lovemaking were very apparent now, the grunting and groaning and moaning easily discernible in the new quiet of the corridor.

"Let's go see what's going on," Victor said.

The Germans captured the UDT men when they tried to set demolition charges on their U-boat submarine. The Axis commander had set up a trap for them and lured them in as easily as tuna fishermen scooping up tuna in their nets. The Germans beat the UDT men until they bled from every orifice. They tortured them until they could no longer take a step, or even raise their arms. They injected them with drugs, scrambled their brains with poisons. But they didn't talk. Not one of them. They revealed no secrets to their enemies.

The German commander grew weary of them and decided to amuse himself by jettisoning them off his submarine by dressing them back in their frogmen gear and packing them into depth charge barrels.

"They tried to attack us from the sea. Let them rot at the bottom of the sea," the German commander said. He barked out his orders and his men shoved the barrels over the side of the submarine and watched them disappear into the deep waters of the Gulf.

Water seeped into the barrels, weighing them down. The barrels slowly sank, swaying slightly to and fro in the water as they descended deeper and deeper.

What no one knew was that life did exist in the

dead zone, but only near the thermal vents far, far below the surface that dotted the floor of the gulf. But this wasn't life that needed any oxygen. This was life that thrived on the hot sulfuric chemicals that spewed forth from the vents that brought up materials from deep within the Earth's crust. These microscopic beings had as strong a will to survive as any other creature, an unquenchable need to continue their existence, to evolve into whatever they needed to be to live. To spread. To expand their territory.

It was a simple matter to ooze into the loose seams of these new items that had entered their world. They moved into the barrels and came upon an interesting find within the metal containers. It was a new form of life. And somehow it was a form of life they could merge with, form a symbiotic relationship with. They spread themselves within these new vessels, moving into the bloodstream, moving into the neural pathways. These new vessels made them feel more secure. They were a protective shell against the other creatures that tried to kill them. They spread themselves within these new vessels, triggering responses that were vital to these new beings they now found themselves partnered with. Triggering their hunger.

"Is there a problem, captain?" Louisa asked as she and Victor moved into the wheelhouse. "Why did we stop?"

Captain Carlyle shook his head. "We didn't stop. We're just slowing down for awhile." He climbed down out of the white leather chair that was positioned in front of the console. Several screens on the console showed different views, radar, sonar, wind speeds. A large wooden wheel was attached to the console, affixed vertically against the wall of the console.

"Why?" Louisa asked.

"There's a storm front a few miles up." Captain Carlyle pointed to the weather radar screen on his console. The screen revealed an image of a bright green glow up ahead of their current position. "It's moving west to east. I just want to let it pass. No sense in sailing into a storm."

Louisa looked beyond the wheelhouse towards the port bow of the ship. Outside, the night was dark. With them being so far from the lights of civilization, the stars in the heaven above were bright and vibrant. The water that surrounded their ship looked as black as ink.

"It'll only be a few hours, then we'll get going again." The captain looked at Victor. "You have any more of that champagne left?"

Louisa looked at Victor curiously. They had chartered the ship and Captain Carlyle, and were paying him quite handsomely for it, but she didn't realize they were including him in their celebration.

"Sure," Victor said. "We've got plenty left. I'll bring you your own bottle."

"Just a glass will do. I do have to eventually steer the ship, you know." Captain Carlyle looked at Louisa. "How would you like to steer the ship?"

Louisa looked at him. "Are you serious?"

"Sure."

"I— I don't know how to steer a ship."

"It's easy. There's the wheel." He pointed to the

large wooden steering wheel in front of the white leather chair. "Keep us steady." Captain Carlyle pointed out of the wheelhouse towards a very bright star up in the sky in the distance. "Just keep on straight at that star."

Louisa looked up at the bright star. "I — okay."

"Just don't hit anything," Victor said.

"Like what?" Louisa asked.

"Like icebergs," Victor said. "Or whales. Please don't hit any whales."

"There's no icebergs in the Gulf of Mexico," Louisa said.

Captain Carlyle patted Louisa gently on the shoulder. "You'll do fine." He motioned to the white chair. "You can even keep my seat warm for me." He turned to Victor. "Now about that champagne…"

The dark figure climbed up over the railing, silently easing himself over the metal bars. His rubber fins had been lost long ago, so he padded along the wooden deck of the yacht in his bare feet. His exposed skin was mottled and gray, withered and shriveled by the water and by the passage of time. He was dressed in a black, skin-tight outfit, the fabric clinging tightly to his body. An oval mask covered his eyes and nose. The mask was damaged, the once-clear faceplate cover looking as if someone had hit it with a bullet and sent dozens of spider-webbing cracks running through it. Cracked Mask creeped stealthily forward, his years of ingrained training pushing his body down into a crouching position as he moved. He did not need to worry about his breathing fogging up his mask because he no longer had the need to take a breath. His mouth was visible, but his lips remained closed, pressed tightly together. He would open his mouth when the time was right. When it was time to feed.

Louisa thought her eyes were playing tricks on her. Was that really a man she just saw climbing over the railing onto the ship? She stared out from the confines of the wheelhouse, still refusing to believe what she had just seen. That wasn't possible. They were in the middle of the Gulf of Mexico. And as far as she knew, there weren't any other ships around for miles. Maybe it was just some weird shadow, some weird reflection bouncing off of the water. The wheelhouse had a few lights positioned outside of it that illuminated a portion of the bow of the ship, but the lights were so soft, so faded from overuse and far overdue for new bulbs that they barely penetrated the inky black dark air of the night.

When the second man climbed aboard to join the first, Louisa knew they were no figments of her imagination. The second man was dressed in swim trunks, with what looked like a snorkeling mask covering his face. His chest was bare. There were horizontal black lines painted on the man's legs and his torso, the stripes separated by about 4 inches between each one. Louisa frowned at the odd sight. What the hell? Was that some kind of camouflage? If so, it was pretty stupid because it wasn't working. She immediately saw a glint of a silver object near the man's waist. My God, was that a knife? She was afraid she knew exactly what she was looking at. Holy crap! She felt her heart start beating a mile a minute and found it hard to catch her breath. She turned away from the sight of the two men and bolted out of the wheelhouse.

Stripes followed Cracked Mask's lead, moving stealthily forward. The horizontal lines on his body had been used as depth gauges on their UDT missions. He could quickly gauge the depth of the water, and the depth of any potential obstacles in it, by looking at where the water level reached a certain stripe on his legs or torso. He could then relay that information to warn incoming vessels, or target certain objects for demolition to remove their threat. The Germans had amused themselves by permanently tattooing the dark stripes on his body.

These were not the slow, plodding zombies so popularized in modern movies and television shows. These were undead creatures of another sort. These were beings who could still move lithely with speed and precision. Their muscle memories were still intact, their years of training ingrained into their reflexes.

They had no vendetta against the human race. They no longer knew what it was to be human. They were something else. There were no guilty. There were no innocent. There was just food.

"Louisa, calm down, we are in the middle of the Gulf of Mexico. Why would there be Somali pirates in the Gulf of Mexico?" Victor asked.

"Shit, I don't know," Louisa said, her voice climbing higher. "I'm telling you I saw someone climb on board! There were at least two of them. They just climbed right onto the ship. One of them looked like he was painted, like a fucking zebra or something. Like some kind of weird camouflage."

"How many glasses of champagne did you have?" Victor asked with a sniggering smile.

A scathing look from Louisa wiped the smirk off Victor's face. "I don't think you would find the knife he had in his belt amusing."

Captain Carlyle frowned at Louisa. "He had a knife?"

Before Louisa could reply, something clicked and beeped and the lights in the wheelhouse went out, plunging them into darkness.

"What the hell?" Victor muttered.

Flippers joined his brothers on the ship, the flat rubber attachments on his feet slapping very faintly against the deck of the yacht. Somehow, even after all these years, his flippers remained on his feet, as if the rubber had somehow permanently melded with his flesh. He was the shortest one on the UDT team, dressed in dark blue swim trunks, his torso also bare. A mask covered his eyes and nose. He moved forward, his flippered feet making soft squishy noises as he walked.

Another click sounded and the lights in the

wheelhouse came back on; they were a lot dimmer than before the main power went out, but they did at least have some illumination.

"The back-up generator kicked on," the captain said, glancing around the area. His face, illuminated in the murky light of the wheelhouse, showed a sense of relief.

"Thank God for back-ups," Louisa muttered. She felt her heart hammering in her chest. They all knew about the importance of back-ups. Everybody working with software knew the vital role back-ups played. They backed up everything four times over when they were working on the app.

"Okay, let's check the ship." Captain Carlyle said. "Grab some flashlights." He pointed to a cupboard nearby. "There's a few in there. You need to crank them to power them up."

"Do you need to call somebody?" Louisa asked. "The Coast Guard or something?"

"And tell them we've been boarded by Somali pirates?" Captain Carlyle shook his head. "I don't think so. We need to check the boat first."

"I'm telling you I saw them! At least two of them," Louisa said, the agitation in her voice very apparent.

Captain Carlyle looked at Louisa. "You can stay here if you want to." He turned to look at Victor, who was busily cranking on a flashlight handle, giving it power.

The light from Victor's flashlight flared on and the beam illuminated two figures who had just stepped into the room. Victor jerked back, letting out a startled yelp. Louisa bit back a scream, immediately biting on the back of her hand to further muffle the shriek that so desperately wanted to explode out of her lungs. The two figures were Jennifer and Liam. Jennifer was a pretty blonde (originally a brunette) with a generous mouth and pronounced cheekbones. Liam was a big swarthy guy, bulging with muscle, his brown hair tight and trim to his head. Jennifer looked frail and weak standing next to her strong boyfriend. Actually, anyone looked frail and weak standing next to Liam.

"Nice of you to scare the shit out of us," Victor said to the couple. "Anybody seen Gregor?"

Jennifer shook her head.

"What's this about pirates?" Liam asked.

Victor turned the flashlight and shined the beam on Louisa. "Ask her."

Louisa squinted under the bright light. "I saw somebody climb aboard."

"Are you serious?" Jennifer asked.

Louisa nodded. "Yes. I saw at least two of them." She raised her hand to block the bright beam. "Do you mind?" she said to Victor.

Liam turned to Captain Carlyle. "Do you have any weapons on this ship? Any guns?"

Captain Carlyle shook his head.

"Not even a spear gun?" Liam asked.

A whistling sound came from just outside the room, and then a loud thunking sound filled the wheelhouse, followed immediately by a thick, meaty sound. Liam grunted and glanced down to see the blood-soaked tip of a spear jutting out from his abdomen. The whistling sound came again, along with another meaty thunk, and a second spear tip exploded out of Liam's gut near the first.

Jennifer threw her hands up to her face and screamed.

"Holy shit!" Victor bolted from the room, clutching his flashlight, racing out the opposite door from where Liam and Jennifer had entered the wheelhouse.

Captain Carlyle grabbed Louisa's wrist and pulled her behind him, racing after Victor.

The fourth member of the UDT frogman team stepped into the wheelhouse. His nickname was Lefty. He wasn't born left-handed, but he quickly became proficient with its use. He had no choice since his right hand had been blown off in a demolition job in Normandy on D-Day. The Navy had sent him home after that, and he could have accepted an honorable discharge, but he wanted to keep up the fight. There was no way he was going to let the guilt of allowing his buddies to continue the war without him overpower his life. And the only way to avoid that guilt was to stay in the battle. He vowed to never stop fighting. He was the only one-handed frogman in the entire Underwater Demolition Team force. He bore his new nickname with pride, and even got a tattoo of 'Lefty' inscribed on his right shoulder.

He also proved to be very adept with the hook they had supplied him with to replace his lost right hand. But he had lost that hook long ago. In its place was a five-pronged piece of coral that had a very crude resemblance to a human hand.

Jennifer stood alone just inside the doorway, staring in shock at Liam as he lay dead on the wheelhouse floor. Lefty raised his right arm and raked his rough-edged coral hand across Jennifer's face, slicing through the flesh of her cheek, drawing thick gouges into her skin. Blood immediately oozed out of the slashes, pouring down her face.

She didn't scream. People usually screamed bloody murder with a wound like that. But she didn't scream. She just whimpered. She was obviously in a state of numbing shock. She put her hand to her ripped flesh and the blood oozed over and through her fingers.

Lefty reached out with his left hand and ripped a piece of loose flesh off her cheek and immediately put it into his mouth and started chewing on it.

Jennifer started to scream after that. And she didn't stop shrieking until Lefty had eaten half of her face.

"Where's Jennifer?" Louisa asked.

Neither of the men answered. The three of them all huddled in the narrow corridor, panting, catching their breaths.

"Is she still back there?" Louisa asked. "You left Jennifer?"

"We *all* left Jennifer," Victor said.

"We have to go back and get her," Louisa said.

The sounds of Jennifer's shrill screams filled the air.

No one moved, except to instinctually huddle even closer together.

The screaming sounds continued.

"We have to help her!" Louisa said.

No one moved.

Victor looked to Captain Carlyle. "You really think it's pirates? What the hell are they doing in the Gulf of Mexico?" He kept his voice in a hushed whisper.

Captain Carlyle said nothing.

"What are we going to do?" Louisa asked, keeping her voice low, the terror clearly audible in her tone. "They killed Liam. And we just left Jennifer in there with them." Louisa looked away from them, back towards the wheelhouse. The sounds of Jennifer screaming continued to rend the air. "Oh my God..." She quickly turned back to the two men cowering with her. "Where's Gregor? Did you see him?"

Victor shook his head. "He was still in his room the last time I saw him."

Louisa turned to look at Captain Carlyle. "*Now* do you think it's fucking time to call the Coast Guard?"

"Yeah, yeah. Call them," Victor said, his head bobbing up and down. "Call the fucking Coast Guard, man."

"The radio's in the wheelhouse," Captain Carlyle said.

"Then we need to go back there," Louisa said.

Again, no one moved. The screaming sounds finally faded away.

"We don't have any weapons," Victor said.

"Then we need to get some fucking weapons," Louisa said.

"Let me order a few from Wal Mart," Victor said. "Just hang on a sec."

"The kitchen," Captain Carlyle said. "There are knives in the kitchen."

"Knives? Like butter knives?" Louisa asked.

"Yes. And some bigger knives. Some butcher knives. At least two. Maybe three. Some pretty sharp steak knives, too. Maybe six or seven of those."

"Yeah? And any forks?" Louisa asked. "Maybe we

can poke their eyes out."

Cracked Mask moved up to Gregor. The chubby man had struggled for quite some time, but eventually tired, and now Stripes and Flippers easily held him captive. Gregor's battered head hung limply and blood dripped down his face. A microbe moved inside Cracked Mask's brain, triggering a memory of the captain he once served under. Captain Bronson. Bronson had been a good commander, a strong man but a fair man. He took no nonsense, nor offered any. Maybe it was the chubby man's portly body, maybe it was the beard, but something inside Cracked Mask triggered a momentary twinge of affection for this piece of meat standing before him. And that ghostly feeling of affection triggered a second memory from deep within his brain. Cracked Mask suddenly felt as if he were back on the farm where he grew up and the time had come to cut up Mister Porker, his favorite pig. He knew he should never have befriended the pig, but he had. There was something about the pig's eyes that just captured his affection. He had cried and wailed and stomped around, begging for his father to let Mister Porker live. He remembered the cruel joke his father had played on him. He had let Mister Porker live, or so he had thought at the time. He had been so happy, dancing around Mister Porker, hugging him, giving him big kisses on his rough hide. Later, his mother had served them the greatest-tasting pork tenderloin he had ever tasted in his life. His father asked him how he liked it. He had told them it was the best piece of pork he ever had. His father popped a tender juicy morsel into his mouth and smiled, nodding. Of course, the pork he had just eaten was the flesh of Mister Porker. Cracked Mask remembered how delicious that pork had been. How tender and juicy. What a fool he had been to fight against his own instincts to feed. All of these memories swirled about in his undead brain without him realizing what was happening. All he knew was that he had a hunger to feed.

Cracked Mask looked over to Gregor, the taste of Mister Porker flooding back into his memories. He grabbed Gregor by the shoulders, leaned in, and took a massive bite out of his neck. Blood sprayed everywhere, splashing against his damaged mask, dripping down the cracked plastic surface.

"This way," Captain Carlyle said, urging them to follow closely behind him with a sharp wave of his hand. Victor still had the flashlight in his hand, but it wasn't illuminating anything. There was enough muted light in the corridor from the back-up generator to let them see where they were going. The three of them moved quickly down the narrow hallway, passing closed stateroom doors as they headed for the kitchen. They rounded a corner and stopped.

Stripes and Flippers stood in the hallway, blocking the end of the corridor.

"Jesus," Victor said. "Is that blood all over them?" He raised the flashlight towards the two figures, but the light didn't shine. He needed to crank the lever on the handle to give it power, but he was too shocked and too scared to remember to do that.

"Who are you?" Captain Carlyle asked, his tone demanding a reply. "What are you doing on my ship?"

Stripes suddenly bolted forward, charging straight at them, drawing his knife from the belt encircling his waist.

"Fuck!" Victor turned to run, pushing and shoving at Louisa to get past her, dropping the flashlight in his frantic haste to flee. Louisa hit the corridor wall hard as Victor shoved her; she grabbed at the gold railing that ran the length of the corridor to prevent herself from falling fully to the floor.

Stripes was on Captain Carlyle so quickly the captain barely had time to raise his hands up in a feeble effort to defend himself. Stripes stabbed his gut repeatedly with his rusted silver blade, plunging the blade in, withdrawing it, then plunging it in, again and again, staining the captain's white uniform a deep crimson. Captain Carlyle grunted and wheezed, doubling over. Then Stripes thrust the blade under the captain's neck and slashed him across the throat to finish the job.

Victor looked back at the scene of carnage to see Captain Carlyle dropping to the floor, his blood spraying everywhere. Louisa gripped the railing, shaking her head dazedly. Victor turned away from the gruesome scene, his breathing ragged, his eyes wide, but he stopped cold as he saw a shape standing in the hallway, the figure of Cracked Mask blocking any exit in the direction he was headed.

Then Lefty stepped out of a stateroom, moving into the hallway right in front of Victor. The UDT men had practiced these types of missions over and over again, so it had become second nature to ascertain the positions of their enemies and formulate a plan of attack. Trapping their food had been child's play. Victor had no time to scream before Lefty gouged him with his coral hand, cutting deep grooves into Victor's face and neck just as he had done to Jennifer. Victor hit the corridor floor and clutched at the bleeding gashes, gurgling grotesquely as blood poured out of the slashes in his cheeks and throat.

Soon, only the screaming woman remained. The four UDT men converged on Louisa.

Cracked Mask grabbed Louisa and pulled her into a stateroom. She tugged and pulled and shouted and cried, but they easily overpowered her, dragging her where they needed her to go. Onto the bed. Cracked Mask roughly pinned her shoulders down on the bed, while Lefty and Stripes each took a leg, gripping her tight, keeping her bucking legs from getting free. They spread her legs wide and Flippers came forward, his rubber flippers slapping against the tiled floor.

Louisa sobbed and pleaded for mercy, but that meant nothing to them. "Please, dear God, please. Stop. Don't do this," Louisa begged. "Don't do this."

Flippers stopped before the bed and stared down at the woman. The microbes squirming about in Flippers' brain triggered a remembered vision of his wife. His wife had been a pretty brunette, too, quite similar in appearance to the woman being held down on the bed. He remembered eating his wife's pussy, remembered how much she enjoyed it, remembered how good that made him feel to hear her moans of pleasure. Flippers lowered himself to his knees and put his face between the woman's legs. He started licking and sucking at the panties that covered her soft folds. The sobbing turned to screaming when he gnawed away the fabric of her underwear and started chewing and biting and tearing flesh.

The UDT men went about the motions of setting charges throughout the yacht, despite having run out of explosives decades ago. The motions were so ingrained in them that they performed them no matter what. They pretended to set charges in the engine room, in the main cabin, on the decks, in the stairwells, all over the ship. It was a ritual they performed after they had fed, signaling mission accomplished.

Once the ritual was complete, they all moved to the edge of the ship and climbed over the guardrail. They waited for a moment, turning to face the ship, gripping the guardrail as their backs faced the water. Their bodies, hands, feet, and masks were all drenched with blood. Then, as if hearing some silent signal only they could hear, they all fell backwards into the dark ocean waters in unison, their bodies hitting the sea with a soft slapping sound. And then they disappeared back into the black depths of the dead zone from whence they had come.

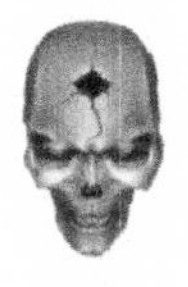

Welcome to the
Land of Fright™
A World of Spine Tingling Stories filled with the Strange, the Eerie, and the Weird
"Step Into Fear!"
Terrorstory
#49
OB
eBooks
Cemetery Dance
A Short Tale of Terror
Jack O'Donnell

TERRORSTORY #49
CEMETERY DANCE

"How you feelin', Rick?"

"You know how the fuck I'm feeling," Rick snapped back. Balls of sweat layered Rick's forehead, like tiny fists curled up into tight water beads of outrage, fatigue, and fear all compressed into shiny miniature orbs.

The torch that Simon held in his hand crackled and spit tiny barbs of flame at the balls of watery sweat on Rick's flesh, the miniature spears of fire clearly eager to attack their enemy from the beginning of time. "I figure you have about an hour left before the poison starts shutting down your heart. After that..." Simon let his voice trail off, then shrugged.

Rick didn't respond. He wiped the back of his hand across his sweaty forehead and blinked away some of the stinging sweat that scratched at his eyes.

The cemetery around the two men was dark, vague outlines of tombstones and mausoleums and spindly trees further blotting the murky landscape with their underlit shapes. There was no moon tonight. Either the satellite that orbited the Earth was too afraid to come out and witness what was going on in the cemetery far below it, or the clouds were just too thick for its light to penetrate. For whatever the reason, the cemetery was very dark. The orangish-yellow-red light from Simon's burning torch was the only light that bathed the hallowed grounds, throwing off a bright sphere of illumination. Simon knew a flashlight would have done the job, or some kind of battery-powered lantern, but a flaming torch just seemed so much more appropriate for the task at hand.

Rick gripped his shovel firmly and continued to dig. He was in his mid-40's, his brown hair cut short, a well-groomed beard covering his chin and jaw and part of his neck. He scooped out half a dozen more clumps of dirt, then the tip of the shovel hit something solid. The resounding thud echoed faintly in the night air.

"Woo wee, looks like you found something," Simon said. "Better hurry." He raised the torch higher and the light flowed down into the hole Rick was in. The hole was about two feet deep and three feet wide.

The light revealed mostly dark patches of earth and rock, some grass that had fallen back into the hole, but then it also illuminated what looked like something white.

Rick raised the shovel high and slammed it down on the exposed object. A cracking sound filled the otherwise eerily quiet cemetery.

"Ooh, I'm not sure I would do that if I were you," Simon said. He shook his head and pursed his lips in a mocking frown. Simon was only a few years older than Rick, but he looked much more haggard; his black hair was longer, wilder, and unkempt. He was overdue for a shave. His face had deeper grooves, his eyes more wrinkles.

Rick gripped the shovel, poised to deliver another strike, but then lowered the tool. He set the shovel down and started to move the dirt away from the exposed object with his hands. Fear immediately gripped at his heart as he excavated more and more of the buried object. It was a forehead. Someone's forehead. Blood oozed from the gouge his striking shovel had just chiseled into it. Rick dropped to his knees in the tight hole and clawed at the dirt, shoving the dirt off of the object, scooping the black particles up in his hands and hurling the clumps into the night. An eye came into view, then part of a nose, then another eye. The second eye was open, staring, vacant.

"Tsk, tsk," Simon said and shook his head. "I think he was still alive before you cracked his skull." Simon shrugged. "I guess we'll never know."

"No," Rick whispered. "No." His voice grew louder as he continued to claw frantically at the dirt. "No! No, you motherfucker, no!" More of the face was revealed. The face of Rick's teenage son Spencer. Rick pushed the dirt away from his son's face.

"You picked the wrong grave," Simon said. "The antidote's not in this one. Better move on."

Fresh sweat streamed down Rick's face, mingling with his older sweat, further muddying his face. He wiped at the sweat, smearing dirt across his forehead and cheeks. "I will kill you," he said, keeping his gaze locked on his son's face.

Simon shook his head. "No you won't. And that's the problem."

Rick said nothing. He stared down at his dead son. His son stared upward with cold, vacant, unmoving eyes.

Simon stared at Rick. "No tears yet? You saving them for later?" Simon nodded. "That makes sense, because there is more."

Rick looked up to glower at Simon.

"In all fairness, I should probably tell you that your wife and daughter are also buried here in the cemetery somewhere," Simon said. He frowned for a quick moment. "Shit. I think I might have honestly forgotten where." Simon cocked his head at Rick and put his finger to his lips. "I *think* they were still alive," he said after a moment of contemplation. He nodded. "Yes, yes. One of them was still alive. Not sure if it was Daphne or Julia, though." He was quiet for a moment. "It's funny. When I was fucking them, sometimes I couldn't tell them apart either. Especially from behind." He grinned at Rick. "They were both pretty tight."

Simon crouched down and moved the torch closer to Rick's face, revealing the torment and rage brewing behind Rick's eyes, the suffering scrunching up his features. "Man, you are good at keeping it all together, aren't you? You saying a silent prayer? Praying for my eternal damnation yet?"

Rick curled his fingers into a fist, but said nothing.

Simon rose back up and the torchlight slithered off of Rick's face, returning his features to a shadowy darkness. "So now you have a real dilemma," Simon said. "In about one hour you will die from the poison that's inside you. Your wife is buried somewhere in the cemetery. Your daughter is buried somewhere in the cemetery. One of them is alive, maybe both. Hell, I don't know." Simon paused. He smacked his head with a grossly exaggerated gesture. "Oh, forgot to tell you." He shook his head disdainfully, staring at the ground. "My mind is really slipping lately." He looked back to Rick. "They are buried on opposite sides of the cemetery, so you would only have time to save one of them, anyway. Or, of course, you could save yourself if you find where the antidote is buried." Simon looked at Rick. "What's it gonna be?"

Rick said nothing.

"What? Now you can't decide what to do? Life or death situation leaving you frozen and indecisive?" Simon asked. "Come on, Rick. You were fast on your feet when you invested all my money in a losing cause. You've always prided yourself on your ability to make quick decisions. You gonna tell me you lost your skills? The magic's all gone just because you bankrupted me?"

Rick looked up at Simon. "How was I supposed to know the world economy was going to tank?"

"Somehow *you* made it through okay," Simon said.

"I didn't know. Nobody knew. Nobody saw it coming," Rick said. "The damn Chinese and the oil glut screwed it up for everyone."

"You made it through okay," Simon repeated.

"I diversified," Rick said.

"You diversified." Simon frowned. "You know what? So did I." Simon smiled, suddenly looking very pleased with himself. "Instead of just torturing you to get a little taste of retribution, I decided to torture your entire family. How's that for diversification?"

Rick said nothing.

"I asked you a question. How's that for diversification?" Simon's voice grew more shrill.

Rick still had no reply.

"Answer the fucking question," Simon said. "How's that for diversification?"

Rick slowly looked up at him. "I would say it has proven to be very effective for you, wouldn't you?"

"Fuckin' A it's effective. Look at you, slobbering and sweating all over yourself. I could probably make you piss and shit yourself, too, if I wanted to."

"It's just money," Rick said. "You can make more. You're a smart guy."

Simon looked down at the dead body in the grave. "It's just life," Simon said. He looked back at Rick. "You can make more. You've got a big dick."

"Help me!" The female voice came out of the night. It was faint, but still audible.

Rick whirled towards the sound. He grabbed the shovel and raced deeper into the cemetery.

"Rick! Someone help me! Rick!"

The voice was coming from under the dirt. Even though the cemetery was dark, Rick had been able to follow the voice to the gravesite. He stumbled over a low tombstone and cracked his shin on the hard granite. His shin ached and throbbed, but he had no time to react to the pain in his leg, or even rub at the site of the soreness. Rick tossed the shovel down and dropped to his knees, clawing and scratching at the earth. "I'm here," he said. "I'm here!"

"Rick!" The voice grew louder. The sound was off to his right, so Rick shifted his position and continued to scratch and claw at the dirt. His fingers touched something that wasn't mud or grass and he continued to dig harder, faster.

Simon slowly came up to the edge of the grave, sauntering casually forward, the torch crackling in his hand, the light washing over Rick as he clawed and scratched at the earth.

Rick's fingers hit something hard. Something smooth and metallic. He dug around its edges and lifted the small speaker into the air. "Rick!" the speaker shouted.

"Wireless," Simon said. "Works great even buried underground."

Rick gritted his teeth and smashed the small speaker against a nearby tombstone. Bits of plastic and electronic components splashed in all directions. He launched himself at Simon, tackling him to the ground. Simon lost his grip on the torch and it fell to the ground nearby, but still continued to burn and crackle. Rick rained blow after blow on Simon's face, the side of his head, his cheeks, his chin, the top of Simon's head.

Simon made no effort to block Rick's punches. He just laughed. Blood trickled out of the cuts on Simon's lips and he just continued to laugh as Rick punched at him. "Use the shovel," Simon goaded. "Bash my skull in."

Rick grabbed the shovel and raised it high above his head. Simon's face glowed in the night, the slithering torchlight smearing his skin with its luminescence in abstract patterns of dark and light. Rick's hands shook as he gripped the shovel. He burned to bring it down square in the center of Simon's face. The sound of Simon's cheek cracking would be a symphonic cymbal clash in his head, a high note of triumph. No, it wouldn't be triumph. At least not for him. It would be a triumph for Simon. His final triumph. Because that's what the fucker wanted. Simon wanted Rick to murder him. Simon wanted his blood to be on Rick's hands.

"Do it," Simon urged. "I tortured your family. Your son is dead because of me." Simon paused. "Well, mostly because of you because you bashed his skull in with that shovel, but I helped it along."

Rick's hands shook.

"I fucked your wife and your daughter. I took my dick out of your wife's pussy and shoved it straight into your daughter. Can you believe that? I mixed your wife's pussy juice with your daughter's. I swirled it around in there good, too. I couldn't believe how wet your daughter was. She was totally digging it."

Rick drove the shovel downward hard and fast. The edge of the shovel sunk into the dirt an inch away from Simon's head.

"You cowardly fuck," Simon said.

Rick leaned against the handle of the shovel, feeling a shortness of breath. His vision swam for a moment, but quickly cleared.

"Damn," Simon said. "In all this excitement, I

forgot you still need to find the antidote. Oh, and your wife and daughter are still buried around here somewhere in this cemetery." He paused. "Or are they?"

Rick tilted his head to look at Simon.

Simon slowly sat up, wincing. He dabbed at the blood dripping from the cuts on his mouth. Bright red welts blotted his left cheek and lower jaw where Rick had pounded his fists into Simon's face. "So you are just going to die and let me live? That's really fucking weak, Rick. Really fucking weak."

Rick said nothing.

"Your immortal soul is more important than the lives of your wife and your daughter?" Simon asked.

"I'm not going to kill you," Rick said.

Simon rose up and shuffled over to Rick. He draped his arm around Rick's shoulder. "Even if I told you I pissed in your son's mouth?"

Rick's jaw tightened.

"He had such a bright future. He was about to graduate college, wasn't he? Already had a job lined up, too, from what I heard." Simon shook his head. "Shame."

Rick angrily shrugged off Simon's arm from his shoulder and moved away from him, taking the shovel with him.

"You should've seen the look on his face when I pulled my dick out of my pants," Simon said. "He probably thought I was going to make him suck it. Imagine his surprise when I just let out a stream of piss right into his face." Simon laughed. "That was the most surprised look I think I've ever seen on someone's face." He paused. "He spit and sputtered, but I'm pretty sure he swallowed some of it."

"You're going to burn in Hell," Rick said.

"Am I?" Simon asked. "What if there is no Hell? What if I'm going to get away with it with no consequences? What if, Rick? What if, huh?"

"You won't get away with it."

Simon scoffed. "Look around you. I *am* getting away with it."

Rick stared at him. "If you're so miserable, just kill yourself. Just run in front of a fucking bus. Step in front of a train. Jump off a building. Blow your fucking brains out."

Simon said nothing.

Rick stared at him for a very long moment. He reached down to the ground and picked up the still-burning torch, moving it closer to Simon's face to illuminate his features. "You're afraid." He looked closer at Simon. "You can't do it. You're afraid to do it. That's weak, Simon. That's real weak."

"Weak? Let's talk about weak." Simon snatched the torch out of Rick's hand. "You're about to die, your entire family is about to die, and you stand there doing nothing!"

Both men stood mutely in the cemetery for a long moment. The torch crackled and burned, spitting off more sparks. "So, you won't kill me and I won't kill myself." Simon paused. "Quite a predicament we have here." He moved the torch closer towards Rick, lighting up his face in the torch's glow. "What other buttons do you have that I can push? What's the secret to making you lose your fucking mind? I thought it was raping and torturing and humiliating your family, but that's clearly not enough for you."

Rick said nothing.

"Okay, I'm gonna help you out because this is

starting to bore me to fucking tears," Simon said.

Rick continued to stare straight ahead, gripping the shovel.

"I set up three tombstones. One to mark where the antidote is buried, one to mark where your wife is buried, and one where your daughter is buried," Simon said. "They have a little white gargoyle figure perched on the top of them, you know, to keep an eye on each one. I always liked gargoyles." Simon looked at Rick. "What about you? You like gargoyles?"

Rick started to race off into the cemetery, scanning, searching, darting from tombstone to tombstone.

"You're cold. So very cold!" Simon shouted after him as Rick began to fade into the gloom.

Rick stopped and headed to the left, moving a bit slower now.

"You're getting warmer!" Simon called out to him. He slowly started to follow Rick, bringing the torch along with him.

Rick suddenly stopped, eyeing a tombstone with a tiny white stone gargoyle perched on the top of its rounded edge.

"Ahh, you found one." Simon walked up to the tombstone and stopped. "Well done. It will take you about half an hour to reach the antidote. I buried it pretty deep. Not as deep as I buried my cock in your daughter's super tight ass, but it's still pretty deep." Simon was quiet for a moment. He glanced around the cemetery, studying their surroundings, then turned back to look at Rick. "What a business, right? Making money off of death. They'll never run out of customers." He glanced around the burial ground.

Sporadic trees broke up the landscape of the cemetery, with slight hills giving the lay of the land some height and depth. All manners of tombstones and grave markers dotted the landscape. Several large mausoleums were visible on a slight rise nearby. "You gotta admit graveyards are kind of cool. All these tombstones. All these dead bodies hidden beneath the surface. Some of them still probably have some flesh on them. And all those skeletons. There must be over a thousand skeletons buried here, if not more than that."

Rick said nothing. He started to dig.

"It makes you nervous, doesn't it?" Simon asked. "Being here. You don't like being here."

"No, I don't."

"You afraid you're going to catch something? Like your death?" Simon laughed at himself.

Rick said nothing as he continued to toss clumps of dirt aside, digging deeper.

"This whole ritual is pretty absurd, don't you think?" Simon asked. "Injecting a dead body with chemicals so it looks pretty and peaceful before shoving it a dozen feet underground in a pretty box filled with a soft cushy lining. Why? The dead don't care. They're dead.

"They're not for the dead. They're for the living."

"Yeah, sure." Simon paused. "We should just grind them up and use them as fertilizer. That's far more useful. Put them back into the dust from whence they came, right? Now, they're just taking up space and providing no benefit to anyone. Well, except for the funeral parlor and cemetery business."

Rick said nothing.

"What if coffins are soul prisons?" Simon asked.

"What if they are all a ploy to prevent souls from reaching heaven? What if they are just cages for your soul? Can you imagine that? What a horrible thing that would be. Trapped for all eternity in a pine box. Actually, some of them are metal these days, too. Oak. Steel. Heck, they're probably made out of fake laminate and plastic, too." He put his hand to his ear, exaggerating his listening gesture, tilting his ear towards the ground. "If you listen close enough, you can hear them crying out to be set free." He straightened back up and lowered his hand.

Rick stopped digging for a moment. "That's just crazy," he said.

"Of course it is. But what if? I like playing *what if*. Like, for example, what if your wife willingly let me fuck her so I wouldn't fuck your daughter? What if that happened? How would that make you feel?"

Rick remained silent.

"Maybe it would make you feel proud of her. Proud that she sacrificed the sanctity of her body to protect your daughter from harm. Or maybe it makes you feel disgusted. Disgusted that she would allow another cock to root around inside her. I came inside her, too. That was nice. I'm thinking she's got a nice little permanent stain on the inside walls of her cunt from my cum. Just think about that. My dick was inside your wife's pussy. And she was fucking wet, too. I don't care what she might tell you later. I mean, if she survives this. She definitely got off on it.

tight. So tight. I have to admit she wasn't very wet. I lied about that earlier. I don't think she enjoyed it as much as your wife did." Simon paused and pointed a finger at Rick. "Ha. I saw the twitch. I saw that little tightness in your jaw. You are trying so hard to stay calm, aren't you? Well, here I am. Right in front of you. Take me down. Go ahead. Take that shovel and bash my skull in. I have no idea what you are waiting for. Your blood's got to be boiling right about now. I mean flowing lava hot inside your fucking head." Simon rubbed thoughtfully at his chin, exaggerating the gesture. "Oh, hold on. I do know what you are waiting for. You are waiting for me to tell you where your daughter is buried." Simon looked at Rick. "Come on, you gotta admit the suspense is killing you. Wait, no, hold on. Not you. The suspense is actually killing your daughter as she slowly suffocates to death. Sorry, my bad."

Rick said nothing.

"So who you gonna save first? Julia or Daphne? Your wife or your daughter?"

Rick didn't answer.

"I asked you a fucking question. Who are you going to save first? Your wife or your daughter? You can't not pick. You have to choose one."

"Daphne, you fuck."

"Interesting," Simon mused. He raised his free hand and waved a finger in the air. "I think we need to discuss why you picked your daughter over your wife first," he said.

Rick gritted his teeth and balled his fingers into a fist.

"Is it because you and your wife have grown apart? She not giving you any anymore? No more hootchie cootchie in the bedroom? No more afternoon blow jobs? Not even a hand job?"

Rick remained mute.

Simon shook his head. "Wow. I didn't know it was that bad. Still, she is your wife. Come on, I need to know. Why did you pick Daphne over Julia? I really need to know."

"That's my business, not yours."

Simon hooted and slapped his thigh with an exaggerated slap. "Hoo whee. This is all *my* business," he said. "The clock is ticking."

"She has her whole life ahead of her."

Simon cocked his head. "Age, huh? That's it? You picked Daphne just because she's younger? Your wife's lived long enough so she's done? Julia's got nothing left to contribute to the future of mankind?" Simon paused. "Wait, she can't, can she? She had the hysterectomy. She's barren. She can't have any more children even if you wanted to."

Rick said nothing.

"And you think your daughter has something to contribute to society?" Simon clucked his tongue. "She's just a socialite snob. What the fuck is Daphne going to contribute to the human race? A new table setting arrangement? Maybe she'll come up with a new color of toenail polish?"

Simon paused, thinking. He pointed a finger and shook it at Rick. "Ahh, she can still breed. I get it. She can still pop out a few more Rick offspring. Keep the ol' Rick gene pool alive and kicking into the next generation." Simon nodded. "I mean, what else is there, right? You can make millions of dollars, reach levels of fame and fortune, but without a biological heir to continue the Rick genes on, you'll just become nothing. Who remembers the rich and famous from two hundred years ago? Nobody. Who were the wealthiest men in the 1700's? Nobody knows or cares. But if they have children, and their children have children, and their children have children, then it does mean something. The legacy lives on. Without that, nothing you do has any lasting meaning or lasting value whatsoever. Everyone's racing around for fame and glory, thinking they are leaving some kind of legacy. It's a false dream, Rick. Unless you are a Newton or an Einstein, nobody cares. And Rick, you ain't no Einstein. Who were the greatest athletes in the 1920's? The smartest businessmen in the 1800's? The funniest comedians in the 1950's? Nobody cares. Oh sure, there are a few historians and some fanatic fan boys, but ninety nine point nine nine nine nine percent of the population don't know and they don't give a rat's ass."

Rick listened.

"You can take away a man's wealth. You can even take away his own life. But take away his children's lives and you have truly defeated him. Especially if you cut his cock off, too." Simon laughed at that. "Oh, did I forget to tell you? Even if you find the antidote, you'll be impotent for the rest of your life. The poison permanently destroys your sperm cell production and utterly destroys your ability to get an erection. Call it the anti-Viagra."

"What do you want, Simon? Tell me!" Rick stepped towards Simon, the muscles in his face twisted with torment. "What do you want?"

"I want you to suffer."

"I *am* suffering, you fuck!"

Simon cocked his head at Rick. "Yeah, I see that."

He was quiet for a moment, then slowly shook his head in a gesture of disappointment. "It's not as satisfying as I thought it would be." He became quiet again for a moment. Then his face brightened and an eager light burned in his eyes. "Let's pull out another surprise right now, shall we?"

Rick froze, only for a second, but Simon saw it.

"Ha, got you again, didn't I? I can hear your ass puckering up from here." Simon made an obscene sucking, slurping sound. "What the fuck else does he have up his sleeve? Right? That's gotta be what you are wondering. What the fuck else does he have? How can this be any fucking worse than it already is? Right? Am I right?"

Rick said nothing.

Simon scowled. "Now you know I want you to answer my question, so I will ask it again." This time his voice was eerily, frightfully calm. "Am I right?"

"Yes. You are right.

"And what am I right about?" Simon asked.

Rick looked at him. "I am wondering how much worse this can get."

Simon nodded in satisfaction. "You must have realized that if I got to your wife and daughter and your son, that I could also get to your granddaughter. That little Cassandra really is cute as a button, isn't she?" Simon kept his expression flat. "That's a rhetorical question. You don't need to answer it."

Rick said nothing.

"Oh, come on!" Simon said, the exasperation clearly coming through. "Your head's gotta be about to burst right about now." He looked at Rick, pushing the torch flame closer to him. The light danced and flickered across Rick's features. "Unless you really just don't care. Maybe you *are* that cold." Simon suddenly jerked backed away from Rick as if Rick had just burst into flames and he wanted to avoid getting burned by the intense heat. Was that a smile he had seen on Rick's face? No, that wasn't possible. Yet he had just seen it. Just a slight quirk of the lips, a barely discernible upturning of the corners of his mouth. "You want them dead," Simon said. "You ruined me because you knew I would come after your family."

Rick said nothing.

Simon put his hand to his forehead, truly aghast at the implications of what he was saying. "You're just putting on a show of concern for me." He lowered his hand and stared at Rick. "Tell me that isn't true."

Rick said nothing. He suddenly felt free. Wonderfully, exhilaratingly free. He could breathe again! For the first time in twenty years he felt like he could actually breathe! He was no longer trapped in a loveless marriage. He no longer felt trapped by the endless demands of parenthood. He was free! He felt giddy. Something in him had changed. Snapped. Broken off. Whatever you want to call it. Maybe it was his sanity. He didn't know. And suddenly he didn't care. The sense of relief he felt was so overwhelming that nothing else mattered. No amount of guilt could stifle the elation he felt coursing through him.

"And here I was thinking *I* was being the monster," Simon said. "You just put me to shame."

Simon snatched at the shovel, ripping it out of Rick's hand, and hurried off deeper into the cemetery.

Rick gave chase, catching up to Simon as he stopped at a grave.

Simon shoved the torch into the ground near the mound and started to dig.

"What are you doing?" Rick asked.

"Not letting you win," Simon said. "I'm getting Julia out."

"I can't let you do that, Simon," Rick said.

"Fuck you. I'm doing it."

"Leave her," Rick said.

Simon stopped shoveling. He stared at Rick. He looked at the white gargoyle atop the gravestone. He leaned closer to the tiny white statuette. "Did you hear that, Julia?" Simon looked over to Rick, then glanced at the gargoyle. "That's a tiny security camera, by the way."

"Yes, I heard." Julia's voice coming from the gargoyle was muted, but still discernible.

Rick stared with confused, unbelieving eyes at the tiny white gargoyle statuette. The gargoyle's wide stone eyes stared at him, its grotesque mouth twisted into a grin.

"They're all still alive," Simon said.

Rick frowned at him.

"Your family," Simon said. "They are all still alive. They're not even here. I locked them up in my shed."

Rick frowned at him. "Spencer. I saw him in that grave…"

Simon shook his head. "That was just a special effects dummy. He's still alive. It was fake," Simon said. "I made a mold of his face. Made a cast and put it on a corpse. I put it on a body that was already dead." He pointed his finger at Rick. "Got you, ha."

Rick just stared at Simon. The torch shoved into the ground nearby still burned, throwing elongated, distorted shadows across Rick's face. "You didn't really poison me, did you?"

"No," Simon said. "But you just poisoned yourself." He handed the shovel back to Rick. "Can't wait for you to be reunited with the family." Simon looked at the white gargoyle statuette, then turned to looked at the man staring vacantly at the shovel in his hand. "How you feelin', Rick?"

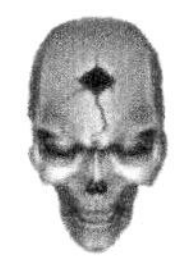

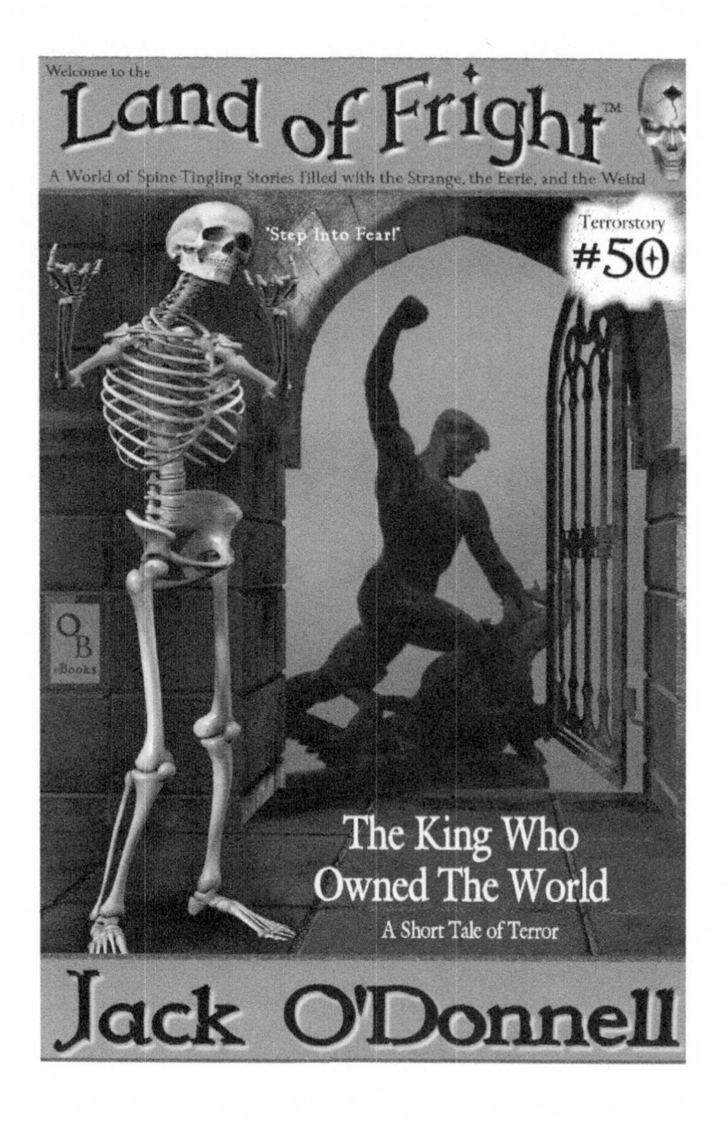
Welcome to the
Land of Fright™
A World of Spine-Tingling Stories filled with the Strange, the Eerie, and the Weird
'Step Into Fear!'
Terrorstory
#50
OB
eBooks
The King Who
Owned The World
A Short Tale of Terror
Jack O'Donnell

TERRORSTORY #50 THE KING WHO OWNED THE WORLD

"It is not enough," Revek said.

Alfihar Grimalt studied his king as he stood before the ornate throne in the royal chamber of Fortress Rohard. "You own the world, my king," Alfihar said.

King Revek was a tall man, thick with muscle, his skin darkened and weathered and scarred from decades of warring in the sun and decades of hard-fought battles. His dark hair had premature streaks of gray running through it, making him look older than he really was. Revek was bare-chested as was his wont; he had chosen Fortress Rohard as his principal stronghold because it was situated in a nearly perpetual moderate climate, with minimal temperature fluctuations throughout the year and mild rainfall patterns, which allowed him the luxury of going shirtless as often as he liked.

A woman dressed in a sheer robe was on her knees before Revek, pleasuring him with her mouth. His loose breeches were pooled on the ground at his bare feet. Both men seemed oblivious of her presence, even Revek.

Revek looked to his advisor. Alfihar was dressed in tight leggings and a baggy white shirt that was too big for his thin frame. A wickedly jagged dagger was stuck into the black leather belt that encircled his advisor's waist. The first time Alfihar had entered the royal chamber he had been dressed in ornate flowing robes. Revek had laughed so hard at the sight of him that Alfihar dared not ever wear the robes again. "It is not enough," Revek said again. His thick muscular arm was draped across one arm of the magnificent golden throne. He leaned forward, staring into the emptiness at the center of the main throne room. Torches flickered on the walls, throwing dancing light on the gleaming marble floor. The outer walls of the room were dotted with spectacular sculptures, lush paintings, various weapons taken from conquered enemies displayed on golden pedestals, but the center of the large expanse was empty.

Alfihar followed Revek's gaze, staring at the vast empty room. The meal tables situated to Alfihar's right were empty, their benches devoid of any guests.

"There is no one left to oppose you, Revek. You have vanquished them all."

Revek frowned. He was quiet for a moment. "Then we must find someone."

Alfihar frowned a deeper frown than his king. "Find someone?"

Revek nodded. "Yes."

"Find someone to oppose you?"

Revek scowled, clearly losing his patience. He turned his head sharply to stare at Alfihar. "Yes."

Alfihar remained quiet for a long moment. "And how are we to do that?"

"You are my advisor, are you not, Alfi?" Revek asked.

Alfihar bristled at the nickname his king had given him, but did his best to ignore it. "I am."

"Then why are you asking *me* to advise *you*?"

"I am only inquiring as to whether you had an idea as to how to accomplish such a thing."

Revek scowled. "Is that not what I pay you handsomely for?"

Alfihar nodded. "It is. It is."

The woman kneeling before Revek bobbed her head up and down, up and down. Both men paid her no heed.

"Gather up your minions and advise me then," Revek said. "I would like to hear your thoughts on this matter tomorrow."

"Tomorrow?" The question came out quickly before Alfihar could stop himself. He nodded and spoke again rapidly. "Of course. Tomorrow I shall bring you a plan."

Revek shook his head. "Not just a plan." Revek again looked at Alfihar with a firm gaze. "Him. Bring him to me."

"H—him?" Alfihar stammered. "Bring the one who will oppose you?"

"Yes. Bring him to me tomorrow."

Alfihar was quiet. He did not move.

Revek looked at him. "You must already have an idea of who he is."

"My king?"

"Otherwise you would not just be standing there like a dolt."

"No, no my king." Alfihar bowed, turned, and scurried from the throne room.

Revek finally looked down at the woman pleasuring him and gently stroked her blonde hair as he closed his eyes and leaned back in his throne.

He was most certainly a brute of a man, Alfihar thought as he studied him. But he knew Hatler's mind was flatter than a field of dandees after a stampede. There was no gleam of intelligence behind his dull brown eyes. There was no hint of a cunning stream of thought running behind the man's skull, nothing that would give Revek the challenge he so desperately craved.

No wonder the opposition in Ulonquin had fallen so quickly. This was their leader? Alfihar only felt a growing contempt for the big man in the dungeon cell. Brute force only took this man Hatler so far in his opposition to Revek's rule, then Revek's guile was his undoing.

Alfihar chided himself for even looking at any of the fallen opposition leaders as possible opponents.

These were men Revek had already utterly defeated once. He would defeat them again.

There were several other defeated men still locked away in the dungeon. Revek kept them alive to parade them out in public every so often when he felt the need to let the people know of the fate of anyone who tried to oppose him. But Alfihar knew this place did not hold the key to unlock the solution to the challenge Revek had thrust upon him. He knew these chained and brow-beaten men did not hold the answer; he would find no worthy challenger here.

Alfihar attended the games in the battle ring, studying the men as they fought each other to the death, studying their techniques, their choice of weapons. There was one man who intrigued him. He used blades as extensions of his bare hands and bare feet. He carried no shield. A thin set of armor covered his legs, his arms, and a small plate covered his chest. He was muscular, but not overly so. The curves of his muscles were there, but lean and tight, not bulging obscenely. The man moved with the quickness of a hungry cat having a mouse dangled before its nose, his hands and feet moving in lunging strikes that were amazing to witness.

Alfihar watched him dispose of three men attacking him in a matter of moments. A triple strike to one man's stomach, was followed with a slashing leg kick to another man's throat. The third man went down in a flurry of punches and kicks, his body laced with slashes and riddled with punctures.

Yes, here was a man who might prove worthy.

Alfihar waited patiently for the answer to his question as the battle man wiped the blood of his opponents off his right arm with a towel. They were in the man's quarters beneath the battle ring arena; it was a room large enough to hold a bed, two tables, a few stools, but not much else. The sounds of a fight being held in the arena above could be heard, but the noises were muffled, distant. Four armed men accompanied Alfihar, one standing near Alfihar, the other armed guard standing closer to the battle man; the remaining two men stood just inside the room, flanking the doorway.

Alfihar knew the battle man's name was LiCru Pesadona; he had gotten the man's name from one of the battle ring workers. LiCru was a tall man, his brown hair cut short and tight to his head. No man who fought in the battle ring had long hair; long hair was far too easy to grab onto and use against its owner. LiCru had been fighting in the battle ring for nearly a month now and had never been beaten. Which, of course, was why the man was still alive. Every fight in the battle ring was to the death.

LiCru Pesadona cocked his head curiously at Alfihar. "You want me to challenge King Revek?"

"Yes."

"Why would I do such a thing?" LiCru asked. "It matters not to me who rules this city."

Alfihar smiled. "You misunderstand the extent of Revek's reign. He doesn't just rule this city. He rules the entire world."

"And you want me to challenge him?"

"Yes," Alfihar said.

LiCru set the bloody towel down on one of the small tables nearby. Blood-stained blades already rested on the table, the weapons that LiCru had used in his latest victory. "I shall repeat my question. Why would I do such a thing?"

"You fight like a man with something to prove. Here is your chance to prove it."

"I fight to prove nothing. I fight to keep on living."

Alfihar smiled softly. "Is that all you want? Simply to keep taking a breath day after day?"

"It has served me well so far." LiCru moved to a nearby stool and sat down to work on removing the armor plates that shielded his muscular legs.

"Yes, well enough for me to take notice of you and give you a chance to improve your lot in life."

LiCru silently continued to remove his leg armor, setting the pieces down on the table next to the bloodied towel. He looked up at Alfihar. "Is this some kind of cruel joke?"

Alfihar frowned at his question.

"I'm a battle ring man," LiCru said. "I fight for myself. How am I supposed to challenge Revek? I would need an army."

Alfihar nodded. "Exactly. Gather all your battle ring brothers together and fight."

LiCru laughed. "No one here is brother to another. We only want to kill each other."

"More than you want to kill Revek?" Alfihar asked. "You want to kill each other more than you want to kill the man who has slaughtered thousands? The man who was conquered your villages, murdered your friends, raped your women, enslaved your children?"

LiCru frowned at Alfihar. "Aren't you one of his advisors? I don't think your king would appreciate you inciting a revolt."

"He is *our* king. And he is the one who sent me. He seeks a… diversion."

LiCru was still for a moment, his face expressionless. Then he returned his attention to removing the armor from his other leg, shaking his head. "You are all mad."

Just then a woman entered the quarters. The guard nearest Alfihar drew his sword and pointed it directly at the intruder. She was a beautiful woman with long, flowing black hair. She was dressed elegantly in a red dress, laced with black fringe, her breasts full and firm. She immediately saw Alfihar and bowed her head. "My apologies for interrupting."

Alfihar caught a glimpse of distress in LiCru's face with the appearance of the woman. It was just a fleeting glimpse, but it was enough to let him know there was something between this man and this woman. "Seize her," Alfihar ordered his men.

The two guards nearest the woman grabbed her and held her tightly, squeezing her slender forearms very firmly. She muffled a startled cry, but did not fight to free herself. The guard near Alfihar kept his sword out, gripping it firmly, clearly ready to use the weapon if called upon.

Alfihar saw LiCru glance at the bloodied blades that were sitting on the table nearby; the weapons were close to the battle man but not within arm's reach.

LiCru stared hard at Alfihar. "You are making a grave mistake."

"Am I?" Alfihar asked, not even bothering to hide

the amusement in his voice.

"Let my sister go."

"Sister?" Alfihar glanced at the woman, then back to LiCru, then back to the woman. Yes, he could see a hint of a resemblance. They shared the same nose and slight hint of a cleft in their chin. But then he saw something else that greatly intrigued him. The woman had a dark teardrop tattoo just below her left eye near her elegant nose. She hailed from Castir, a far off land beyond the swirling sands of Valakesh. A land known for its dark magic. Revek had declared all the mages of Valakesh wiped out a decade ago, decimated with the brute force and overwhelming number of soldiers Revek commanded, but the appearance of this woman made Alfihar realize not all of them had been destroyed. He looked back to LiCru. "She will be treated well."

"LiCru, what is going on?" Sheyla Pesadona looked to Alfihar, then to LiCru. "Who are these men?"

"They want me to challenge Revek."

A flash of fear crossed Sheyla's features. "What? Why?"

Alfihar shook his head at LiCru. "No, not just you. An army. You must raise an army and attack the city."

"What? Don't listen to him, LiCru," Sheyla said. "This is crazy."

"Yes. It is," LiCru said.

Alfihar wiggled his fingers at the guards holding Sheyla. "Take her to the fortress. She is proving to be a bad influence on her brother."

"You'd best take care with her," LiCru said, the warning in his tone clear. "She has the blood of the Old Ones in her veins."

Sheyla snapped her head towards her brother. "LiCru!"

LiCru closed his mouth and looked away from his sister, lowering his head.

The two guards moved out of the room, half dragging, half carrying Sheyla along with them.

Alfihar turned back to LiCru. "Perhaps you are not the one I was looking for." He paused. "Tell me more about your sister."

The opulence of Fortress Rohard was overwhelming. Everything seemed to glitter and glisten with gold. Immaculately dressed servants scurried about everywhere. The smell of fresh cooked meat filled the hallway. Sheyla's mouth began to water and her stomach rumbled.

The two guards had released their tight grips on her and allowed her to walk in front of them as they guided her in which way to turn and move through the massive hallways of the fortress. They approached a large opening on their right and, even though she had never been in the fortress before, she somehow instinctively knew that led to the massive throne room. They reached the opening just as a tall muscular man strode out of the throne room, nearly colliding into them.

"A thousand pardons, my king," one of the guards said, his words fumbling from his lips. Sheyla could almost see the fear wrapped around each word as it spilled out of her captor's mouth.

Revek said nothing. He stared at Sheyla, raking her face and body with his gaze. "What has she done?" he asked the guards.

Both guards hesitated. "Nothing," one of the guards finally said.

"Nothing?" Revek kept his gaze on her. "Yet you lead her through the palace as though she were a prisoner?"

"She *is* a prisoner, my king."

Revek turned to the guard. "How can she be a prisoner and yet she has done nothing?"

"Alfihar's orders."

Revek looked at Sheyla. "And what did you do to my friend to make him treat you thus?"

Sheyla did not answer.

One of the guards poked her hard. "Your king has asked you a question."

"Nothing," she said, the word nearly spitting out of her mouth.

"Nothing," Revek mused. "These men say you have done nothing and you say you have done nothing, yet you are being treated as a prisoner. Surely, someone is lying to me." He looked hard at the two guards. "I don't appreciate anyone lying to me."

"She's his sister," one of the guards blurted.

"Whose sister?" Revek asked.

"The sister of the man who is going to challenge you."

Revek broke out into a wide smile. "Ahh." He looked back to Sheyla. "This is very exciting. Very exciting." He looked to the two guards. "Leave us."

The guards hesitated, but only for the briefest of moments, then turned and headed away from them.

Revek reached out and grabbed Sheyla by the hand. She tried to pull her hand away from him, but

Revek held her tight. "Come, you must tell me all about your brother."

"You say he commands ten thousand men?" Revek was nearly giddy with excitement. He raised his golden goblet and took a heavy sip of his warm wine. He had been lounging on a couch, laying on his side, watching the woman who called herself Sheyla, but her words caused him to sit up straight and pay closer attention to her. She sat primly upright in the couch across from him. Between them, a heavy fur pelt covered the marble floor. A fire crackled and burned in the hearth nearby. Pedestals dotted the area, several of them holding trays of food filled with sliced fruit, dried meats, nuts, and cheeses. A servant woman stood a dozen yards away, waiting to be summoned for whatever Revek needed.

Revek immediately lusted after this woman called Sheyla, yet something inside him told him not to touch her. She sat in the chair, her elegant red dress flowing down her legs, her face demure, her eyes watching him. She sipped gently on a goblet of nectar and her lips glistened with its dew in the firelight. This was madness. He released himself from his breeches, pulling his cock out to hold it in his hand.

The woman gasped despite herself. He knew she hadn't meant to react that way, but she had gasped anyway.

He stroked himself, running his hand up and down his shaft, enjoying the feeling of his fingers on his flesh. He gritted his teeth, fighting back the urge to stomp over to her, rip off her pretty little red dress and fuck her hard and deep right on the bear rug in front of the fire. "Ten thousand," Revek repeated. "That is a battle that may last weeks." He smiled.

Sheyla cradled the golden goblet in her hands, rolling it between her fingers, but she did not take another drink. She avoided looking in his direction.

"And they fight with blades tied to their hands and feet, you say? Oh, that is rich. What a spectacle that will be!" Revek took another drink, draining the goblet. "And they wear minimal armor? I must hold my archers in reserve then. That wouldn't be a fair fight." He held his goblet out and the servant woman scurried over to him to refill it. Revek looked at Sheyla as he continued to stroke himself. "There is nothing more tedious than a lopsided fight. Then it is simply a slaughter, not a battle. I have no stomach for slaughter."

Sheyla said nothing.

"I apologize. I am being rude." He spit into his palm to give himself some lubrication and returned his moistened hand to his hardened cock. He continued to stroke himself, feeling himself lengthen and thicken in his hand. "Only asking of your brother. And what of you? Are you one of his advisors? You seem to have a keen intellect."

She turned her head away, as if trying to hide her embarrassed face from him, but he didn't care. He could still see her. It did not matter if she looked at him at all. He could still see the soft lines of her cheekbones, the creamy smoothness of her skin. The curves of her breasts were obvious beneath her dress and he was pretty certain he could see the hardened points of her nipples beneath the fabric.

"I am just a sister who worries about her little

brother," Sheyla said.

Revek nodded. "As I worry about my sisters."

She glanced at him. "You have sisters?" She quickly looked away.

Revek laughed. "Too many of them. Eighteen. I have eighteen sisters. None of them are here at Rohard right now, though. They are all helping me rule some portion of the world that needs ruling."

"Eighteen sisters?"

"My father was a busy man." Revek laughed again. "His seven wives bore him eighteen girls and one boy — me." He looked at her, releasing his grip on his cock to wave his fingers at her. "Come, tell me more of you. What else? Surely, you are more than just a sister."

Behind Sheyla, the fire in the hearth crackled as it continued to feast on the logs contained within the stone enclosure. He saw her glance about the room, as if looking for an exit, but there were none. The doors were closed, guarded by men just outside. The only other person in the room was the servant woman who was laying out dishes on the table nearby, continuing to prepare the food for their main meal. Revek wasn't quite certain what the servant woman's name was and he didn't want to call her by the wrong name, so he summoned her to his side as best he knew how. "Woman," he said to her. "Come and take care of this."

The servant woman looked over to him and betrayed no emotion as she saw his enlarged member in his hand, his fingers stroking its pink flesh up and down. "Yes, my king." She set the serving bowl she had been holding down on the table and moved over to Revek.

Revek caught Sheyla slightly turning her gaze towards him to see what was happening. He smiled. Her curiosity was getting the better of her dignity.

The servant woman moved to her knees in front of Revek and started licking the underside of his balls as he continued to stroke himself. He immediately thought of the Sheyla woman doing the same to him and he had to release his grip on his cock lest he unleash the white rain that threatened to pour out of him.

The servant woman moved her tongue up his shaft, licking and kissing at his cock. She took the head of his manhood into her mouth and started to suck on him. She moved her warm mouth up and down over his head, taking half his shaft into her mouth, stopping only when she couldn't fit any more in without choking on his large cock.

Revek kept his gaze locked on the woman in the red dress. Sheyla seemed to be frozen in place, unsure of where to go, what to do, or even where she should look. Her face was still mostly turned away from him, but he could see the lines of her neck, the luscious bounty of her black silken hair, the curves of her shoulders. Her slender fingers still held the goblet in her hand, the drink within the cup apparently forgotten for now.

Finally, Sheyla spoke. "Must you do this?" She looked at the servant woman, who now had her buttocks bared, her serving uniform dress hiked up past her waist.

"It is either her or you," Revek said.

"It will *not* be me," Sheyla said, her voice firm.

Revek moved behind the servant woman and moved into position on his knees behind her. He gripped her sides, guiding his stiff cock towards her waiting wetness with decades of experience. He easily found her wet folds and pushed inside of her, gliding into her warmth. The servant woman moaned with delight.

Sheyla turned away.

Revek started to thrust, moving slowly in and out of the servant woman, not pulling all of the way out but taking nearly half the head of his cock out of her before plunging back inside of her. He kept his gaze firmly riveted on the woman seated in the chair before him as he fucked the servant woman a mere few feet away. He wondered how many men this Sheyla had had. He wondered how wet she would be for him. How tight. Did she have skills like some of the other women? Would she be able to grip him and milk him with her muscles? Some of the servant women were very expert at doing that, and that was something he greatly enjoyed.

The servant woman came with a breathy moan as he continued to thrust himself in and out of her now very wet folds.

Revek saw Sheyla look at the servant woman as the woman moaned heavily with pleasure, again unable to stop herself from sneaking a glance.

And then this dark mysterious beauty named Sheyla looked at him, capturing him with her stare. Her eyes mesmerized him, captivated him, tormented him. They were a deep blue, a blue that made her eyes shine with some kind of inner light. There was no fighting their effect on him. He exploded inside the servant woman, sending a gushing blast of his seed deep into her belly.

And then the woman named Sheyla did something

that actually unnerved him. She smiled at him. It was just a hint of a smile, just a slight turning up of the corners of her mouth, but he was certain he had seen it. And it wasn't a shy smile. It was a clever, cunning smile. She slowly raised her goblet to her lips and took a gentle sip of her nectar.

"She has magic in her," Alfihar said to Revek. "Her brother has confirmed this to be true." The two men walked through the outdoor training yard. Around them, men and women practiced swordplay, their metal blades clanging and clashing against each other as they struck and parried.

"Have you seen her beauty? She'll soon have my cock in her, too," Revek said. "I can confirm *that* to be true."

Alfihar looked at his king with a clear warning in his gaze. "Be careful of her, Revek. Women and magic can be a dangerous mix."

"I surely hope so," Revek said. "Isn't that the point of this entire exercise? To bring me some danger? Some *real* danger?"

"She is an artist, too, my king," Alfihar said.

Revek threw back his head and laughed. He looked at his advisor. "An artist, too? Now I surely must quake in my boots. Perhaps she'll slay me with her paintbrush."

Alfihar shook his head. "She does not paint. She is a master of metal and glass."

"A sculptor?" Revek asked. "Or perhaps a weapons maker? A woman who makes weapons. Now that is something I would like to see. What does she make? Daggers? Surely she does not make swords. I cannot see a man wielding a sword forged by a woman."

"No, she does not make weapons."

Revek waited for Alfihar to elaborate but his advisor did not continue. "Well, out with it, Alfi," Revek said, his tone insistent. "What does she make?"

"Yes, I am an artist," Sheyla said, quickly raising the goblet she held in her hand to take a sip of the warm nectar it contained.

Revek nodded his head in approval. He had summoned Sheyla to join him in the throne room to discuss her talents. "Alfihar said as much. I do enjoy good art." From his seated position on his throne, he motioned to all the spectacular sculptures, the lush paintings, the numerous ornamentations that filled the throne room.

Sheyla glanced about the room, taking in all the stunning pieces, then looked back to him. "You do? Where is it?" She took another sip from her goblet, peering at him over the rim of the golden cup.

He stared at her for a long moment, then burst out laughing. "Ah, a funny sister." He pointed at her. "That's what you are. Is that your art? To be funny? To amuse people?"

She shook her head. "That's just an extra bonus I bring." She paused. "I make things. I make things with glass and metals."

"What manner of things?"

"Mirrors mostly," she said.

"Mirrors?"

She nodded. She again looked about the room. "I do not see any mirrors in here. Surely, a king as great as yourself would want to gaze upon your own magnificence at least a few times during the day."

Revek looked at her for a quiet moment, slightly cocking his head as he stared at her. "This is true," he finally said.

"I can make one for you."

"Why?"

"You are the king," Sheyla said.

"*The* king. Not *my* king?"

"You are my king," Sheyla said immediately with no hesitation.

Revek nodded. "Yes. Yes, you will bring me one of these mirrors. Let's see how great of an artist you really are."

"Where is my challenger?" Revek asked. He made no effort to hide his annoyance. Several days had passed and Alfihar still had brought him no word of his challenger. He sat on his throne, too bored to even have a servant woman work between his legs.

Alfihar pointed to the large object situated on the throne room floor. It was a rectangular object nearly seven feet high, a few inches taller than Revek, covered by a cloth. It rested on the throne room floor a few feet away from the raised dais where the throne was located. "Beneath that cloth, my king."

"Let me see him. Damn you for being such a tease, Alfi."

Alfihar moved to the object and pulled the cloth away, revealing the item that lay beneath. "It is an enchanted mirror, my king. The lady Sheyla created it just for you."

"And that is where my greatest threat lies?" Revek gripped the handle of his sword, staring at a reflection of himself, watching his mirror image grip its sword along with him. The mirror was ornately bordered by a dark metal frame, intricate patterns and shapes and words etched all along the lengths of the frame.

Alfihar nodded.

"I see nothing but a black mirror."

"You must step closer, my king. Gaze into it."

"Is this some sort of wizard's trick, Alfihar?"

Alfihar nodded.

Revek rose up out of his throne, moved down the few steps that led away from the dais, and strode forward to stop directly in front of the mirror. "I only see a reflection of myself."

Alfihar nodded. "A man's greatest enemy is usually himself."

Revek looked askance at his advisor with an annoyed expression, then looked back to the black mirror. Odd, wispy streams of blue light appeared to flow out of his body and into the mirror. Revek glanced down but saw no such light radiating out from his body; the streams of light were only visible in the mirror, as if seeping out from his own body and moving into the reflective image of himself in the dark glass. He gritted his teeth. "This is what you bring me? This is my greatest threat? Myself?" Revek stared at his reflection with a tightened jaw. He drew his blade and smashed the butt end of the sword's handle into the mirror with a savage strike, smashing the shards into a dozen pieces.

"No!" Alfihar shouted, raising his hands in alarm.

The shards of the black mirror fell to the floor, breaking into even smaller pieces, skittering across the hard marble.

"No!" Alfihar shouted again, his widening eyes filling with cold fear.

The throne room went quiet for a moment. Both men stared at the broken shards of mirror that littered the floor. Images of Revek were visible in each shard, as if his image had been locked into each piece of the broken glass. And then the reflections of Revek began taking physical form, bursting forth from the enchanted pieces of glass as if being born from some darkly enchanted womb. But these creatures being born were no infants. They were of all manner of sizes, some two feet tall, one three feet tall. Many others were only a foot tall. And some of these miniature Reveks were even less tall than that, barely reaching the height of a few inches. They all shared Revek's features. Each of their bodies, despite their different heights, were all thick with muscle, their skin darkened and weathered and scarred. Each one of the mirrorlings had a dark head of hair, the same premature streaks of gray running through them that colored Revek's head. Within moments, twenty-seven versions of Revek in all now stood in the large chamber, twenty-seven miniature versions of the great king, each armed with a sword in their left hand, each gripping their weapon in the mirror-opposite hand.

Revek stared at the mirrorlings for a long moment, his face grim, his sword gripped in his right hand. And then he burst out laughing, throwing his head back to let out a hearty rumble. "Oh, this is rich, Alfi. You have outdone yourself!"

Alfihar opened his mouth to say something, but

then recovered and pressed his lips together. He took a brief moment to compose himself, then bowed towards Revek. "I am glad you are pleased, my king."

Suddenly, Revek stumbled, as if he had just been pushed by some unseen force. He looked as if he had just stepped forth from a tavern after a heavy night of drinking and fucking. "What manner of Hell is this?" Revek asked. He stared dumbfounded at the mirrorlings that filled the throne room. He felt an unpleasantness in his head, a lightheadedness that made him feel tired. It was a feeling he was not used to. It was a feeling he did not enjoy. He was never tired in the middle of the day, yet here he felt as if he needed to go to sleep. His arms felt heavy, which made the lightheaded feeling all that more uncomfortable and unpleasant. The sword in his right hand felt as if it weighed a hundred pounds. His body felt in complete disarray.

"There was only supposed to be one of you," Alfihar said. "Only one." Alfihar looked to one of the servant women standing nearby. "Fetch me that woman from Castir. Bring Sheyla here."

The servant woman did not move. She seemed frozen in fear, staring wide-eyed at all of the mirrorling copies of King Revek.

Alfihar stalked over to the servant woman and shook her roughly, pushing her towards the throne room doorway. "Now! Bring her here!"

The servant woman stumbled and fell to the floor. Three of the mirrorlings moved in her direction, one two-foot tall mirrorling reaching out its hand to help her. The servant woman muffled a shriek at the diminutive version of her king and scrambled to her feet, racing out of the room. Two of the Revek mirrorlings, each one only about a foot tall, chased after her, racing out of the throne room.

"Stop them, you fools!" Alfihar shouted at the two guards stationed just inside the throne room. The guards hesitated, then hurried after the two mirrorlings.

Five more of the mirrorlings raced out of the throne room as if obeying Alfihar's desperate command as well. These mirrorlings ranged in height from a mere six inches to one mirrorling that was about three feet tall. It was quite the odd sight to watch them all run across the marble floor, each one a different height, yet each one a mirror image of the king. Each one clutched a sword that was scaled in size appropriately to their height.

Despite his best effort, Alfihar could not hide the fright that had filtered into his eyes. He turned to look at Revek. "I suggest you go find Sheyla yourself, my king."

Revek frowned at his advisor. "Why?"

"She may be in danger."

"From myself?" He shook his head. "I have no desire to harm her. I only want to fuck her." He shook his head again, but this time more in an effort to clear his muddled thoughts than to respond to his advisor.

"As do they," Alfihar said.

Revek shook his head. "They are too small to hurt her."

"A rat can kill a man if he catches him in the throat unawares," Alfihar said. "Even a spider's bite can still kill a man." Alfihar paused. "They are all armed."

Revek stared at the twenty versions of himself that

remained in the throne room, forcing himself to focus. The shattered remains of the mirror and its frame lay scattered about the floor. He squeezed his eyes tight, then opened them. He just wanted to rest, just for a little while. These — things — were, indeed, all armed, but each mirrorling was holding his sword in his left hand instead of his right. It really was like looking at a reflection of himself, but the reflections were not perfectly opposite duplicates of him. There were some distortions in some of their faces, in their bodies, even in some of the swords they held. They were him, but twisted variations of him.

He looked at one of the larger mirrorlings standing to his left. This one was nearly four feet in size, perhaps a little less. But there was something wrong with him. No, not him. *It.* It was not human. It was a thing. There was something twisted and gnarled about its features. Its arms hung at an odd angle. Its left eye was higher than its right eye. Its mouth was twisted into something that looked like a smile and a grimace at the same time. Its legs and feet seemed normal. It was just the upper half of it that somehow had come out of the enchanted mirror in a distorted fashion. It tried to grip its sword, but its fingers were so misshapen it had a hard time keeping its grip on the handle. The sword kept falling out of its left hand and clattering to the ground. It quickly grabbed at the weapon and picked the sword back up, only to drop the sword a moment later as it lost its grip on the weapon again.

Revek saw it try to speak, but it couldn't move its lips to make any form of comprehensible words. It just spewed nonsensical gibberish. Saliva oozed out of its mouth and this grotesque thing didn't look as if it could do anything about it; its lips were so misaligned that there was a permanent gap that allowed its saliva to just continue dripping out of it mouth. It was the most unpleasant thing Revek had ever seen in his life. A horribly grotesque version of himself. A version he couldn't have imagined even in his worst nightmares.

Again, the deformed mirrorling dropped the sword and the weapon clattered to the ground. It fumbled at the blade and managed to pick the weapon back up. It held the sword up in front of itself defensively. This… this thing had no means of launching an attack against him, Revek realized. All it could do was pathetically try to defend itself.

The tears were what set Revek off. He watched them form and pool in the corner of the thing's eyes. He watched them come free of their position and drag themselves down the creature's misaligned cheeks. The tears glistened and sparkled in the torchlight. The creature wailed and whimpered as it dropped the sword again. This time, it didn't try to pick up the sword again. It just looked down at the blade laying inert on the marble floor, then looked back up at Revek. The tears were flowing heavier now, raining down from its eyes in a torrent of sobbing the likes of which Revek had never seen before, not even from a woman mourning the loss of her beloved or her stillborn child. He felt the rage brewing inside him, growing red hot. This… thing had come from within him? This thing was born out of a reflection of himself? This thing was showing some horribly twisted version of some weakness he had inside him? It sickened him and that only fueled Revek's rage. He took a few strides forward and swung his blade, lopping the thing's head off with one clean strike. The body stayed upright for just a moment as the head rolled across the marble floor, blood spraying out in a geyser of redness, but then toppled to the side and flopped spasmodically on the floor.

Revek watched with amazement as a soft swirl of blue light, some form of energy, rose up out of the dead mirrorling he had just slain and moved towards him. He slashed at this blob of light, but his sword just passed harmlessly through it like he was trying to cut through a ray of light given off by a torch. The amorphous cloud of light sank into Revek's chest and he felt an immediate sensation of energy and strength and clarity.

Revek could feel them, sense them. He was connected somehow to all of the mirrorlings. They were part of him, after all. They had come from him. He realized they had taken some of his energy and strength from him. That is where the flash of weakness and fatigue had come from; they had taken some of his life force from him. And he also now knew that when he killed one of them, he could feel part of his strength return, as if their deaths restored the energy they had stolen from him.

He found himself breathing hard, his hand clenching his sword so tightly that his fingers ached. He knew he must kill them all and re-absorb their energy back in to him. Especially before any of his enemies got wind of his weakened state.

Revek looked at the decapitated body with disgust. I need to burn it, he thought. Wipe away any trace that it had ever existed. He glanced around for the severed head, following the trail of blood along the marble floor with his gaze. But he stopped searching for the head when he saw what happened next.

One of the mirrorlings just slid along the smooth marble floor of the throne room, as if the bottoms of its boots were oiled and a rope was attached about its waist and someone was pulling it. Yet, there was no oil on its boots. There was no rope attached about its waist. It just glided along the floor towards a much larger mirrorling. And then the small mirrorling was just sucked up by the larger mirrorling, the mirrorlings acting like two drops of water rolling towards each other and merging into one when they struck each other. The larger mirrorling flared with a bright light for a brief moment, then the light faded away. Revek had battled sorceresses and dragons and ogres and giant lizards and odd creatures of all types, but he had never seen an enemy that absorbed other creatures into itself.

To Revek, it looked as if the larger mirrorling grew a bit taller, its body widened out a bit thicker. It had absorbed the energy from the small mirrorling just as he had absorbed the life force of the mirrorling he had just slain. Somehow, even the breeches on the mirrorling seemed to have lengthened, as well as the sword it held. Everything about these reflections of himself was enchanted, from their bodies to the blades they wielded. These creatures stole the energy that belongs to me. I have to kill them all, Revek realized. I have to kill them all now! The thrill of the hunt, the promise of many battles, stirred his blood. Revek smiled a grim smile.

But the mirrorlings, possessing the same mind, or at least a version of Revek's mind that held many of the same thoughts, had the same realization as King Revek did. They all scattered, racing away from each other, moving in all directions. Three of them raced towards the throne room doorway, but two of them were absorbed into a larger one as they got too close to it, so by the time they reached the doorway, there was only one mirrorling actually racing out of the room.

Within a matter of moments, Revek found himself staring at a throne room empty of anyone but Alfihar, the decapitated body of the mirrorling, and himself. He turned to Alfihar. "Well, my friend, not quite the challenge I expected. I will have to give you a healthy bonus of coin this year on your naming day." He slapped Alfihar on the back and laughed. "If we survive that long."

Sheyla stared at the three-foot Revek mirrorling who now stood in her room. Moments earlier, she had heard shouting out in the hallway, heard the clashing of swords, but she had remained in her room, not knowing what the cause of the commotion was. What had happened to him? She knew of no magic that would shrink a man. If she had, she would have shrunk many a buffoon down to size long ago. Such a thing was not possible. "What happened to you?" she finally asked aloud.

The three-foot Revek mirrorling pointed his sword at her. "You caused this," the man said. His voice was not as deep as Revek's, but it was still strong despite the man's diminutive size. The tip of his sword dripped with blood, and a wet, red streak ran along the blade's length. More smears of dark blood were visible on his arm and stained his pants; his bare chest was slashed in several places.

She noticed he was carrying the blade in his left hand and she suddenly began to understand what had happened. Revek was right handed.

"That damned mirror caused this," the little man king said, confirming her suspicions.

"I was ordered to create it by your pale friend," Sheyla said. "I had no choice. You are holding my little brother captive."

"Did Alfihar tell you to curse it?"

"Yes. He said you craved a challenge." She looked at him and smiled. "Well, now you have one." She looked at the Revek mirrorling and paused for a moment. "Well, not you actually. Him. Now Revek has a real challenge in front of him."

The three-foot Revek mirrorling took a few steps closer to her, keeping his sword at the ready. Blood continued to drip down the blade. "And what of me?"

Sheyla shrugged. "What of you? You are nothing but a toy. An amusement for your king."

"I am no toy."

"Then what are you?" Sheyla pointed at him. "Look at you. You're half a man. You are a toy. You're an aberration. You're a creature of magic. You were born of dark light and dark energy, twisted into some inhuman shape."

The Revek mirrorling gritted his teeth. "I am no toy."

Sheyla said nothing.

The Revek mirrorling stepped closer to her, re-gripping the handle of his sword "You made me. What am I?"

Sheyla shook her head. "No, Revek made you. Go

and ask him what you are."

"You had best temper your tone with me, woman. I can still gut you like a fish. There may be many of me running around, but there is only one of you."

Sheyla looked at him, hesitated for a moment, and then smiled a cunning smile. "Is there?"

The three-foot Revek mirrorling gritted his teeth. "Let's go find this brother of yours. Alfihar told me he wasn't very cooperative, so he sent him to the dungeon." He raised the bloody sword. "Maybe he'll be more cooperative with me."

Revek stood in the doorway to Sheyla's room, staring at the empty space. "She is not here."

Alfihar stood silently behind him.

Revek glanced back out into the hallway. Several small pools of blood dotted the floor, along with several small mirrorling corpses. Revek moved back into the hallway. He crouched down and picked up several small swords, each one a different size. He showed them to Alfihar.

"One of them is starting to take control," Alfihar said.

"One of them is taking the life that belongs to me," Revek said. He threw the small swords down in disgust and they clattered along the floor. He pointed to the small dead bodies. "I want those burned to ash. And then I want the ash dumped into the gong pits. I want no trace of them to remain."

Alfihar nodded. "Though I do not know why he is killing them instead of absorbing them."

"I suspect I know why," Revek said immediately.

"He probably feared he was going to be absorbed, so he killed them first. I would have no desire to be absorbed into another. I would do the same."

Alfihar just nodded.

"Where would he take her?" Revek asked.

"He needs allies," Alfihar said. "He'll be smart enough to realize that."

"And where would he go to find those?"

"That is a simple question to answer, Revek." Alfihar looked at his king. "Where would *you* go?"

"What manner of dark magic is this?" LiCru asked. He stared at the diminutive version of Revek standing before the open cell door. The tiny man looked almost comical to him.

"Do you not want Revek dead?" the diminutive mirrorling of Revek asked.

"But you *are* Revek." LiCru said.

"I am of Revek, but I am not Revek. I am not the man who put you in here and sentenced you to fight in the battle ring."

LiCru just stared at the mirrorling. "And what would you have me do, little man?" LiCru finally asked.

"Find Revek and kill him. Kill all the versions of Revek you come across. And then you will earn your freedom and riches beyond your wild imaginings."

LiCru looked at the open cell door. "It seems to me that I already have my freedom." LiCru moved with amazing and surprising speed. He grabbed the Revek mirrorling by the arm and threw him hard against the stone wall of the cell, dazing him. The

Revek mirrorling grabbed at his side and wheezed out a struggling breath as blood trickled down from his skull. Parts of his brain were exposed where a sharp piece of stone had taken out a chunk of his skull. His dropped sword lay on the cell floor, out of easy reach.

"Damn you are hard to kill, even when you are one half of your normal size." LiCru grabbed the mirrorling's arm and flung him hard against the wall again.

This time, the mirrorling did not get up.

LiCru stomped on the mirrorling's head for good measure, splattering his brains all across the floor of the cell. LiCru raised his bloodied foot to look at the results and smiled with grim satisfaction. "*Now* he's dead. What the hell happened to him?" He looked up at his sister, who had remained quiet and still during the altercation. "He said he was *of* Revek, but wasn't Revek. What does that mean?"

Sheyla looked at the bloodied corpse of the Revek mirrorling, then turned to look at her brother. "He came out of a black mirror," Sheyla said.

"One of yours?" LiCru asked.

Sheyla nodded. "Revek wanted some amusement to challenge him." She paused. "So I gave him some."

LiCru looked at the smashed and smushed body of the Revek mirrorling for a moment, then turned to Sheyla and smiled a grim smile. "Yes, you did."

"Let's go home to Castir," Sheyla said. "I grow weary of this place. I am sorry I did not rescue you from the battle ring earlier, LiCru."

LiCru shrugged. "I was doing well." He followed Sheyla out of the prison cell and into the hallway beyond. "What about the real Revek?"

Sheyla stood in the dungeon corridor, moving her

gaze over several closed cell doors. "I know of a way to keep him busy."

Revek and Alfihar walked through the dungeon, passing empty prison cell after empty prison cell, every door thrust open wide. Several dead guards lay motionless in the corridor.

"Are you getting nervous yet, Alfihar?" Revek asked.

"I must admit my apprehension is growing, yes," Alfihar said.

Revek laughed. He slapped Alfihar on the back. "You have so greatly outdone yourself, Alfihar. Whatever you desire will be yours. If—"

"—we survive this," Alfihar said, for the first time interrupting his king and finishing his words for him.

Revek laughed again, and once more slapped Alfihar heartily on the back. "Yes, *if*."

Alfihar did not join in Revek's laughter. "I need to rest, my king, and eat."

Revek nodded to his advisor. "Yes. We must eat. And then I need sleep. These damned things you brought into the world have sapped some of my strength. A tired fighter most often becomes a dead fighter."

Revek's sleep was fitful. Images of his shattered selves somehow filtered into his mind. The dreams were macabre, ghastly nightmares the likes of which Revek had never experienced before in his life. He found himself inhabiting the bodies of the mirrorlings and experiencing what they were experiencing. His mind was somehow attached to theirs and his fevered dreams forced him to live as they lived, feel what they felt.

One of the mirrorlings died a horrible death at the mercy of one of the castle cats. The calico cat had caught him unawares as he rounded a corner. The huge paw came seemingly out of nowhere, swiping him across the side of his head and his shoulder, sending him sprawling to the stone floor of the corridor. He lost his grip on his sword and it went clattering across the stones. He staggered to his feet, feeling a warm wetness on his face, dripping down his shoulder. The cat had ripped into his flesh with its claws, gouging his skin. He looked about for his blade, and saw it on the floor a few feet away. He lunged for the sword, but the cat flattened him to the ground with a crushing paw. He glanced up over his shoulder to see the cat's open jaw and massive sharp teeth descending straight towards him. Darkness filled his world and he saw nothing after that.

Revek scowled in his sleep. He never liked that calico cat. He knew that cat always had it in for him. There were seven or eight other cats in the fortress, and he enjoyed the company of all of them. He felt a kindred spirit with their aloofness. But this was one cat he had never warmed to, and the cat had never warmed to him, either. They were just not meant to be companions for whatever the reason. And now the blasted beast had ate him. The damn infernal calico had eaten him! It was most likely purring up a storm right about now as it licked its lips and cleaned *his* blood from its paws.

Is this what Alfihar had intended all along? To

have him conquered by the most unlikeliest of enemies - a cat? No, he didn't think so. Alfihar seemed genuinely horrified when he had smashed the mirror. He didn't think this was part of Alfihar's plan.

How many mirrorlings were there? How many copies of himself? He had seen dozens of shards on the throne room floor and more than two dozen of these infernal copies of himself. But were there more than that? Were there hundreds of him running around the fortress now? And were they all plotting to kill him?

His fevered dreams continued. One small mirrorling who was merely a few inches tall had fallen off a ledge and fell into a bucket of water. The walls of the bucket were too smooth, the rim too high for him to reach. He was trapped in the cold water with no means of escape. He fought valiantly to stay afloat, but fatigue eventually claimed him and he drowned in a smothering wave of blackness.

Revek immediately transitioned to the body of another mirrorling in his dreams. This mirrorling was even smaller than the last, barely the size of an ant. He got caught in a spider's web. The spider crawled closer along the web, its brown body bristling with tiny hairs. The mirrorling twisted and turned but could not break free of the sticky web. The spider crawled over his body and injected him with a paralyzing poison. He watched himself get eaten alive by the spider.

Revek woke up feverish and sweating. He waved his arms about wildly, very afraid of not being able to move his limbs, truly terrified of being paralyzed. He knew he had to destroy all of the mirrorlings to rid himself of these horrible nightmares; they would continue as long as one of the mirrorlings lived. He needed to destroy every last one. These odd fears were starting to overwhelm his thoughts, and that was something he knew he could not let continue.

LiCru took a step forward, putting an arm out protectively in front of Sheyla. "We set you free," he said to the motley gang of four newly released prisoners who stood in the hallway. "Let us pass." Nothing was going as planned. Instead of running off to cause chaos throughout the fortress with the other dozen prisoners they had released, these four prisoners had decided to follow them and torment their would-be rescuers.

"Give us the woman and you can go. We don't need what you have between your legs. We've got plenty of those," the bald man with the pug nose said. He was the obvious leader of the group.

"Be on your way," LiCru said to them. "Or this will end badly."

Pug-Nose nodded. "Yes, it will. For you. I know about you, LiCru." The man glanced at LiCru's hands and feet, then looked back up to his face with a scornful scowl. "You don't have your fancy little blades. I don't think you'll amount to much of a challenge without those."

"Just go, LiCru," Sheyla said. "I've handled worse than the likes of these."

LiCru looked at her with utter disbelief. "Don't be stupid. I am not leaving you."

"I've taken ten men at once. I can take these four."

Pug-Nose shook his head as if trying to shake off a

tidal wave of disbelief. "Ten at once? Oh, this is getting better by the minute." His smile grew bright and wide.

Sheyla looked at the criminals. "I prefer five. Two holes, two hands, and one mouth, you know. But you four will have to do."

Pug-Nose looked at LiCru. "You really should have introduced us sooner."

LiCru looked hard at Sheyla. "What the hell are you doing?" he asked her, his voice whispered but harsh.

She turned her body away from the criminals and looked at LiCru, speaking so softly that only he could hear her. "Making them stupid. Now get out of here and circle around them and kill them." She whirled away from him and turned back to face the criminals. "He is leaving."

"That's funny, 'cause his feet ain't moving." Pug-Nose started to step closer.

Sheyla raised her hand, motioning for him to stop. "Ah, ah. Not yet. Give him a few minutes to get clear."

Pug-Nose stopped. A dark frown clouded his face.

Sheyla smiled at him. "Don't worry. I'll entertain you." She turned aside to LiCru. "Go!"

LiCru hesitated, but then turned and moved quickly back down the hallway, walking rapidly away from them.

Sheyla looked back to the criminals. "Now where were we? Oh, yes. I was about to take my clothes off for you." She started to dance to a silent tune, rhythmically weaving her body about, gyrating her hips, running her hands up and down her arms, across her breasts, between her legs.

The criminals watched, mesmerized by this stunning vision of beauty displaying herself to them, flaunting the power the female body had over them. They couldn't look away. They didn't want to look away.

The servant woman set a bowl of stew down in front of Revek. He was in his throne room, sitting before the meal table the servants loaded with food twice a day for meals. He ripped off a chunk of bread from a nearby loaf and dipped the piece into the thick broth. He tore off a large bite and hungrily chewed at the tasty morsel of bread. He saw a slight movement out of the corner of his eye and saw a small spider crawling along the table. He felt a sudden, irrational flash of fear at the sight of the eight-legged arachnid. His nightmare flashed through his mind, and he remembered the paralyzing fear that had gripped him. He fought against the frozen state threatening to still his moments and smashed angrily at the spider with his fist. He glowered at a nearby servant woman. "Rid this fortress of every spider!" he demanded. "Search every corner, every crack. I want them all destroyed!"

The servant woman hesitated.

Revek smashed his fist again on the scarred wooden table. "Now!"

"Yes, my king," the servant woman said. She bowed her head and scurried off to do his bidding.

Sheyla looked past the criminals as she continued to dance and sway, waiting for LiCru to appear at any moment. She had exposed one of her ample breasts to the men and that had appeased them for a few more moments, but she knew she couldn't do this for much longer. She could see the wolfish desire in their faces turn into an even more animalistic lust. She was only fueling the flames, she knew, but she was just trying to buy some more time.

She pulled her dress down further, revealing her other breast to the hungry gazes of the men.

Pug-Nose started to stalk closer, but Sheyla held her hand up to him. "I haven't shown you the best part," she said.

"I don't want to see it," the man growled. "I want to fuck it."

"Don't you want to taste it before your men sour it with their seeds?"

Pug-Nose stared at her. He wasn't used to a woman being so boldly brazen with her body. They usually cowered before him. Didn't she realize he could snap her neck with very little effort? Didn't she understand that he just needed to raise a finger and two of his men would come forward and sever her pretty head from her slender neck?

She was a beautiful creature. Long, slender legs. Sleek black hair that fell halfway down her back. She had softly curved shoulders, an ample chest, hips he could grab onto. She had a mouth that always seemed to be moist, and just slightly parted, as if she were in a constant state of sensual arousal. But it was her eyes that really trapped him. Those infernal eyes that wouldn't let him go. They drew his gaze in, as if they had some kind of magnetic pull on him.

She had her legs spread, her dress hiked up to show him the soft furriness that lay between them where her thighs joined. The folds within glistened in the torchlight that burned in the corridor, the moisture of her desire twinkling at him like stars in the dark sky. He felt himself grow large, engorged with lust. He strode forward towards her. He would split her in two.

She closed her legs as he neared.

Pug-Nose frowned. He reached down and grabbed her knees, easily forcing her legs apart to reveal the wet folds between her thighs. He thrust his hand between her legs, roughly grabbing at her. Sheyla put her hand on his chest, pushing him back. "Not yet," she said to him. "Taste me first."

Pug-Nose looked down at her, his face squinting.

She studied him for a moment. "Surely you've tasted a woman down there before," she said. "And if not, it's something you should learn to do properly."

He said nothing.

She searched his face, looking for an answer in the silent lines of his expression. Then she looked beyond his shoulder at the three men eagerly awaiting their turn with her. She looked beyond, deeper into the corridor, willing the shape of LiCru to appear, hoping that he would burst upon the scene and start cutting these men down.

LiCru never came out of the darkness.

But someone else did.

It was over in a matter of moments. All four men lay dead in the corridor, their blood splashed across both stone walls, across the tiled floor, across her dress, her arms, her face. He had come out of the darkness, his blade already swinging before he was even visible. The first two died without even having a chance to deliver a counter-blow; one lost his head in a clean strike straight through his neck, and the second fell clutching at the intestines that poured out of the huge gash in his gut. The third man drew his blade and managed to swing a few good strikes at his attacker, but the attacker easily parried the blows and then sunk his bloodied blade into the man's belly, slashing the sword sideways through him, opening up a large rip in his stomach.

Pug-Nose had his face buried between Sheyla's legs when the commotion started. She squeezed her thighs tight, locking his head between her legs. Those few seconds were enough to give her rescuer time to dispose of the other three men before Pug-Nose freed himself from her grip. His mouth and cheeks were wet with his slobbering lust as he fumbled for his sword which lay on the ground nearby.

Revek put his blade straight through Pug-Nose's open, surprised mouth. The sharp end of the blade erupted out of his neck with a meaty sound. Blood sprayed out, splashing up against the stone wall, joining the dripping blood of his fellow escapees.

And then it was quiet in the corridor.

Sheyla stared up at her rescuer. She immediately realized he wasn't the true Revek. He was too short by about a foot. And he wielded his blade in his left hand, instead of his right. Of course, Revek could be proficient with the blade with both hands, but she knew fighters almost always preferred their natural, strong hand when in close quarters battle. This man standing before her preferred his left hand. He had come from her black mirror. She reached out a hand to him, wondering how he would respond to it.

The Revek mirrorling reached down and took her hand, gently helping her to her feet. "Are you all right?" he asked.

She was surprised by the genuine sincerity in his voice, but managed a normal response. "Yes," she said. "Thank you." She glanced down the dim hallway. "Have you seen my brother?"

The Revek mirrorling squinted in confusion.

"LiCru. My brother. Have you seen him? Did you see another man in the hallways?"

"No. I saw no one."

Sheyla stared into the dark hallway. Where was LiCru? She knew she didn't have time to dwell on that. She turned to the mirrorling, trying to form a plan of action in her mind before she spoke. "Come with me," Sheyla finally said to the Revek mirrorling. "You don't belong here."

The Revek mirrorling frowned at her. "Where do you think I belong?"

She hesitated. "Not here," she said.

He shook his head. "No. This is where I belong."

Sheyla looked at him. "You're not real."

His frown deepened. "I feel real. I stand here and take a breath." He opened and closed his right hand, squeezing and releasing his fingers. "I can feel this."

She shook her head softly. "I am sorry. As long as the first Revek lives, you cannot call yourself a real man."

"Then he must die."

"You are not strong enough," Sheyla said. She hesitated for a moment. "You need to find some of the… others… and join forces…"

The Revek mirrorling looked at her.

Revek sat brooding at one of the meal tables in the throne room. But he didn't have long to dwell on his current situation before several people entered the throne room. Several of his guards stepped forward to block the new arrivals. "Stand fast," Revek called out to the guards. "Let them approach." Revek rose from the meal table and motioned for the servants to clear it all away. He moved up the steps that led to his throne as the servants scurried about removing the chairs and the meal table from the area.

Revek sat silently in the large chair, waiting for the visitors to approach. Sheyla approached him, flanked by four mirrorlings of various heights. The tallest of the mirrorlings was about five feet in height; the others varied from a foot in height to three feet in height. They stayed far enough away from each other so as not to be absorbed by each other. Sheyla stopped before the seven steps that led up to the dais and the throne upon which Revek sat. "Have you enjoyed your latest challenge?" Sheyla asked him.

Revek looked at her curiously. He leaned forward in his throne and grinned at her. "Yes." He looked to the mirrorlings behind her. "And what have you brought me here?"

Sheyla looked over her shoulder, as if absently realizing the mirrorlings were still standing there. "Oh, them? They're here to kill you."

As if on cue, the three of the smaller mirrorlings moved closer to the five-foot mirrorling. As each one drew close to the larger mirrorling, the larger mirrorling absorbed them into his body, growing taller and stouter with each mirrorling he absorbed. Within moments, the mirrorling was a near perfect replica of Revek in height and width and appearance.

Revek slowly rose up out his throne. He looked at his guards. "No one interferes." He looked back to the mirrorling, then glanced at Sheyla. "I suggest you step away, Sheyla." He paused. "Unless you enjoy being covered in blood." He drew his sword.

"As long as it's your blood," Sheyla said. She remained where she stood.

The two Reveks circled each other in the middle of the throne room, both gripping their swords tight, Revek gripping his in his right hand, the mirrorling gripping his sword in his left.

The mirrorling tossed his sword from his left hand to his right hand and struck at Revek, delivering a very skilled blow. He was clearly as adept at using his right hand as he was with his left. Revek blocked the strike and the two men circled each other, striking, parrying, slashing, dodging glinting steel as it sought out flesh. It only took a matter of moments of the men twisting and turning and ducking and changing sword hands and battling about the room before it was impossible to tell which of the men was the real Revek and which was the mirrorling.

"What is the meaning of this?" Alfihar demanded as he strode into the throne room to witness the two Reveks dueling with their swords. He looked at the guards positioned nearby. "Kill the imposter."

None of the guards moved, ignoring Alfihar's order.

But they did move when the dozen escaped prisoners suddenly burst upon the scene. The guards immediately enjoined the released prisoners in fresh battles. One guard protected Alfihar from a potentially deadly strike by yanking him out of the way of a slashing dagger. Swords clanged over and over again, the metal biting sounds echoing through the large chamber. Blood spilled. Voices shrieked in pain. Men died.

Alfihar slowly backed away into the shadows, moving behind a large golden sculpture of Revek that was positioned near a corner of the vast room. He watched with a growing sense of dread as the throne room became a chaotic swirl of bodies and blades, blood and hacked bone.

The two Reveks danced on the marble floor, their blades screeching and spitting sparks as they collided again and again, each man battling with furious intensity to get the upper hand over the other.

Sheyla watched the battles from the raised platform. She saw a guard take out two of the escaped prisoners with expert slashes across their throats. Another prisoner stabbed a guard in the back, then stole the guard's sword from his dying fingers.

She looked at the two Reveks battling in the middle of the room, thinking she knew who the true Revek was at one moment, but then doubting herself seconds later.

She glanced about for an avenue of escape, but the only exit she knew of was through the main doors that led into the throne room. She knew she could never make it safely through the chaos of the battles raging all around her.

In the chaos of the battle, Alfihar had made his way to Sheyla, unnoticed by her. He got close enough to her to grab her and pin her arms behind her back. He held her tightly against him, keeping a very firm grip on her as they watched the battles unfold before them. He glanced at the criminals battling the guards. "I suspect that was your doing," he said to her. "Too bad the only reward they will give you in the end is a blade through your belly."

Sheyla stiffened in his grip. But then a most welcome sight brought a cunning smile to her lips. "I don't think this is going to turn out the way you expect."

Alfihar followed Sheyla's gaze to see LiCru standing on the threshold of the throne room in the distance. His hands and feet were now adorned with his wicked killing blades, the blades that had brought him great renown and respect in the battle ring. LiCru paused for only a moment as he assessed the situation before him. He locked gazes with Sheyla and gave her a relieved, reassuring smile. And then he went to work.

Any escaped criminal LiCru came across was easy prey. It often only took one slashing kick across a man's abdomen to open up his belly and send his intestines pooling to the marble floor. He managed to accomplish that with three of the prisoners they had released.

In the midst of the battle, LiCru found himself near the throne and near his sister. "I'm sorry, Sheyla," he called out to her. "I got lost in those damn dark hallways." He lifted one of his arms, showing off the bloodied blade attached to his hand. "But at least I have these now."

"Don't worry about me," Sheyla said to him. She didn't even bother to struggle against Alfihar's grip on her. "Just kill them all."

LiCru was forced to turn his attention back to the fight as men converged on him. He killed four more escaped prisoners with slashing strikes to their throats. The blades attached to his hands and feet were mere extensions of his own limbs; he was so accustomed to wielding them that it was as if they actually were his hands and feet.

Soon, there were no more prisoners left alive and only two guards remained. The two guards proved to be tougher opponents, but they were still no real threat to LiCru and his blades. He dispatched them both, but one guard did manage to cut his shoulder. LiCru ignored the pain and the blood.

Alfihar clutched Sheyla as he watched the two Reveks battle. Even he was not certain which Revek was his true king. Both men kept switching their swords from hand to hand, wielding them with expert precision regardless of which hand they held the blade in. Then one of the Reveks slipped in an unexpected pool of blood, causing him to stagger. That's all it took to turn the tide of the battle. One second of imbalance. The stumbling Revek tried to block the strike, but he could not do it cleanly. The blade hit him in the throat, cutting deep into his flesh. Blood spurted. The attacking Revek did not hesitate; he struck again and again, delivering the final death blow with a solid driving thrust to the fallen Revek's chest.

Alfihar knew the fallen Revek was dead because the blue orb of light flitted out of its fresh corpse and swirled into the chest of the victorious Revek. "Behind you!" Alfihar shouted.

Revek turned just in time to block LiCru's slashing hand-blade.

Alfihar frowned deeply. He could see that fatigue had settled in heavily on the king. Even with the extra life energy he had just absorbed from the slain Revek, there was an obvious exhaustion etched deeply into every sun-baked wrinkle on his aging face.

LiCru unleashed a volley of savage kicks, the blades on his feet flashing hotly as the torchlight reflected off their gleaming surfaces. Revek blocked two of the strikes, but not the third. The blade on LiCru's left foot slashed across Revek's forearm, drawing blood. Revek gritted his teeth and battled on.

But then a most curious sight brought a twisted smile to Alfihar's lips. "I don't think this is going to turn out the way you expect," Alfihar said to Sheyla, throwing her words right back at her.

Sheyla frowned at him and Alfihar pointed past her shoulder. Sheyla turned to see three small shapes charging into the room. It was the last of the Revek mirrorlings. She turned back to Alfihar. "Perhaps," she said to him. "But whose side will they choose?"

The warped smile left Alfihar's lips.

Sheyla called out to her brother. "LiCru, make them your allies."

LiCru looked away from his sister to stare at the three Revek mirrorlings standing before them. "Fight with me," LiCru said. "He has vowed to destroy you," LiCru said to them. He moved his glance from one little Revek mirrorling to the next. "All of you."

All of the little Revek mirrorlings nodded their little heads. "We know," one of them said, his voice low and barely discernible, but somehow still deep. "But he is of us and we are of him."

LiCru shook his head. "Not any more. You are now your own— men." LiCru struggled to find the right word, what to call them, but they were still men despite their diminutive size. "Do you not want to continue to take a breath in this world?"

A determination set in the eyes of each of the Revek mirrorlings. They gripped their swords and moved towards King Revek.

Revek watched the mirrorlings approach him. They were only a foot high each. One of them had a left leg longer than its right leg, so it walked with an odd, loping limp. Each one clutched a blade. They were not fighting each other. Somehow these three had decided to work together. They stood far enough apart not to be absorbed by each other.

"There is only room for one Revek in this world," one of the Revek mirrorlings said.

And then they did something that made Revek proud. Almost in unison, they set their blades down on the ground and moved to one knee, bowing their heads to him. Offering themselves to him. Revek stared at these tiny men. He knew exactly what they were thinking. They could not win. Even if they defeated him, they could not win in the end. They could never rule the world as he did. They would not even be able to hold the heavy gold jewel-encrusted crown in their hands. They were just too small. He silently thanked them for their sacrifice, and quickly and efficiently ended their lives with three quick strikes of his blade.

Then the life essences of the three mirrorlings rose up out of their tiny bodies, the swirling balls of light spinning above their corpses. The orbs of energy whooshed through the air and penetrated Revek's chest, returning some of his stolen life force back to him. He sucked in a deep breath, feeling this second surge of energy returning to him, exhilaration running through him. Revek rose up tall and turned his full attention to the man wielding the deadly blades on his hands and feet.

The ballad of the battle between King Revek and LiCru would be a song handed down from generation to generation. The king and the battle ring champion fought an epic battle. They rolled over the meal tables, crashed into sculptures, slit holes in tapestries. They moved throughout the entire throne room, striking and slashing, blocking and ducking. They slipped in pools of blood. They tripped over fallen corpses. They stumbled over splattered intestines. LiCru fought well, masterfully using his hand-blades and feet-blades, but in the end he was no match for the raw fury of King Revek. The cuts and slashes LiCru inflicted on King Revek did nothing to slow him down; the level of Revek's explosive rage remained high throughout their fight and only seemed to increase as the battle raged on. Revek lopped off one of LiCru's arms, severing it at the elbow. After that, LiCru had no chance. King Revek finished him off with a decapitating blow that sent his head rolling up to the edge of the raised stairs that led up to the throne.

Sheyla screamed as she stared into the lifeless eyes of her brother. Only then did Alfihar release his grip on her.

King Revek mounted the stairs of the platform, moving up to the dais. His body was streaked with blood and cuts, but he stood tall and strong. He glanced over at Alfihar. "Thank you, Alfihar. That was quite satisfying."

Alfihar bowed a slight bow.

King Revek turned to look at Sheyla. He reached up his left hand and caressed Sheyla's cheek, leaving a smear of his blood on her smooth skin. "Now where were we?"

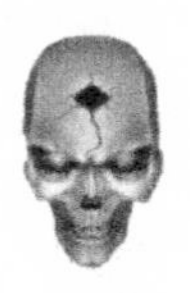

A NOTE FROM JACK O'DONNELL

Thanks for joining me on this fifth tour of that shadowy realm of fear known as Land of Fright™. I'm glad you decided to travel along those twisted paths with me.

I grew up in the suburbs of Illinois on a steady diet of comic books, Creature Features, WWII movies, Hammer horror movies, used paperbacks, James Bond, Edgar Rice Burroughs, the Don Pendleton Executioner series, and giant bug movies. Some favorite guilty pleasures are The Warriors, John Carpenter's The Thing, Von Ryan's Express with Frank Sinatra, and the original Planet of the Apes with Charlton Heston.

My one claim to fame (so far) is that I co-wrote and co-produced the movie Stephen King's The Night Flier, based on his short story.

Visit www.landoffright.com and subscribe to stay up-to-date on the latest new stories in the Land of Fright™ series of horror short stories.

Please visit my author page on Amazon at www.amazon.com/author/jodonnell to see the newest releases in the Land of Fright™ series, or to see what else I might be up to.

-JACK

MORE LAND OF FRIGHT™ COLLECTIONS ARE AVAILABLE NOW!

Turn the page and step into fear!

Land of Fright™ terrorstories contained in Collection I:

#1 - Whirring Blades: A simple late-night trip to the mall for a father and his son turns into a struggle for survival when they are attacked by a deadly swarm of toy helicopters.
#2 - The Big Leagues: A scorned young baseball player shows his teammates he really knows how to play ball with the best of them.
#3 - Snowflakes: In the land of Frawst, special snowflakes are a gift from the gods, capable of transferring the knowledge of the Ancients. A young woman searches the skies with breathless anticipation for her snowflake, but finds something far more dark and dangerous instead.
#4 - End of the Rainbow: In Medieval England, a warrior and his woman find the end of a massive rainbow that has filled the sky and discover the dark secret of its power.
#5 - Trophy Wives: An enigmatic sculptor meets a beautiful woman whom he vows will be his next subject. But things may not turn out the way he plans...
#6 - Die-orama: A petty thief finds out that a WWII model diorama in his local hobby shop holds much more than just plastic vehicles and plastic soldiers.
#7 - Creature in the Creek: A lonely young woman finds her favorite secluded spot inhabited by a monster from her past.
#8 - The Emperor of Fear: In ancient Rome, two coliseum workers encounter a mysterious crate containing an unearthly creature. Just in time for the next gladiator games…
#9 - The Towers That Fell From The Sky: Two analysts race to uncover the secret purpose of the giant alien towers that have thundered down out of the skies.
#10 - God Save The Queen: An exterminator piloting an ant-sized robot comes face to face with the queen of a nest he has been assigned to destroy.

Land of Fright™ terrorstories contained in Collection II:

#11 - Special Announcement: A fraud investigator discovers the disturbing truth behind the messages on a community announcement board.
#12 - Poisoned Land: Savage hunters patrol the Poisoned Lands, demanding appeasement from the three survivors trapped in a surrounded building. How far will each one of them go to survive?
#13 - Pool of Light: A mysterious wave of dark energy from space washes over the Earth, trapping a woman and her friends in pools of light. Beyond the edges of the light, deep pockets of darkness hold much more than just empty blackness.
#14 - Ghosts of Pompeii: A woman on a tour of Italy with her son unwittingly awakens the ghosts of Pompeii.
#15 - Sparklers: A child's sparkler opens a doorway to another dimension and a father must enter it to save his family and his neighborhood from the ominous threat that lays beyond.
#16 - The Grid: An interstellar salvage crew activates a mysterious grid on an abandoned vessel floating in space, unleashing a deadly force.
#17 - The Barn: An empty barn beckons an amateur photographer to step through its dark entrance, whispering promises of a once-in-a-lifetime shoot.
#18 - Sands of the Colosseum: A businessman in Rome gets to experience the dream of a lifetime when he visits the great Colosseum — until he finds himself standing on the arena floor.
#19 - Flipbook: A man sees a dark future of his family in jeopardy when he watches the tiny animations of a flipbook play out in his hand.
#20 - Day of the Hoppers: Two boys flee for their lives when their friendly neighborhood grasshoppers turn into deadly projectiles.

Land of Fright™ terrorstories contained in Collection III:

#21 - The Prospector: In the 1800's, a lonely prospector finds the body parts of a woman as he pans for gold in the wilds of California.
#22 - The Boy In The Yearbook: Two middle-aged women are tormented by a mysterious photograph in their high school yearbook.
#23 - Shot Glass: A man discovers the shot glasses in his great-grandfather's collection can do much more than just hold a mouthful of liquor.
#24 - The Champion: An actor in a medieval renaissance re-enactment show becomes the unbeatable champion he has longed to be.
#25 - Hitler's Graveyard: American soldiers in WWII uncover a nefarious Nazi plan to resurrect their dead heroes so they can rejoin the war.
#26 - Out of Ink: Colonists on a remote planet resort to desperate measures to ward off an attack from wild alien animals.
#27 - Dung Beetles: Mutant dung beetles attack a family on a remote Pennsylvania highway. Yes, it's as disgusting as it sounds.
#28 - The Tinies: A beleaguered office worker encounters a strange alien armada in the sub-basement of his office building.
#29 - Hammer of Charon: In ancient Rome, it is the duty of a special man to make sure gravely wounded gladiators are given a quick death after a gladiator fight. He serves his position quietly with honor. Until they try to take his hammer away from him…
#30 - Pharaoh's Cat: In ancient Egypt, the pharaoh is dying. His trusted advisors want his favorite cat to be buried with him. The cat has other plans…

Land of Fright™ terrorstories contained in Collection IV:

#31 - The Throw-Aways: A washed-up writer of action-adventure thrillers is menaced by the ghosts of the characters he has created.
#32 - Everlasting Death: The souls of the newly deceased take on solid form and the Earth fills with immovable statues of death...
#33 - Bite the Bullet: In the Wild West, a desperate outlaw clings to a bullet cursed by a Gypsy... because the bullet has his name on it.
#34 - Road Rage: A senseless accident on a rural highway sets off a frightening chain of events.
#35 - The Controller: A detective investigates a bank robbery that appears to have been carried out by a zombie.
#36 - The Notebook: An enchanted notebook helps a floundering author finish her story. But the unnatural fuel that stokes the power of the mysterious writing journal leads her down a disturbing path...
#37 - The Candy Striper and the Captain: American WWII soldiers in the Philippines scare superstitious enemy soldiers with corpses they dress up to look like vampire victims. The vampire bites might be fake, but what comes out of the jungle is not...
#38 - Clothes Make the Man: A young man steals a magical suit off of a corpse, hoping some of its power will rub off on him.
#39 - Memory Market: The cryptic process of memory storage in the human brain has been decoded and now memories are bought and sold in the memory market. But with every legitimate commercial endeavor there comes a black market, and the memory market is no exception...
#40 - The Demon Who Ate Screams: A young martial artist battles a vicious demon who feeds on the tormented screams and dying whimpers of his victims.

Land of Fright™ terrorstories contained in Collection VI:

#51 - Zombie Carnival: Two couples stumble upon a zombie-themed carnival and decide to join the fun.
#52 - Going Green: Drug runners trying to double cross their boss get a taste of strong voodoo magic.
#53 - Message In A Bottle: A bottle floats onto the beach of a private secluded island with an unnerving message trapped inside.
#54 - The Chase: In 18th century England, a desperate chase is on as a monstrous beast charges after a fleeing wagon, a wagon occupied by too many people...
#55 - Who's Your Daddy?: A lonely schoolteacher is disturbed by how much all of the students in her class look alike. A visit by a mysterious man sheds some light on the curious situation.
#56 - Beheaded: In 14th century England, a daughter vows revenge upon those who beheaded her father. She partners with a lascivious young warlock to restore her family's honor.
#57 - Hold Your Breath: A divorced mother of one confronts the horrible truth behind the myth of holding one's breath when driving past a cemetery.
#58 - Viral: What makes a civilization fall? Volcanoes, earthquakes, or other forces of nature? Barbarous invasions or assaults from hostile forces? Decline from within due to decadence and moral decay? Or could it be something more insidious?
#59 - Top Secret: A special forces agent confronts the villainous characters from his past, but discovers something even more dangerous.
#60 - Immortals Must Die: There is no more life force left in the universe. The attainment of immortality has depleted the world of available souls. So what do you do if you are desperate to have a child?

AND LOOK FOR EVEN MORE LAND OF FRIGHT™ STORIES COMING SOON!

THANKS AGAIN FOR READING.

Visit www.landoffright.com

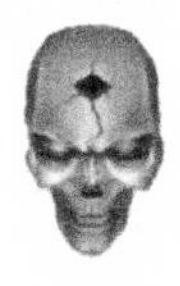

Made in the USA
Las Vegas, NV
03 March 2023